THE RAMAGE HAWK

THE RAMAGE HAWK

John Pilkington

severn House

This first world edition published in Great Britain 2004 by
SEVERN HOUSE PUBLISHERS LTD of
9–15 High Street, Sutton, Surrey SM1 1DF.
This first world edition published in the USA 2004 by
SEVERN HOUSE PUBLISHERS INC of
595 Madison Avenue, New York, N.Y. 10022.

Copyright © 2004 by John Pilkington.

British Library Cataloguing in Publication Data

Pilkington, John, 1948 June 11-
    The ramage hawk. - (A Thomas the falconer mystery)
    1.   Thomas the Falconer (Fictitious character) - Fiction
    2.   Great Britain - history - Elizabeth, 1558-1603 - Fiction
    3.   Detective and mystery stories
    I.   Title
    823.9'14 [F]

    ISBN 0-7278-6087-9

Typeset by Palimpsest Book Production Ltd.,
Polmont, Stirlingshire, Scotland.
Printed and bound in Great Britain by
MPG Books Ltd., Bodmin, Cornwall.

Prologue

John Tyrrell was dying.

The other prisoners in the Twopenny Ward – as close to the Hole as a man may be while still counting himself a cut above its wretched, groaning inmates – began to avoid him, stepping around what had become Tyrrell's section of the wall. Gaol fever: they knew the signs. And the ragged, shivering, foul-smelling man who had once called himself Master Tyrrell, student of St Johns, Cambridge, knew them too.

In this first week of August, in the year 1590, when the heat and stench inside the Wood Street Counter – the debtors' prison nearest St Paul's – had become all but unbearable, a new face appeared in the Twopenny Ward. Simon Pepper was the name he gave. Within hours, for some reason none could fathom, he had befriended John Tyrrell, brought him a tarred leather mug of sack and a dish of pease and watched him drink greedily, though he could not swallow the food. When Tyrrell had drained the last of the poor, watered sack, he spoke in a voice choked with phlegm and weak from starvation.

'Why have you done this for me?' His filmy eyes searched the dark-bearded face, seeing a man who looked somewhat well fed and a little too well dressed to be clapped up in the Counter.

'I'm a friend of your catamite – Will Pygot,' Pepper answered.

Tyrrell's whole body jerked. 'You've seen him?'

Pepper wore a sombre look. 'He's dead.'

Tyrrell gave a cough. 'When?'

Though Pepper still looked concerned, he seemed to be

hiding a smile, as if unable to believe that it was going to be this easy. He leaned a little closer. 'I killed him.'

Tyrrell began shaking.

'No one knows,' Pepper told him quietly. 'To all appearances he was drunk and fell down the Blackfriars Stairs, breaking his empty head. The verdict will be mischance, not murder.'

'You spoke with him . . .' Tyrrell began hoarsely. 'So you know something, or you wouldn't be here—'

'Stop.' Pepper's voice, though soft, bore the unmistakeable note of authority. 'I will lay the tale before you.'

Tyrrell sank back against the crumbling mortar.

'It begins with you,' Pepper told him, and shook his head sadly. 'What dumps you put your poor mother in, John Tyrrell. A man of good family, who went to the University – such bright hopes she had for you. You might have come home to Salisbury, married well and given her grandchildren. Instead, you repay her by abandoning your studies and forsaking the company of women for the rough bodies of boys . . . men like Will Pygot, dice-player and as crooked a purser as ever sailed out of harbour – or sailed into harbour. As he did three years back, on the twenty-sixth of June 1587, when the whole of Plymouth turned out in celebration to see Drake bring the *San Felipe* into port.' Pepper stopped for a moment.

'You and Pygot,' he sneered. 'Two lusty lads who can't keep their hands off each other. Lying spent in some waterfront tavern after you have foined each other raw, you fall to fanciful talk, as all lovers do. And Pygot's a bold one: he tells you of the riches aboard the *San Felipe* – that glorious treasure ship Drake has plucked from the Spanish . . . the jewels, plate and bullion, the chests of gold double-ducats that amount, it's said, to more than a hundred thousand English pounds. And more, he tells you how he has an armlock on one of the guards who fears for his post; and how he may bribe another, if only someone he can trust will despatch a third – then you and he may come at a portion of the *San Felipe*'s riches. And nailed up in a barrel, which may be rolled down the gangplank in broad daylight while

2

the business of the port goes forth about it, you and he may make away with your portion. And dividing it up into panniers, with packhorses ready, you may set forth from Devon, never to return. And Arcadia awaits you!'

Tyrrell turned a haggard face towards Simon Pepper, but the other refused to meet his gaze. 'Your scheme fadged well, did it not?' Pepper said. 'By the time the theft was discovered you were gone. And besides, no man could vouch for certain what had happened.. . . . a guard knocked on the head, another pinned from behind, his head covered so that he saw no one . . . if any man wondered at the timely disappearance of one of Sir Francis's pursers, none seems to have given voice to his suspicion.'

Pepper turned slightly and gave Tyrrell an admiring look. 'It was a wondrous crime, John. Would that you had had the sense to take ship for some other land . . .'

A cry that was almost a yelp came from Tyrrell's lips. 'I had a plan, disguises – all was ready!' he croaked. 'In Italy we could have lived like lords for the rest of our days – why wait? It was not folly, but madness!' He raised a shaking hand to his face. 'But Will said he was known to too many seamen . . . we would be discovered.' He shook his head. 'Why did I let him rule me?'

Pepper laid a comforting hand on his arm. 'He was all to you, was he not?'

Tears rolled from Tyrrell's eyes. Then he frowned suddenly. 'And you killed him?'

'He betrayed you,' Pepper answered smoothly. 'Why did he not come with the money he promised? You and he have a fortune hidden away!'

Tyrrell sniffed. 'We vowed we would not touch it until the matter was long past,' he mumbled. 'When it was safe, we would recover it, and . . .' He swung his head towards Pepper. 'If he'd told you where it was, you wouldn't have come here!'

Pepper gave a bland smile, as one who is glad to come to the nub of things at last. 'Now you see your course. Rather, you see the choice, and it is but a simple one. Tell me where it is, and you walk free of the Counter. Tell me nothing, and

I'll leave you to die here. Because nobody knows you *are* here, John Tyrrell. No one will pay your debts, for Pygot disowned you. He was ready to leave for Wiltshire and take up your prize.'

Tyrrell started. 'And I'm the only one who knows where it is!'

'I said, you may walk out of here,' Pepper went on. 'In the morning I pay the Keepers what they have asked, and one will escort us both to Silver Street. You have remembered an old friend who'll settle your debts. Once we are there, the Keeper will turn aside for a moment, as I have paid him to, and we will make our escape through Cripplegate. In St Giles Without we will go to a house I know, where we can rest and make ready for our journey.'

Tyrrell's senses were reeling. It was no bluff; people did pay the Keepers to take them out sometimes. If you had the money, you could get anything in the Counter. He swallowed, wincing at the pain in his swollen throat. 'A physician,' he muttered. 'I need physic . . .'

'You'll have it,' Pepper answered. 'Then once you're fit to travel, we go to Wiltshire and recover the prize, which we divide in two. Then we part, forever. Agreed?'

Tyrrell gave a long sigh. He could rest now. In the morning . . . He coughed, then nodded feebly.

Pepper smiled – a real smile now, of mingled pleasure, anticipation, even friendliness. 'Good John Tyrrell,' he murmured, 'put yourself in my hands, and you will be free.'

But Tyrrell's eyes were already closing, and his head fell forward.

It was the last real sleep he would know.

Two days later, Simon Pepper left a semi-derelict tenement in St Giles and made his way round the Walls towards Holborn Bridge. With him was a stout, very muscular man wearing a hood, who carried their belongings in a shoulder pack. It was he, playing at first the unlikely part of the physician, who had taken hold of the broken body of John Tyrrell the night before, and wrung the last scrap of information from his sorry, wasted frame before despatching him with a single blow to the skull. By the end, Tyrrell had been more than ready to spill all he knew. In the hands of such an inquisitor he begged to tell more – anything that would bring oblivion and an end to his suffering.

The heavy man wore no expression; his features had long since lost the ability to register emotion. But his master breathed the sweet air of the fields west of the City, felt the morning sun on his back, and smiled to himself. All his life he had waited for an opportunity like the one that now lay before him. And the ease with which it had fallen into his lap, after a chance talk with a maudlin sailor in a Plymouth alehouse, made him want to laugh aloud. An old, half-forgotten air from his boyhood drifted into his mind, and he began to whistle it softly. To the irritation of his burly servant he was still whistling it at dinnertime when the two men, now mounted, broke their journey at Uxbridge on the West Road, their first stop on the way to distant Wiltshire, and the home of John Tyrrell's aunt. A half-mad, painted spinster in her middle years, who dressed like a young maid and still waited for a handsome gallant to wed her, she had no idea at all of the existence of the treasure from the *San Felipe*, which had lain hidden in her house for the past three years.

One

The harvesters, coming home from the hayfields in a body, paused at the crossroads as a tall rider on a bright sorrel horse approached them from the north. As he reined in, they saw he bore a hooded hawk on his wrist. Their leader, John Cardmaker the hayward, half raised a hand in greeting. Falconers were common enough on the Downs, especially about the village of East Everley, where the Queen's own falconer, Sir Ralph Sadler, had built the fine manor house and trained his hawks until his sad death three years back – though happily his son Henry carried on the tradition. Tradition was everything here on the hills that gave on to Salisbury Plain, stretching away to the south-west. As far as most people were concerned, life in east Wiltshire had changed little since Doomsday. And that, most said, was how it should be.

The tall rider, russet-bearded with grey, far-seeing eyes, gazed down upon the group of men and nodded in return.

'Looks like you've done a hard day's work.' He smiled.

'That we have, master,' Cardmaker answered. 'Hay harvest is a late one this year.' He was a little man with an officious manner that did not sit well with his brawny arms and deeply suntanned face. 'Are you seeking the manor of Everley?'

Thomas the Falconer, who had ridden twenty miles from his west Berkshire home since noon, shook his head. 'I'm seeking the manor of Chilbourne. The seat of Sir Giles Buckridge. Can you point me toward it?'

There was a snort from one of the harvesters. One or two others shrugged. It was left to Cardmaker to act as spokesman.

'It's no distance, for one who's mounted,' he said a little stiffly. He pointed eastwards to the little stone church that stood back from the crossroads. 'Past the church, follow the path downhill to the river, then a mile downstream you'll see Chilbourne beyond a clump of beech.'

Thomas murmured his thanks. As he did so the fine hawk on his wrist, which had been motionless as a statue, shifted slightly, looking as if she were about to bate. Instinctively Thomas took the reins in his teeth, leaving his right hand free to stroke the bird, all the while talking softly under his breath. She quietened at once.

The village men watched in silence. Used to falconers here on the Downs, nevertheless they seldom saw one who had such a way with birds. With horses too, perhaps, for the sleek sorrel gelding, in which many might have noted a choleric temperament, seemed content to stand patiently until Thomas took the reins up again and made ready to ride.

'I'm obliged, master,' he said, and allowed his eyes to settle on Cardmaker's plain features. 'Who am I addressing?'

Cardmaker gave his name and his station, then clearly felt it was his right to ask the other man his business.

'Thomas Finbow, falconer to Sir Robert Vicary at the manor of Petbury,' Thomas told him. He gave a wry smile. 'I'm but a hired man like yourselves, who's been loaned to Sir Giles like the bird here.'

The men relaxed a little now. One or two even smiled back.

'You'll have your work cut out then, maister,' one volunteered. 'There used to be more than eighty servants at Chilbourne – now there's barely twenty.'

Thomas raised an eyebrow. Cardmaker, clearly a man who disliked gossip, showed his disapproval. But another spoke up.

'And if what village folk hear be true, none of them's been paid in months!'

Cardmaker rounded on the man, who looked away and spat into the dry ditch beside the road. But when he glanced back at Thomas he saw the falconer regarding him with a look of understanding. He too, Cardmaker realized, was not given to idle talk.

'Then I'd best look to my own business,' Thomas said.

He gave the reins a twitch, and half turned the gelding. But before taking his leave he pointed with his chin towards the thatched roofs of the village, dark against the sunset.

'At least tell me there's an inn here, where a man might find a welcome,' he said.

The hayward relaxed somewhat. 'There is, Master Finbow,' he replied. 'The White Hound – the largest house there, where the ground rises.'

Thomas nodded. 'Then I shall come in when I may, and buy you a mug for your information,' he said. He clicked his tongue, touched his boot heels to the gelding's flanks, and rode off in the direction he had been given.

The harvesters watched him disappear, then shouldered their hooks and pitchforks and resumed their trudge homewards, wondering what Sir Robert Vicary – whoever he was – was doing loaning a falconer of that calibre to the impoverished, debt-ridden – indeed rather ridiculous – Sir Giles Buckridge, whose very name had become a byword for failure on the Everley Downs.

For Thomas it was a less than auspicious end to his journey, and one that threatened to confirm his worst fears.

It was only a matter of days since Sir Robert, in one of his rare fits of generosity, had ordered him to travel to Chilbourne to aid his old hunting friend, though admitting that he had not set eyes on him for years. Thomas, who had more than enough work on his hands this summer, hid his displeasure, merely asking what his master wished him to do for Sir Giles. When the reply came, that he was to instruct Sir Giles's nineteen-year-old ward, a bookish lad named Gervase Lambert, in the arts of falconry, his heart sank.

'Is there no one there who might perform such a task, Sir Robert?' he had muttered, standing beside the falcons' mews with a frisky young hawk on his arm, both of them eager to be out on the Downs.

Sir Robert had been somewhat evasive that morning. 'Sir Giles's own falconers have left his service, I hear,' he answered, gazing into the distance. 'Besides, the task requires a man of sympathy and patience, like yourself.'

Refusing to rise to the obvious flattery, Thomas persisted. 'Is the young gentleman then such an unwilling pupil?' he asked, unable to avoid the depressing thought that someone who had not mastered the basic tenets of falconry by the age of nineteen could hardly be enamoured of the sport at best. At worst, he might be utterly unsuited to it.

'You choose to ignore – as is your custom, Thomas, when it suits you – the fact that Chilbourne lies in one of the finest parts of England for falconry,' Sir Robert told him. 'You must make the best of your stay. See now, surely you might trap a couple of passage hawks before the September migration?'

Thomas nodded. 'With luck, that I may, sir,' he answered.

'Then the matter's settled.' Sir Robert, short on patience as usual, turned to take his leave. 'I have sent word to Sir Giles that you will arrive a week before Lammas Day. You may ride Cob, the new gelding.'

Thomas inclined his head, surprised. Cob was a fine horse.

'And . . .' Sir Robert looked away. 'Take Tamora with you.'

Tamora was one of his master's best falcons – a princess of a bird, and a favourite with everyone at Petbury. Why was his master being so generous? Thomas opened his mouth, then closed it. He sensed he was being softened up for the worst.

'There's one other matter . . .' Sir Robert said, rather too briskly. 'Sir Giles has need of someone to tame one of his birds – someone highly skilled, like yourself.'

Thomas understood. 'A ramage hawk.'

Sir Robert sniffed. 'A young hawk, it's true,' he murmured. 'Taken rather late in the season, perhaps . . .'

Thomas nodded grimly. Ramage hawks – those that had been allowed to fly wild for some months – were notoriously difficult to reclaim, let alone train for the sport. How many days had he spent since his youth, crashing about in the bushes trying to recover such a bird, which hopped from branch to branch just outside his grasp and seemed to mock him with every step he took?

'I see the picture, Sir Robert,' he said. His master looked him in the eye at last, not without amusement.

9

'Good,' he replied. 'I will commend you to Sir Giles's service until September. The Petbury men must manage without you.' He lifted a purse from his belt and held it out. 'This should last for the duration. If you are in dire need, you may send word to me for further payment.'

In dire need . . .? Thomas had taken the purse, a number of questions forming in his mind, but at once his master had stalked off towards the house; a little too quickly, Thomas thought. Now he began to understand why.

Sir Robert was helping out a country knight like himself, one who had nothing like his station or influence – and, it seemed, nothing approaching his wealth. If indeed, he had much wealth at all.

From the moment he dismounted in the weed-choked stable yard and no groom came out to take his horse, he knew his stay here would be a difficult one.

Chilbourne, he saw, had once been a rather grand house, well built in the local manner of grey stone infilled with knapped flint. But in recent years it had been allowed to decay. One of the outer gates hung off its hinges, while the park beyond was untended. The only sign of habitation, apart from smoke from the kitchen chimney, was a small horse herd in a rudely fenced paddock. From the manor itself came no sound.

Thomas placed the falcon on a stump beside the door then led Cob into the stable, where he received a greater shock. From the gloom within came a stifled shriek and a rustling sound. Peering about, he saw two pale figures in the corner, half hidden in a pile of straw.

'Who's there?' he asked, feeling rather foolish. He could guess what was afoot. There was a silence, then a male voice called: 'Who's asking?'

'Thomas, falconer to Sir Robert Vicary, come to serve Sir Giles,' he answered, and waited.

There was more muttering, until finally a big, heavy-set man with long nut-brown hair and a thick beard stepped out of the straw and came forward. With one hand he wiped his sweaty face, while the other held up his grimy-looking breeches. He was naked to the waist, with a crow's nest of dark hair on his chest.

'I'm Judd Chalkhill,' the man mumbled. 'Slaughterman.'

Thomas, aware now of the weariness in his limbs, gazed at him without expression. 'Is there no one to look after my horse?' he enquired. 'I've ridden the best part of twenty miles.'

Judd Chalkhill looked both Thomas and the horse up and down. 'I reckon I better do 'ee. Seeing as there's no one else.'

Thomas looked past the heavy frame of the slaughterman to the crouching figure beyond. He had no wish to start by making enemies.

'I ask pardon for startling you,' he said. 'It's no business of mine what a man does in the stable after sunset.'

But Chalkhill merely scowled. 'Right enough it's not. And what business do a falconer have here, anyways?'

Thomas made no reply until the silence was broken by the sound of more rustling. Finally a female form emerged from the straw pile in the corner. Thomas saw a plain, fair-haired woman in her mid-twenties, wearing a soiled shift. Far from displaying any embarrassment, she gazed at him with frank curiosity.

'It's him as come to teach Master Gervase,' the woman said. 'Don't you remember nothing?'

Chalkhill looked less sure of himself. 'No one in that 'ouse tells me nothing,' he said.

Thomas raised an eyebrow and held forth the reins. After a moment, having made sure his breeches weren't about to take leave of his waist, the slaughterman took them from him. 'I didn't mean no disrespect,' he muttered.

Thomas nodded. 'I ask you to take good care of Cob. He's a favourite of my master's.' When the man grunted his acquiescence, he added, 'Is your master at home?'

Before Chalkhill could answer, the woman spoke. 'I'll take ye inside, falconer. I'll guess Master Oakes will receive you. He's butler to Sir Giles.'

Thomas smiled his thanks, and the woman met his gaze with a sudden flush of awkwardness. She began to speak

quickly, as if now embarrassed at the manner of their intro-
duction.

'I'm Nan Greenwood, washerwoman. We was expecting
you yesternight, only Master Oakes said it could be today,
and he's never wrong about nothing. You'll likely stay in
the groom's loft, above here. No one's used it since Ned
Tree skipped off with the best harness . . .' She clapped a
hand to her mouth abruptly, so like a child that Thomas
wanted to laugh.

But Chalkhill spoke up in irritation. 'Lord stop your great
mouth, Nan,' he growled. 'You can no more hold your
tongue than a ram can shave his horns.' He looked askance
at Thomas. 'It's not a good place, this,' he said. 'There's no
money for wages, nor barely enough to feed the household,
nor even the beasts. I killed the last breeding bull for flesh
. . . It's mutton for supper, when there's any meat at all.' He
brightened suddenly. 'Here – you'm a falconer, you can hunt
for the pot, can't ye? Partridge . . . rail . . . a few pigeons
would go down fine!'

Thomas nodded and turned away. 'Mayhap I can help,'
he answered. 'For now, all I want is a mug and a bite of
supper, and somewhere to lay my head.'

Nan Greenwood had moved to the straw in the corner and
found a plain kirtle, which she quickly pulled over her head.
Straightening herself as best she could, she retrieved a pair
of old walking shoes, pulled them on and stepped forward
to show that she was ready.

Leaving Judd Chalkhill to look after Cob, who seemed to
accept his fate with indifference, Thomas followed her
outside. The mighty Tamora, hearing him approach under
her hood, stiffened and half raised her wings.

Nan stared. 'Jesu – be that an eagle?'

Thomas stooped to take the falcon on to his gauntlet. 'If
she was, she'd be a mite bigger,' he replied. 'Is there somewhere quiet I can set her for the night?'

With a nod, Nan led him away from the stables, round a
crumbling wall and pointed to a low, open-fronted hut made
of willow hurdles.

'That's where the falconers used to keep their hawks,' she

said. 'Before they up and left. There's only one bird there now. 'Twas a gift to the master from Henry Sadler up at Everley manor. Judd's been giving 'er water and scraps. He's not the skill to fly her – no one has.'

She waited while Thomas walked softly towards the weathering, peered into the darkness within, and saw the ramage hawk. He stopped dead.

The young bird seemed to have been waiting for him. Still in her first year's plumage, she shifted on her perch, caught his eye and held it. Thomas gazed back, seeing at once the task that lay ahead. He was known as a friend to beasts, but the ramage hawk stared back at him unflinchingly, the challenge plain in her baleful gaze: *tame me if you can* . . .

With a sigh Thomas looked away, noting that at least the bird was tethered properly and had a bowl of water nearby. Outside the weathering he found another perch, and settled Tamora so that she and the ramage hawk would be kept separated. Then he walked back to where Nan was waiting.

'I'm ready,' he said.

Sir Giles Buckridge, for all his shortcomings – which seemed to multiply in Thomas's mind with every minute he had so far spent at Chilbourne – was, it seemed, not a man who stood on ceremony. Perhaps in his circumstances he had found it easier to dispense with many of the formalities of his rank and status, for in a very few minutes Thomas found himself, still in his dusty riding clothes, being shown into the Great Chamber where the family were at their supper. Sir Giles himself – a tall, thin-faced man in a duck-green doublet – rose from the high table at once and called out.

'Falconer! Come forward, pray! We shan't bite!'

The chatter at the top table – which seemed to be occupied mostly by ladies – ceased momentarily as, feeling very self-conscious, Thomas approached, then stopped and made a bow before the company.

There was a stifled gasp from a young girl to his left. 'By the Lord, but he's handsome!' she whispered, loudly enough to be heard in the kitchens. Sir Giles, wearing a pained look, swung his head in the girl's direction.

'Hold your foolish tongue, Margaret!'

The child – for she was barely a dozen years old – ducked her head, stifling a giggle. Her neighbour, an older girl in a faded sky-blue gown, smiled to herself.

'Master Finbow, you are welcome!' boomed Sir Giles. 'How is my dear friend, Sir Robert?'

'He's well, thank you sir,' Thomas answered. 'He sends his warmest greetings, and commends me to your service.'

'Splendid. We will have work aplenty for you, make no mistake!' Sir Giles paused, clearly feeling that introductions were necessary. Not without pride he presented his family, one by one. Thomas, tired and aching from his journey, bowed to each in turn, making a mental note of their features, for the Buckridges had three girls – and he had no desire, in the days ahead, to get one of their names wrong.

With Lady Katherine – an elegant though painfully thin woman with prematurely grey hair – there could hardly be any mistake. Her face was lined, her mouth drawn down at the corners, though Thomas guessed she was still less than forty years old. She nodded to him in an uninterested manner. The doings of falconers, he sensed, ranked somewhat low on her list of concerns.

Then came the daughters: Margaret, the youngest, a pretty, lively child in a plain old-fashioned hood; Emma, the one in the blue gown, rather too knowing for one of fourteen or fifteen years; and finally Jane, the eldest at perhaps eighteen years, who was not merely pretty – she was quite simply beautiful. This, Thomas guessed, was what the girl's mother had once looked like, before child-bearing, financial strain and the cares of running such a household had taken their toll. Every inch the chaste and dutiful daughter, Jane smiled modestly at him, then lowered her blue eyes at once and gazed down at the table.

There was another at the table: a young man in a dusty-pink doublet, with delicate features and a thin, neatly trimmed beard. Then he remembered: Sir Giles's ward – his pupil.

'Master Lambert!' Sir Giles announced. 'Behold your tutor!'

Thomas met the young man's soft brown eyes, reading

14

neither ill will nor friendliness in his gaze – rather, boredom. Gervase Lambert, he saw, was being pushed into learning the art of falconry, perhaps in the hope that it would make a hawking man of him – which, Thomas feared, was something he would never be. As if to confirm his impression, Margaret Buckridge called out suddenly: 'Now see father, how we have all grown serious again! Cannot Gervase play for us?'

There were murmurs of agreement, and Lady Katherine spoke quietly into her husband's ear. Clearly used to being overruled, Sir Giles gave a nod then turned back towards Thomas.

'We will speak tomorrow, falconer,' he called. 'The cook will give you a supper, and no doubt someone will show you where you may lodge.'

He gestured vaguely, and Thomas, highly relieved to be dismissed, made his bow and retreated at once to the far door. As he went out, he glanced back to see Gervase Lambert seating himself on a stool some distance from the table. In his hands was an instrument of some kind. As Thomas gained the stone-flagged passage outside, the strains of a lute, played skilfully enough, rose to fill the Great Chamber, which, he realized suddenly, had been quite empty of attendants.

He found them in the kitchen, as disgruntled a bunch of house servants as he had met anywhere.

Nan was not among them, nor was Judd Chalkhill. Their domain was not the Great House but the outbuildings. As he stepped into the wide room, warm from the dying fire where the remains of a roasted sheep still hung, he looked about at the faces that turned towards him, and met a wall of blank stares.

Finally a balding man with strands of blond hair about his cheeks roused himself from a joined stool in the chimney corner and announced himself as the usher, Richard Hawkes.

'There's a pottage of pease and barley for you, and a mug of small beer,' he said with a jerk of his head. 'That's more than some have had this night.'

Thomas raised an eyebrow. 'Will you not have the left-overs, when the company leaves the Chamber?' he enquired.

Hawkes, who clearly disliked Thomas's tone, frowned. But a big man in a dirty apron, who had been leaning over a cluttered table in the middle of the room, gave a loud snort. 'That we will, such as they are – but they must serve for tomorrow's breakfast and dinner too.' His voice rose. 'And I'm to make panniers for the harvesters in the fields, and find enough flour to bake pies, and put out scraps for the dogs, and—'

'Spare us your whining, Master Clyffe!' a reedy voice spoke up from the far wall. Thomas saw an elderly man in a good but old-fashioned suit of dark blue, watching him steadily. After a moment the man got up from his bench and came forward, dragging one leg in a clumsy fashion. Indeed, the entire left side of his body seemed out of harmony with the right, for the arm too hung limply at his side.

'I'm Redmund Oakes, butler to Sir Giles,' he said. 'And you are the falconer.'

Thomas nodded and gave his name. Seeking for some way to ease the tension, he thought of Judd Chalkhill's words, and added: 'Mayhap I can bring in some game to help fill the pot, Master Oakes. Partridges, pheasants, snipe, perhaps . . .'

There was a stirring in the room. Clyffe, the cook, frowned at Thomas but there was a gleam in his eye.

'Could you bring down a few quail?'

Thomas shrugged. 'If there are any about.'

Hawkes spoke up from his corner. 'A great bustard would feed us all for a day or two.' He was smiling, a very thin smile. Thomas saw the malice in his eyes, and found himself on the alert.

'I haven't seen one of those for a good while,' he answered in a conversational tone. 'Mayhap they're more common hereabouts . . .'

'You may find them, if you venture out on to the Plain,' Hawkes told him. 'Though they run fast. Can you handle a crossbow, falconer?'

Thomas shook his head and looked away.

But Clyffe, he sensed, was warming to him. 'You're to teach Sir Giles's ward how to fly a falcon – is't not so?' he asked. Before Thomas could reply, he went on: 'I've heard

16

how two goodly hawks may act as one, and so bring down a bird far bigger than themselves – even a bustard! What say you to that?'

Thomas blinked. The great bustard, the biggest bird in England . . . rare now, but still found on the Downlands . . . Bigger than the turkeys of the Americas he'd heard about; a bird with a six-foot wingspan that could weigh more than thirty pounds. Did the fellow really think it was fair game for falconing?

He shook his head. 'I'll see what I can do.'

Clyffe nodded in a deliberate sort of way, picked up a mug from the table, drained it in one, then gave a loud belch. The other men looked away. Only then did Thomas realize that the cook was drunk.

Redmund Oakes had been observing Thomas as if to get the measure of his man. Now he addressed him in a kinder tone than before. 'You're weary from your journey,' he said. 'Take your supper, then I'll find a servingman – we still had a few of them somewhere, last time I counted – to show you where you are to sleep.'

Thomas favoured the elderly butler with a grateful smile. And though he already knew the way back to the stables and the groom's empty loft, he kept silent and nodded his thanks.

'Tomorrow, then.'

From the chimney corner, Hawkes watched him without blinking.

17

Two

Thomas woke at dawn, roused himself from his straw pallet in the bare stable loft and, as was his custom, went out at once to exercise the falcon. The ramage hawk would have to wait.

It was a fair morning with the promise of another warm day. As he left the outer park of Chilbourne and climbed the gentle slopes above the river Bourne – a shallow chalk stream fringed with gentian and yellow wort – the sweet air of the Downs filled his lungs. Rabbits scampered away, while larks and plovers called to each other above his head. Tamora turned under her hood.

'Soon enough, my lady,' he said, and stroked her long wing feathers. The bird responded by a twitch of her head.

There was not a tree in sight. Ahead of him fields of hay and corn stretched into the distance, before giving on to the open Plain where he could make out tiny dots that he knew were grazing sheep. The hay fields, mostly cut down to stubble now, lay in long strips, divided by no more than a line of chalk here and there. Most of the crop, he guessed, was held by the village folk, but some no doubt belonged to Sir Giles, or to Everley Manor. He followed a narrow path westwards, still climbing. Ahead and to his right, the roofs of East Everley village appeared, caught in the first rays of the rising sun. No doubt the harvesters would soon be moving out. He loosed the thongs and slipped Tamora's hood from her head. As he did so, a movement caught his eye some distance away, amid a field of uncut hay. Tamora, of course, saw it too, and tensed on his gauntlet.

'Easy,' he murmured, keeping a firm hold of the leash, looped between his second and third fingers. He stared. A thin haze lay above the hay crop, diffusing the early-morning light. Then his eyes narrowed, for there could be no mistake: someone was moving through the hay field parallel to the path, bending low, trying to keep out of sight.

Thomas took a few paces forward until he was barely a dozen yards from the mysterious figure, then halted and called out cheerfully: 'Good morning! I hope I did not startle you?'

There was a short silence, then a man in a rough brown jerkin raised himself slowly from the hay and stood up, looking decidedly sheepish.

'Morning to you,' he called back after a pause. He had something in his hand, which he seemed to be trying to conceal. Thomas heard it drop softly into the hay at his feet.

'You're early for the harvesting,' Thomas said, feeling inclined to smile. 'Where are all the others?'

The man shrugged and looked away. Then, as if tired of the game, he walked through the hay until he stood on the path before Thomas. He was a man of the outdoors, tanned and fit-looking, with a reddish-brown beard and sun-bleached hair. And now Thomas saw the look in his eye – one of mingled defiance and amusement.

'A fine bird,' the man said with a nod towards the falcon. Thomas nodded, meeting the other's eye. 'You'll forgive my fancy, only I thought you had a boundary marker in your hands, back there in the hay crop.'

The man stared back without expression. 'Did you so?'

'I did.' Thomas nodded. 'I seem to recall such a thing happened on the West Berkshire Downs, where I come from. A fellow was caught moving the boundary posts by night. On the Lammas strips, that is – the tenth of the crop due to his master. If you move the markers a few inches at a time no one notices, do they? Only the outcome was, his master got a deal less than the portion that was his by right.'

The man still returned his stare. Then he gave a shrug. 'Mayhap his master had less need of the crop than the villagers who broke their backs sowing and reaping it for him. Who gave up their time to work the fields in return for holding their own bit of poor land, for a man who lies abed all morning, before rousing himself to ride out and watch them at work.'

Thomas said nothing. After a moment, the other added: 'But then, falconers ride along with the gentry and their ladies, and share their discourse, and enjoy their favours. They have small need to bend their backs in toil. Is't not so?'

Thomas opened his mouth to reply, but at that moment there was a sudden whirring of wings, and from little more than twenty feet away, a partridge that had been cowering in the stubble beside the path suddenly took flight. At once Thomas loosed the jesses from the leash, raised his arm quickly and watched as the mighty Tamora spread her wings and soared, following the flight of her quarry. In seconds she had overtaken it and was hovering above the luckless bird, which flew this way and that before dropping to the ground in a futile attempt at concealment. Tamora, the tinkling of her bells audible even at this distance, dropped upon the partridge like a stone, then rose, holding the limp bird in her talons. Then she flew back to Thomas, dropped the catch at his feet, settled squarely upon his outstretched arm and folded her wings. The whole business had lasted little more than a minute.

'One for the supper table,' Thomas said quietly as he picked up the bird. He glanced at the blond man, who was staring at the hawk. 'I guess even falconers have their uses.'

To his surprise, the man grinned. 'Mayhap they do.' He came forward and stretched out his hand. 'Edward Birch, cottager of East Everley.'

Thomas stowed the partridge in the pouch of his belt and took the man's hand – and at once regretted it. For the other's fingers closed about his own in a grip of steel, and held fast, tightening by slow degrees. He faced Edward Birch, trying to appear unperturbed for the falcon's sake. Tamora shifted slightly on his gauntlet.

'If you wish to fight me, at least let me release the bird,' he said between his teeth.

Birch's smile widened, but his grip tightened even further. 'Why would I want to fight you, falconer?' he enquired innocently. 'I won the wrestling bout between East and West Everley, last Harvest Home. You think you could match me?'

'Then what is it you want from me?' Thomas asked, trying to ignore the pain in his hand, which worsened by the instant.

Birch seemed to consider. 'I would venture I want you to forget you saw me in the fields this morning.'

But the falcon, her senses highly tuned in the sharp morning air, had felt the tension in Thomas's arm through the gauntlet. Sharply she turned her head and half raised a talon.

Birch was wary. His glance strayed from the falconer to his bird, and Thomas saw his chance. Shifting his left arm slightly as if about to release the falcon, he threw his right foot out, hooked it behind Birch's leg and thrust him backwards with all his strength. With a look of surprise, Birch let go of Thomas's hand and toppled to the ground, sprawling on his backside. A faint wisp of chalk dust rose from the path.

Thomas gazed down at him, breathing deeply. 'My trouble is, I have too good a memory,' he said. He glanced at his throbbing right hand, which was bright red, and worked the fingers, wincing at their soreness.

Birch regarded him from the sitting position, then slowly got to his feet, dusting off his breeches. 'One hitch to you,' he muttered.

Thomas felt for the small dagger at his belt. 'You guessed aright that I'm no wrestler,' he said. 'You come at me, I'll spoil your hand.'

But Birch showed no sign of resuming the offensive. 'Nay, master falconer,' he said, with a half-smile. 'I see you're no slouch either. I ask pardon for tweaking your fingers.'

Thomas eyed him warily. 'No bones broken,' he allowed.

Birch turned as if to go, then hesitated. 'You reason well. The Lammas strips along the edge of this field, and the next, and still others hereabouts, belong to Sir Giles Buckridge. A man who couldn't find the points to unlace his own breeches – who's ruined more good land than anyone I know with his foolish schemes . . .' He broke off, as if feeling he was wasting his time. 'But you do what you must. I will not deny what I did.'

21

Thomas gazed back at Birch and saw the plain courage in his face. One who would not plead for mercy, but stand his ground and take the consequences.

'I'm a stranger here,' he said after a moment. 'Mayhap I don't know the fields so well as those that work them.'

Birch's eyes narrowed, but he remained silent.

'And I have work of my own to do,' Thomas added. 'I'd best be about it.'

He took a step along the path towards the open Downs beyond the fields. The other stood aside to let him pass. But he had barely taken a dozen paces before Birch called after him.

'If you come to East Everley of an evening, take a bite with me and mine, and I'll tell ye more tales of Chilbourne,' he shouted. 'Last cottage in the village, nearest the inn.'

Thomas gave a nod, which might have meant acceptance of the invitation, or merely consideration of it. Turning back, he strode uphill as the sun's warm rays broke across his shoulders.

It was past dinnertime before he received his first instructions, with little enthusiasm: he was to take Gervase Lambert out to begin his falconry lessons.

He stood in the long gallery that stretched along the entire south front of the Great House. Dusty portraits of long-dead members of the Buckridge family hung from the walls. There was little furniture, and only stale rushes on the floor. Neglect seemed to permeate every part of Chilbourne Manor.

Sir Giles was looking somewhat harassed. 'I know 'tis no easy task to lay upon you, falconer,' he mumbled, walking to and fro before the traceried windows. Thomas's gaze wandered outside to the figure of Nan Greenwood, who was spreading bed sheets on the grass to dry.

'I have strived to turn the lad into a gentleman. How else will he be fit to marry well – I mean here in Wiltshire, where a man with no appetite for the chase is less than worthless?' He cleared his throat. 'God's heart and thighs, I despair at times . . . It's all anyone can do to tear him away from his books.'

22

Thomas managed a sympathetic smile. 'I will do my best, sir. But I hold little hope of progress if Master Gervase has no liking for the sport . . .'

Sir Giles turned upon him with a pained expression. 'Would that you and I might change places, falconer. I would like nothing more than to spend my days tending hawks, rather than play shepherd to a flock of daughters who flout my authority at every turn . . .' He hesitated, like one who wishes to confide in another yet is unsure of his ground. 'A man with no sons, who has been dogged by . . . a degree of ill luck, may find himself hard-pressed to provide dowries,' he said, staring absently at the nearest portrait. 'Which is why my eldest daughter, Jane, is betrothed to a man many years older than she . . .' He paused, embarrassed by his own words, then went on more briskly. 'My ward, Gervase, is an orphan, the son of one of my dearest friends, who died when the boy was scarce old enough to walk. I had in mind to make him the son I never had . . . to raise him a gentleman fit to marry into one of the great Downland families – the Hungerfords, the Hunts or the Danvers. He is handsome enough, is he not? With the right accomplishments – and I mean not merely the ability to sing and play that blasted lute . . .' Sir Giles broke off, a look of irritation on his features. Thomas turned to see Gervase Lambert entering by the door at the far end of the gallery.

The young man was wearing a saffron-coloured doublet trimmed with blue and green, yellow-striped breeches and silver-pointed shoes. Thomas swallowed, and made his brief bow.

Sir Giles stared, a look of helplessness on his face. 'Is that what you propose to wear for hawking?'

Gervase looked the very picture of innocence. 'Does my suit displease you, sir? Then I shall change it at once.'

Sir Giles made no reply, but glanced towards Thomas for assistance. It was his part, Thomas saw, to take the reins. 'No matter, Sir Giles,' he said in as reassuring a tone as he could muster. 'Today's lesson will not take us far from the house, nor will it spoil Master Lambert's suit 'Tis but a matter of putting on the gauntlet.'

Sir Giles nodded with some relief. 'Then I will place the

pupil in your capable hands.' As he turned to go, he added: 'Allow him no special treatment. I hope to see some progress in a week's time.'

Thomas bowed as Sir Giles strode out of the gallery. Gervase bowed too, and as he did so, Thomas caught a look in the young man's eye that unsettled him – a look of some amusement. Not the ideal pupil, he thought. He straightened up and raised an eyebrow at his charge, who returned his gaze unflinchingly.

'Well, falconer,' he said. 'Shall we take a turn outdoors?'

Thomas nodded, and led the way.

A quarter of an hour later they walked from the falcons' mews, uphill towards open ground. Thomas carried Tamora, hooded on his fist. Gervase wore the gauntlet Thomas had given him over the yellow sleeve of his doublet.

As they walked, Thomas talked a little about the sport. He recounted the old adage: *a tercel gentle for a prince; a falcon for a duke or an earl; a bastard hawk for a baron, a saker for a knight; a merlin for a lady, a hobby for a young man* . . . Then, turning to his charge, he found this particular young man's eyes fixed upon him. 'What bird for an impostor?' he enquired. When Thomas made no reply, he added: 'Come, Master Finbow, you are no man's fool. You know I have no desire for this.'

Thomas halted and faced the other squarely. 'Yet I am ordered to instruct you, sir. What else can I do?'

Gervase shrugged. 'We can make a show of it, if you must. Sir Giles will not blame you if he sees little in the way of progress, for he expects little. Of me, that is.'

Thomas frowned. 'Then why not speak plainly with him? Why trouble us both with this . . .'

'Comedy?' Gervase finished the sentence for him. 'Let's say that I would prefer to humour him.' He paused, then gave Thomas a smile – considerably warmer than before. 'You will understand more, the longer you spend at Chilbourne,' he said. 'Sir Giles will soon forget to ask how our lessons go forth. He has too many other matters preying on his mind.'

24

Thomas considered this. Then, feeling Tamora twitch on the gauntlet, he drew off her hood. Watched by Gervase, he loosed the jesses, raised his arm and allowed her to take flight. In a very short time she had mounted to a great height, found the warm air currents and floated, little more than a speck far above their heads.

After a moment, he turned back to Gervase. He had the feeling the young man wanted to unburden himself in some way. Having watched the falcon for a moment, he looked Thomas in the eye.

'Tell me, falconer. Has our sovereign Queen, God bless her, levied any forced loans upon your master, Sir Robert?'

Thomas blinked. 'It's not my place to speak of such matters, sir,' he began, but Gervase waved a hand in a gesture of impatience.

'Come, 'tis no secret,' he said. 'The Queen levied crippling loans upon her nobler subjects two years back, to raise money for the war against the Spanish. Now, having failed to repay the last loans, she levies more. This time to help the French, I hear. Whatever the cause, there are some who have been left in debt, if not in stark penury.' He nodded towards the Great House, which lay peacefully on the sward, bathed in a warm afternoon haze. 'One with a sharp eye like yours must have noticed the poor straits we are come to at Chilbourne.'

After a moment, Thomas nodded. 'It would explain why the servants are so few.'

'And so sullen,' Gervase added. He turned sharply towards Thomas. 'Come, falconer. Speak plainly with me, and I will do all I can to make your stay here bearable.'

Thomas stared, but could detect no ill will in the other man's demeanour. 'What is it you desire of me, sir?' he asked.

'Your friendship,' Gervase answered. 'You have no heart for your task – I understand that. Hence, let us make a show of going forth to our lessons; once out of sight of the house, you may go where you will – and I may go where I will. And when you leave here, you'll have a couple of angels for your trouble. Is that not a fair bargain?'

Thomas was silent, liking the bargain not at all. 'Would you have me lie to Sir Giles?' he asked finally. 'A friend of my master's – the man who is like a father to you?'

Gervase shook his head vehemently. 'No! I love Sir Giles, as if he were truly my father. Yet . . .' he dropped his gaze. 'There are others to consider.' He raised his eyes again. 'If I told you that in time the matter will become clear, and you will see why I ask this of you, would that be enough?'

Thomas returned the young man's gaze. 'No, sir, I don't believe it would.'

But now, having expected Gervase to display irritation, he was surprised when the other said, 'Very well. You are an honest man, and as such you deserve plain dealing.' He gestured uphill. 'Shall we walk a little?'

Thomas nodded, and with one eye on Tamora hanging in the warm, still air, he and Gervase walked up the gentle valley slope and topped a low hill. East Everley was away to their right. Ahead, the fields stretched to the Plain beyond, but they were now filled with activity. The harvest was in full spate: figures toiled at the hay crop, bodies swinging from side to side in the practised motion of harvesters everywhere. A hundred yards away a cart drawn by a plodding workhorse halted and figures gathered round, pitching hay into its bed.

Thomas recalled, with some unease, his meeting that morning with the wily Edward Birch. But now Gervase spoke, and drove the matter from his mind.

'This family,' he said, 'is sinking like a holed vessel. Sir Giles struggles to keep it afloat, yet I fear he has not the strength, nor the wit, to save it. He is laughed at by men of his station. He dare not go to Court, for fear he would be treated like a buffoon. Though there are others in as dire need as he, most have sons to marry off, bringing dowried girls into the family. Sir Giles has only daughters. Hence . . .' The young man hesitated.

Thomas, recalling his conversation with Sir Giles, added his own words. 'Hence, the betrothal of Lady Jane to an older man . . .'

Gervase gave a curt nod. 'More than forty years older. Stephen Ridley, already twice a widower. A man of great wealth, from many sources – wool-dealing, dyeing, lead mines in the Midlands, a fleet of merchant ships that ply between Bristol and the East . . .' He broke off, but Thomas nodded in reply.

'Great wealth, but no wife.'

'Indeed. And in sore need of a son and heir. Especially one with the noble ancestry that he lacks himself.'

Thomas frowned. It was a common enough arrangement, yet one he had never been able to like.

'My dear sister,' Gervase continued, gazing into the distance, 'for I deem her, and Emma and Margaret my sisters, accepts the match. For she is a dutiful daughter, who would die rather than displease her father. Yet I know how unhappy she is – as are all those at Chilbourne who care for her. And I have sworn to do all I can to help her.'

Thomas looked hard at him. 'What can you do?'

Gervase took a breath. 'I am writing a book of melodies,' he said.

Thomas blinked.

'A book of sweet airs,' Gervase continued, 'for young ladies of accomplishment to play upon the virginals or the lute. It is almost completed. When it is done, I shall beg leave to present it at Court, to the Queen herself. I venture to hope she will receive it well, and value its merits. And reward me, perhaps with a pension – even a royal appointment.'

Thomas strove to keep expression from his face. 'But . . . how might that help your sister?'

Gervase gazed at him with an air of triumph. 'Do you not see? I shall be famous – celebrated. I shall be able to obtain credit and help Sir Giles pay his debts – as well as persuading Her Majesty to repay him what he is owed. Hence he will not need Ridley's money, but will be able to provide Jane with a dowry of her own . . .' He broke off, as if suddenly aware that he was confiding too much to a falconer – let alone one that he scarcely knew. 'See now, Thomas,' he said haltingly. 'I fear I have spoken too freely.'

'Mayhap you have, Master Gervase,' Thomas replied. He shaded his eyes and stared upwards to where Tamora wheeled in the empty sky. Would that he were home on Lambourn Down, he thought to himself, hunting rabbits for dinner.

'Then I ask pardon,' Gervase said, and took a deep breath. 'It was wrong of me to burden you so. If I come to my lessons when I can, and agree to be ruled by you, will you in turn forget all that I have told you today?'

Thomas allowed himself a small sigh of relief. Keeping a straight face he answered: 'I have forgotten already, sir.'

But he had not, and knew that he would not.

At sunset, only too aware that he could put the matter off no longer, Thomas walked up to the falcons' mews, turning his attention to the ramage hawk.

Tamora, well fed and exercised, sat quietly atop her perch where he had left her after his first, disconcerting session with Gervase. Mercifully, after his earlier revelations, the young man had been as good as his word and proved a docile pupil, listening as Thomas spoke to him of the falconer's art. He had even allowed him to place Tamora on his gauntlet for a short while – hooded, of course. Then they had parted, Thomas to hunt a few birds for the cook, Gervase no doubt to return to his musical compositions.

The night was clear, and no rain was expected, so he knew Tamora could be left safely outdoors. He walked past her through the unmown dry grass, rounded the wall of bent willows, then stopped dead. The ramage hawk was gone.

He swallowed, then stepped forward to examine the bow perch where she had been tethered. There were old chicken bones about it, the remains of her last few meals, as well as pellets of muting – but no feathers that spoke of any kind of struggle. Stooping, he frowned: the leash was still tied to the perch. He lifted the end, and saw the leather jesses were still attached. With a silent curse he moved out from under the low roof then straightened up, staring about.

The bird had been stolen. He gazed at the empty Downs, their receding shapes lost in the fading light, as if he might see her somewhere close by. Apart from small Downland birds twittering softly, and crows flying to lower ground in search of trees to roost in, there was nothing.

He frowned to himself again. Who would want to steal a ramage hawk? Especially one whose very demeanour spoke of the hard work needed to turn her into anything like a hunting bird. The notion came to him with stark clarity: someone had released her. Why else were the leash and jesses left behind? Anyone with even a rudimentary knowledge of falconry would have simply hooded the bird, untied the leash from the perch and taken everything.

With a last, futile glance about him, Thomas turned and walked downhill towards the house. By the time he had reached the kitchen door, he realized that his step had lightened considerably, in spite of whatever disciplinary fate might lie in store for him.

In fact, he found that he was smiling.

Three

A short time later Thomas faced a frowning Sir Giles, who sat at the high table in the dimly lit Great Chamber with the half-cleared remains of supper and a flagon of malmsey before him. This time there were no daughters present, nor was there any sign of Gervase or his lute. Instead, Richard Hawkes and Redmund Oakes sat a short distance down the table, each with a cup and trencher before him. Lady Katherine was at Sir Giles's right hand, and beside her was a dark-haired woman in her mid-twenties, apparently a lady-in-waiting, whom Thomas had not seen before. As his gaze scanned the assembled company, he caught her eye – and received a shock through the lower half of his body; almost as if he had stepped into a cold stream. And though the woman was looking pointedly in another direction, he was left in no doubt as to what it meant.

Cap in hand, and feeling something of a charlatan, Thomas spoke in grave tones of his discovery. When he had finished, he found all eyes upon him save those of the dark-haired woman. *Well*, he thought, *she has no need. She has begun the dance, and my part is but to follow like a ram to the tup*.

Mentally he shook himself, for Sir Giles was speaking.

'Do you understand the import of your words, falconer?' he muttered, more in puzzlement than in anger. 'You've scarce set foot in my house, and you've lost a bird already!'

Gently, Thomas voiced his suspicions. There was a ripple of surprise round the table. Then Richard Hawkes, whom he had not seen all day, spoke in a hard voice. 'No one here would do such a thing,' he said. 'Master Finbow seeks to deflect the blame on to others.'

Thomas kept his eyes on Sir Giles, who winced as if the matter were becoming more distasteful by the minute.

'I can make my own deductions, Master usher,' he said in a tone more defensive than authoritative. 'Let us consider the matter carefully before we fall to accusations.'

There was a short silence, whereupon Thomas made bold enough to explain about the leash and the jesses. A half-wild bird would not have allowed itself to be released, then tied again in such a manner, he reasoned. There were muted reactions from the company before Redmund Oakes spoke up in his thin voice.

'The falconer speaks truly, Sir Giles. I do not believe we harbour a thief at Chilbourne – not since the groom fled.'

Sir Giles looked as if he did not wish to dwell on that particular indignity, whereupon the butler added: 'If you so wish, you might question the household . . .'

'No.'

Thomas glanced from Oakes to the still figure of Lady Katherine, realizing that it was the first time he had heard her speak.

'Let there be no such investigation, sir,' she said in a low voice, addressing her husband directly. 'At least for the present. Have we not enough to think on with our guest arriving tomorrow?'

Sir Giles looked like a man forced to recall something he had managed to overlook. 'That's true enough,' he answered, then looked at Thomas. 'We will have need of your services tomorrow, falconer. My daughter's betrothed comes to visit, and will expect a day's sport.'

Thomas nodded, relieved at the turn of events. 'I will not disappoint him, Sir Giles.'

'Indeed you will not.' It was Hawkes, making no attempt to mask his hostility. 'Your part is to serve, and speak when given leave to do so.'

Keeping his feelings in check, Thomas made a slight bow that had only a hint of irony about it. Was it his fancy, or did he detect a trace of amusement just then in the eye of Redmund Oakes?

But it was Lady Katherine's eyes that rested upon him,

31

before looking away and addressing her husband. 'It grows late. Shall we not leave this for another time? I would speak with our daughter about tomorrow.'

Sir Giles nodded, somewhat absent-mindedly, and raised his cup to his lips. Then he gestured to Thomas to indicate that the interview was at an end. 'Be ready in the morning, falconer. You may understand that I am giving you a chance to redeem yourself.'

Thomas bowed and turned to walk from the Chamber. Only when he was outside the door did the murmur of voices commence. But the last thing he was aware of was the briefest of glances from Lady Katherine's lady-in-waiting, who seemed intent on leaving no possible doubt in his mind as to what she desired of him – as if it wasn't plain enough already.

Relieved to be outdoors, he drank deeply of the sweet night air before going to his pallet in the stable.

He awoke with a start, breaking a dream of towering falcons, mockingly dancing above his head yet refusing to come to the gauntlet. To his chagrin he found that he had his arm up, as if he were truly at his work. With a yawn, he raised himself on an elbow. Stars were still visible through the holes in the thatch. Then he started, knowing at once what had woken him. From the stable beneath came a muffled sound.

Silently he thrust aside the coverlet, stood up and moved barefoot across the rough boards towards the ladder-head in the corner. Then he sat down a few feet away and waited. He was not mistaken: footfalls, light and hesitant, ascended the ladder. Finally a head appeared at floor level, barely visible in the windowless room.

The head turned, reflecting starlight off a patch of thick blonde hair. Thomas, who had been holding his breath, allowed himself a sigh of . . . What? Disappointment? Had his dreams included some fancy of a dark-haired lady-in-waiting stealing softly to his bed? Berating himself for the notion, he spoke aloud. 'What do you want, Nan?'

Nan Greenwood gave a yelp, and nearly lost her grip on the ladder. Her head snapped round in his direction. 'Lord Jesu, you gave me a frit! What you playing at, maister?'

Thomas roused himself, came forward and offered his hand. Nan took it, scrambled up the last couple of rungs, and allowed Thomas to heave her up on to the floor. There she sat, a surprisingly bulky figure in a pale smock, peering at him through the gloom.

'Isn't it me should ask what you're playing at?' he enquired. Then he sensed rather than saw that Nan was smiling.

'Thought you might want a little company,' she said in a softer tone.

Thomas said nothing.

'Chilbourne maids got to earn a crust any way they can,' Nan added. In the dark he saw her put a hand to her neck and heard the faint sound of a lace being drawn. 'What shall we say – fourpence?'

Thomas sighed, and smiled ruefully at his own presumptions. It was business, of course. Why should it be otherwise? He yawned, then exhaled deeply.

'Keep your shift on, Nan,' he said. 'I'm weary, and must be up at dawn.'

But Nan shuffled towards him across the boards, kneeling so that her breath was on his face. It smelled faintly of ripe fruit. 'So must I, falconer,' she murmured, and put out a hand to touch his cheek. 'So let us fall to while we may. You'll sleep sound as a blind mole after I'm done with ye.'

Thomas took her hand. 'I doubt it not,' he smiled. 'But . . .'

Nan stiffened. 'I'm not good enough for ye, be it so?'

'Nay,' Thomas said gently, and squeezed her hand. 'You are fair – fit for the Lord Sheriff himself . . .'

Nan caught her breath, then gave a snort of laughter. 'By heaven, you're a flattering cove!' She paused, then added: 'I'd guess you was expecting it for free. Your sort always does!'

'I do not,' Thomas countered, and surprised himself by adding, 'Nor do I lie with whores in stables.'

Nan drew in her breath. 'Whore! You runagate knave!' She withdrew her hand and raised it, but Thomas caught it and held it.

'I ask pardon,' he said. 'Another night, mayhap . . .' He

33

trailed off, unsure of his own emotions, and released her hand.

Nan peered at him though the gloom. 'You are in love, then? I might have guessed as much.'

Thomas shook his head. 'Nay . . .' He sought for some suitable words, but none would come. These days, a widower now for seven years, he tended to put thoughts of love – and marriage, too – aside. A fifteen-year-old daughter and his work were enough for any man – were they not?

Nan was silent for a moment. Then to his surprise she leaned forward and planted a kiss on his mouth. 'No matter, my duck. I have customers enough . . . Some that would surprise you, I venture.' She smiled, sensing his eyes upon her in the dark. 'Yon gentleman servants aren't too picky when they get sight of my thighs.'

'I doubt it not,' Thomas replied, feeling a deal more relaxed.

'There's talk about you, did you know?' Nan told him. 'Strangers are few here. Come to that, servants are few enough, compared to how it was.'

'I heard as much,' Thomas told her. Seizing the opportunity, he remarked: 'I seem to have ruffled Master Hawkes' feathers already.'

Nan sniffed, and sat down on her haunches. 'He's a bitter fellow, everyone knows it.' She yawned suddenly. 'The one you should watch is Lady Jane's betrothed. Master Ridley.'

Thomas grew alert. 'Why? Is he . . .?'

Nan put her fingertips to his mouth. 'He's many things, my handsome, but I guess you'll find out tomorrow.' She yawned again, then arched her back in a luxurious stretch. 'You need not fear to oversleep, for he has a long ride to reach here – all the way from Marlborough. He's a townsman, through and through.'

She got herself up on her knees. 'I'd best leave you to your bachelor's couch,' she said with a trace of pique. Then she crawled to the ladder-head, manoeuvred her ample haunches into position and placed a foot on the top rung. As she climbed down she added, in a different tone: 'You're a fool to yourself, maister. For I'd fain have let you tumble me for free this night, did ye not know that?'

Thomas sat in the dark and watched her disappear through the floor.

Early in the morning, after a bowl of porridge and a mug of well-watered ale in the kitchen, he went out to exercise Tamora and make ready for a day's hawking. The only man he had seen was Redmund Oakes, who told him that Master Ridley would be accompanied by his own falconer with a brace of birds. Sir Giles would hunt with Tamora.

'Little for me to do, then,' Thomas murmured, standing in the kitchen yard as the sun poked over the rooftops.

The butler had swivelled his crippled frame towards Thomas, and fixed him with a pair of watery blue eyes. 'I would not wager on that, Master Finbow,' he said, and turned away.

Now he stood on Everley Down and watched the harvesters already toiling at the last of the hay crop. Today, he recalled, was Saturday, the seventh day of August. By Lammas Day – the twelfth – the hay would be in and most of the corn harvest too. After that date the fields would be turned over to common pasture, through the winter until next seedtime, as had been the practice since anyone could remember. No doubt folk would celebrate Harvest Home here, he mused, as they did back in Berkshire. Then the village would be hung with green boughs, and there would be dancing and drinking . . . The notion cheered Thomas a little. So far he had found small welcome – at Chilbourne Manor, at least.

He glanced at the sun and realized he should be getting back; the company would be here soon. And though it was not his custom to call a falcon down – as astringers often did their goshawks and sparrowhawks – he put fingers to mouth and gave a piercing whistle. Tamora wheeled and began to drift downwards in the warm air. A minute later she settled on his gauntlet and allowed herself to be hooded.

Then, as Thomas turned to take the path, a large bird flew suddenly into his field of vision from behind. He froze, squinting in the bright sunlight, as the bird gained height rapidly and soared away, beyond the distant tower of Everley Church. Soon it was but a speck, and then it was lost to sight.

Thomas's heart was beating as if he had been running. It was a wild falcon, certainly . . . He gritted his teeth, settled Tamora against his body and began the trudge downhill towards Chilbourne. There were other passage hawks on the Plain, he told himself – and other ramage hawks . . .

But he knew that the notion was fixed in his mind, and would remain there until such time as he took his leave of this place. The bird released from the mews was roaming just beyond his reach, and mocking him still.

Half an hour later he stood respectfully with a little group of attendants near the house while the hawking party mounted and made ready.

Judd Chalkhill, in an old green jerkin that had clearly once belonged to a real falconer and was far too tight for him, was to assist for the day. So was a gangling kitchen lad, ill at ease in borrowed clothes and clearly unsure of his duties. The last man, who had given Thomas his name and said not a word more, was Stephen Ridley's falconer, John Steer.

Steer was a surprise. Knowing of Ridley's wealth, Thomas had expected someone impressive. But this man, who stood beside Thomas and Tamora with a fine hooded peregrine on his own arm, was barely five feet tall and thin as a rake, with a sparse beard and wisps of black hair sticking out from beneath his cap. He had a nervous air about him, Thomas thought – a man constantly on watch.

The party was not quite what Thomas had expected, though he was relieved to learn that Master Gervase had pleaded a stomach ache, and would not ride today. Lady Jane would, however. To Thomas's surprise she bore a fine lanner falcon on her embroidered gauntlet. Then he guessed that it was a gift from her betrothed, Master Stephen Ridley.

Ridley, dressed in a fine hunting suit and tooled leather boots, stood some distance away beside a beautiful Neapolitan horse, talking with a somewhat subdued Lady Katherine. Thomas tried to put aside the judgements he had already

36

begun to make about a man he did not know. Yet it was difficult not to feel repelled by the thought that this stooped, white-haired, unsmiling widower of at least sixty years was the future husband of Lady Jane Buckridge.

The ladies, in fact, made up the bulk of the party. Seated on a dappled-grey mare beside Jane, Lady Katherine and her middle daughter Emma, all mounted on brown jennets, was the dark-haired woman who had already occupied Thomas's thoughts more than he cared to admit.

'Is that Lady Katherine's waiting-woman?' he asked Judd Chalkhill in a casual tone.

The slaughterman nodded. 'Mistress Eliza Willett.' He sniffed loudly, then caught Thomas's eye and leered. 'Best put aside any notion of getting your paws on that one. Though the notion's kept my hand busy on many a lonely night.'

Thomas gave him a wry look and turned his attention to Sir Giles and Ridley, who were now mounting their horses. Sir Giles, peering above the heads of the ladies, caught his eye and beckoned him forward.

Thomas approached and, as Sir Giles reached down, placed Tamora on his gauntlet. The knight, affecting an expansive mood this morning, smiled admiringly at the falcon, straightened up in the saddle and turned towards Ridley.

'How do you like my bird, friend Stephen?'

Ridley, who was signalling Steer to bring up his own falcon, paused, then laughed suddenly – a cracked, humourless laugh that raised the hackles on Thomas's neck in an instant.

'Yours, Sir Giles? Away with your theatrics! All of Wiltshire knows your falconers fled Chilbourne weeks ago, taking their birds with them. What sentimental old friend have you called upon now to help you save face?'

Thomas, standing silently beside Sir Giles, was moved to pity, for he saw the look of mingled shame and helplessness that passed across the knight's features. Glancing towards Ridley, he saw the stark cruelty in the man's eye – then realized it was fixed upon him.

'Whom do you serve, falconer?' Ridley asked sharply. 'Come, out with it!'

'Sir Robert Vicary, sir,' Thomas answered in a neutral tone.

Ridley grunted. 'Berkshire man, isn't it?'

'The manor of Petbury, sir.'

'Aye. And that's his bird.' Ridley was pointing at Tamora with a gloved hand. When Thomas did not respond, he looked him up and down briefly and added: 'You look like you know your craft. See that we have a fine day's sport, and there's a crown for you at the end of it.'

Before Thomas could react, Ridley gave a jerk of his head and glared down at the willowy figure of Steer, who was standing patiently beside his stirrup, holding his falcon. 'Up!' he snapped.

Steer raised the bird, but Ridley did not offer his gauntlet. Aware that a hush had fallen, he seemed bent on humiliating his servant before the entire company.

'Higher, you dolt!'

Steer raised the falcon higher, until he was almost standing on tiptoe. All eyes were now fixed upon the ugly little scene. Sir Giles, struggling to redeem both himself and the situation, cleared his throat loudly and called: 'Come, Master Stephen, the morning will be over before we have even flown a bird!'

Ridley half turned and threw another of his parchment-thin smiles at his host. 'Fear not, sir. There'll be a full pot at supper tonight. My Callisto can outmatch any bird in the county.'

And, after what had seemed an age, he lowered his arm and graciously permitted his falconer to place his charge on the fine gauntlet of green leather. Its tassles hung so long, it was all Steer could do to avoid them whipping his face as Ridley raised the falcon aloft for all to see. Touching his spurs to the horse, he walked it towards Jane Buckridge, who sat stock-still in the saddle.

'My bird and yours, working in harmony, shall outshine any in the field, my dear,' he announced. Jane gave a shy smile, and kept her eyes on the reins in her hand.

Thomas glanced around, taking a crumb of comfort from the knowledge that, as far as he could judge, everyone present

38

seemed to feel as he did. Even the kitchen lad was staring dumbly, seemingly in sympathy with Sir Giles, who bore his humiliation in silence. Then he clicked his tongue to his horse and led the way uphill, away from the house. The rest of the party followed – Lady Katherine with Emma and Eliza Willett, Ridley in the rear, riding stirrup to stirrup with Lady Jane.

Thomas rejoined the other men, who followed on foot. Steer came up quietly behind them and was surprised when Judd Chalkhill stopped, put out a meaty hand and clapped the little man on the back.

'By Christ,' growled the slaughterman, 'I wouldn't change places with you for a feather bed with a pair of perfumed trulls in it.'

Steer threw him a quick half-smile, then trotted off after the riders.

It was a long, hot day. The party drifted out on to the Downs and the Plain beyond, further than Thomas had been before. Despite his feelings towards Ridley, he had to admit that the man was not given to idle boasting. His falcon, skilfully handled with support from the nimble Steer, brought down a bagful of game birds within the first hour. Tamora hunted well too, as did the sleek little grey-brown lanner that Jane Buckridge had passed on to her mother after a short time. Thomas paid the matter small mind, noting that though the girl had handled a bird before, no doubt instructed by her father, she had only a passing interest in the sport. But Lady Katherine, with no bird of her own, surprised him with her energy. Taking the falcon on her gauntlet, she spurred her mare forward as if suddenly unleashed, and rode swiftly to join Sir Giles, who was hunting alone some way ahead. As the lanner left the fist and soared to join Tamora in the cloudless sky above, she reined in beside her husband. Together they slowed to a walk, talking quietly. And though they were too far off for anyone to hear, Thomas fancied he saw Sir Giles's shoulders sag as they spoke.

A familiar voice at his elbow startled him. 'Sleep sound in your straw up in the loft, do ye?' Judd Chalkhill asked.

There was a look of amusement on the slaughterman's face. Though he had loosened his clothing as far as decency permitted, he was sweating profusely in the heat. At his waist was a pouch of dead birds.

'I sleep sound wherever I am,' Thomas told him.

'Not what I heard.' Judd grinned.

'I wouldn't pay too much mind to things you hear,' Thomas said, with the growing certainty that he was going to lose this argument.

'Now, Thomas,' Judd said, lowering his voice, 'Nan do spread herself about – everyone knows that. But she ain't nobody's callett. Not poxed, nor ever bore a bastard child, and that's Lord's truth.'

Thomas was watching Ridley some fifty yards away, still keeping close to Lady Jane. Such a man would never give her a moment's peace, he thought. Then as Judd's words sank home, he turned upon him. 'What is it you're trying to say to me?' he asked sharply.

'You heard me plain enough,' Judd muttered. 'If she tried to live by a washerwoman's wage here, she'd starve to death within a year.'

'I can believe that,' Thomas answered. Peering into the man's rough features he saw no ill will . . . Rather, to his surprise, a look of concern, even anxiety.

'Have I offended her?' he asked, dropping all pretence of ignorance. 'Because I would not take her to my bed?'

Judd sniffed, then spat. 'Nay,' he answered after a moment. 'Rather . . . I should thank 'ee.'

Thomas blinked. But, misreading his expression, Judd scowled suddenly. 'You thought I was her bawd? Taking a cut of what she earns on her back?'

Thomas shook his head. 'I had no such notion.'

Judd stared at him, then relaxed. 'It's well then. By Christ, I'm getting twitchy as a hare these days. I been thinking every man's getting his hands on her paps.'

Thomas found a laugh rising from somewhere in his gut. 'Be easy with yourself, knifeman,' he said. 'I've a woman to warm my own bed back home, who's more than enough for any man.' It was true enough, though he seldom confided it to anyone. Nell, the red-haired cook at Petbury – whom his master had hired against all advice, since it had always been a man's place to rule the kitchens of great houses – had been his off-and-on sweetheart for the past year. Though when she touched upon the subject of his making a wife of her, he always had to hurry off to tend his falcons. Such a circumstance could not last much longer, he knew.

Judd's face softened into the familiar leer. 'Pleased to hear that,' he said. ''Twouldn't be a fair match, you and the best wrestler on the Downs, if I had to fight 'ee.'

Thomas frowned. 'That's an odd matter,' he said. 'I met a man only yesterday, told me he was the best wrestler here.'

Judd's head went up like a startled buck. 'Birch!' he spat. 'You been talking to him!'

'That was the name,' Thomas allowed, managing to suppress the smile that threatened to break forth.

'Well you wait, Master Thomas,' Judd said, raising one massive fist and waving it in the air. 'Come Harvest Home there'll be a wrestling match 'tween East and West Everley like there is every year – and then ye'll see who lifts the prize!'

Thomas nodded soberly. 'That will be worth waiting for.'

And so it would, he mused, as Judd, tense about the neck now, glared at him before rotating his huge frame deliberately and stalking away across the dry grass.

So his first day's hawking as Sir Giles's borrowed falconer ended as the party rode homewards in the late-afternoon sun. Most of the day had been spent on the vast, treeless emptiness of the eastern reaches of Salisbury Plain. But on the outward and return journeys they crossed the upper valley of the Little Avon, another chalk stream very like the Bourne, with a string of small farms and villages along its length from Rushall in the north, down to Bulford in the south and still farther, to distant Amesbury. While the party of riders and their weary foot-servants were ascending the eastern slopes of the valley near the hamlet of Haxton, something so unforeseen occurred that it was a long time before anyone even noticed.

41

Sir Giles, looking somewhat tired and drawn, was in the lead. Alongside him, talking amiably, rode his future son-in-law Ridley, a man almost twenty years his senior. Ridley appeared to have adopted a magnanimous manner, as if wishing to seem gracious to a defeated opponent. Thomas, Steer and the other men now had charge of the birds, and plodded along in a weary group a little behind their masters. The ladies followed at a walk, Emma in conversation with Eliza Willett, and Lady Katherine at the rear. Hence, it transpired later, no one quite knew how long it had been since they had sight of Lady Jane Buckridge. Indeed, they had crossed the vast hare warrens south-west of Chilbourne, scattering dozens of the frantic, leaping animals in their path, before anyone chanced to look behind. Then came the discovery. And of all people, it was the keen-eyed little falconer, John Steer, who stopped abruptly, shading his eyes and peering about, before running quickly to Sir Giles.

'Sir! Your eldest daughter . . . I fear she is missing!'

Four

The search began at once.

At first there was confusion, then disbelief, and finally alarm as Sir Giles, Ridley and their servants began back-tracking, on horseback and on foot, in search of Lady Jane. Lady Katherine, after a hurried conference with Sir Giles, rode on to Chilbourne with Emma and her lady-in-waiting. Redmund Oakes would be instructed to call in men from the fields and the surrounding farms to assist in the search.

On Salisbury Plain, a rider who climbs to the summit of even a small hill may see for miles in any direction. So it was that Sir Giles, visibly uneasy now, sat in his saddle on the nearest rise and peered about for some minutes. Then he touched spurs, wheeled his mount and rode swiftly back to the little group of men who stood, out of breath and sweating, awaiting his orders.

'The valley,' he said, pointing in the direction of the Avon, a distant gash of dark green against the brown plain. 'There is the only cover – she must be somewhere along the river!'

Hoof-beats sounded, and Stephen Ridley, red-faced and furious, came galloping up, reining in so sharply that his horse whinnied and snapped its head back.

'By the good Christ!' he shouted. 'There's some mischief here! And I shall discover it, make no mistake!'

Sir Giles, tired and anxious, turned to him. 'What do you mean?'

'You think me a fool, sir?' Ridley threw back, his eyes blazing. 'It's beyond belief that she could have got herself lost here – any halfwit may see that. She has run away!'

The same notion had already occurred to Thomas. From the corner of his eye he saw Judd Chalkhill, rivulets of sweat running down his face and neck, smile grimly to himself as if to voice all their thoughts. *Small wonder, with you for a husband-to-be . . .*

But Sir Giles, to everyone's surprise and no little satisfaction, bristled and glared at Ridley.

'Jane would do no such thing! She is an obedient daughter—'

'She's a sly little filly, and as spirited as any I know, had you the eye to see it!' Ridley countered. 'Mayhap I know her better than you think.' Before Sir Giles could answer, he went on, 'We had not quarrelled, nor had she shown any signs of displeasure all day. I believe she has planned this – chosen her moment well, and seen it through. Now think, Sir Giles, and think hard. Where would she go?'

Larks called from above, while the falcons sat hooded and docile on the wrists of Thomas, Judd and John Steer. Sir Giles opened his mouth, closed it again, then seemed to gather his faculties. Passing a hand across his well-creased brow, he turned aside and looked down at the men on foot.

'I have a notion,' he said at last, to no one in particular.

Ridley glowered impatiently at him. 'Well?'

'Cracked Oak,' Sir Giles muttered, and looked away. Thomas saw the knowing look that passed between Judd Chalkhill and the kitchen lad, and frowned. The name clearly had some import to Chilbourne folk.

Ridley was still staring, awaiting an explanation.

'It's . . . several miles upriver,' Sir Giles told him with a jerk of his head towards the distant Avon valley. He looked down again at the tired falconers and their helpers. 'The servants are exhausted. We must send for horses—'

'What!' Ridley shouted. 'You would spare their legs rather than find my Jane?'

His tone was dangerously close to one of contempt. While the other men shifted uneasily, Sir Giles faced Ridley with surprising calm.

'She is not yet *your* Jane, sir,' he replied, and some felt a small surge of pleasure to hear him say it. 'And mayhap it's you who should start thinking, with less bluster about it.'

44

It was Ridley's turn to open his mouth, fail to find a suitable reply, then close it again. He merely glared.

'The evening draws on,' Sir Giles continued, 'and she has been riding for most of the day. She cannot travel far – nor, I am certain, would she wish to. If she is where I think she is, she will remain there for the night. So, refreshed and remounted, we may ride over later and . . .' He trailed off, finishing somewhat lamely, 'And discover why she has acted in such a precipitate manner. It is most unlike her.'

Ridley hesitated, then glanced towards his falconer, who met his eyes briefly before looking at the ground. At last he spoke, managing a gentler tone than before.

'Forgive my harsh words, sir,' he said with an effort. 'I merely fear for the safety of my dear betrothed.' When Sir Giles said nothing he continued, 'Shall we ride back to the house together? You may tell me of this place you think she has gone to, and why.'

Sir Giles returned the briefest of nods, touched spurs to his horse, and led the way.

An hour later, a large party of men gathered in the stable yard at Chilbourne. It seemed another, smaller group, had already gone out to search the area around the village, unaware that their action was almost certainly useless. Sir Giles, on his return, had asked folk to await his instructions before moving off. Richard Hawkes, it seemed, rather than the aged butler, was the one who had been so swift to act after Lady Katherine had raised the alarm, summoning men from the fields and from East Everley village. And though there had been some grumbling and a few excuses, most had rallied to the call to aid Sir Giles in his distress.

Leading the main group of villagers was John Cardmaker the hayward, whom Thomas had not seen since his arrival two days previously. Nodding a greeting, the man approached him and at once began to speak of the disappearance. Already it seemed gossip was rife in the village.

'Tongues are running free,' the hayward said, then hesitated. 'If I'm to speak plain, there's some as wish the girl

Godspeed, seeing as who her betrothed is.' He looked away. 'I wouldn't hold with such talk, myself.'

'Nor I,' Thomas agreed, catching the look in the other man's eye. He glanced across the yard to where Judd Chalkhill was saddling a horse for Sir Giles. Fresh ones had been brought up from the paddock. All those who had been out on the hawking party, both gentlefolk and servants, had been glad to eat, drink and rest briefly before setting forth again.

There was a commotion from the direction of the house and Sir Giles appeared, striding across the yard with Stephen Ridley. At once a silence fell.

'I thank you with all my heart for coming so swiftly to my aid,' Sir Giles called out as the men gathered round. His features looked taut, even in the soft glow of sunset. 'Yet I fear you will not be needed – at least, not for some time.' Seeing the looks of consternation, he added: 'I have a few miles' ride ahead of me, which may well render your service unnecessary. However, if it prove fruitless . . .' He looked around. No one spoke. 'If it prove fruitless, then a full search must be made – and those who are able to obtain horses will be most needed.'

There was stirring, and the village men began muttering to each other. Thomas, standing to one side with Cardmaker, could guess what was being said. *How many horses does he think folk like us can put our hands on?*

'I will furnish what mounts I can, for those that ride,' Sir Giles said as if in answer, raising his voice above the hubbub. 'As for the rest . . .' He broke off as if the thought had just occurred to him, then announced: 'Tomorrow is the Sabbath. With the rector's blessing, I will speak to you all in the church after service, about . . . about what may be required.' He made the vague gesture that Thomas was beginning to find familiar, as if it explained everything else. But the matter was plain enough: Lady Jane, wherever she was, was not close enough to be found by any foot party, so they might as well go home. Relief broke over the entire group then, and Thomas heard the name of the White Hound from several different directions. And who could blame them, he thought. *Would that I could join them in a mug myself . . .*

46

Sir Giles, followed by Ridley, who had remained tight-lipped throughout the entire business, walked over to the horses. Then Richard Hawkes appeared, leading another horse up from the paddock. These three, it seemed, were enough to form the search party Sir Giles had in mind. His curiosity aroused, Thomas turned to Cardmaker.

'What's the Cracked Oak?' he enquired, then raised an eyebrow as the other man gave a snort.

'Cracked Oak,' the hayward replied, 'is where Sir Giles's first cousin lives – Lady Euphemia Hart.' Then, with a shake of his head, he added: 'And an oak tree bain't the only thing there that's cracked!'

Before Thomas could ask more, the man turned to go. Others were starting to move away. Sir Giles was in the saddle, Ridley too, both of them impatient with Hawkes, who was still preparing to mount. Dusk was now falling. Then, while Hawkes placed his boot in the stirrup, there came a distant shout. Other voices were raised, and men peered past the distant gate of Chilbourne, from whence the sound had come.

'Torches!' someone exclaimed. Thomas looked into the distance and saw flickering lights coming through the outer park towards the stables. Sir Giles spurred his horse forward, followed by Ridley and several men on foot. There was an air of growing excitement. As Thomas watched, the lights separated and resolved themselves into flaming rush wands, held aloft by two or three running men. Behind them came others.

'It's Birch and his fellows,' Cardmaker said. Thomas guessed that this was the other party that had set forth earlier in too much haste. Following Sir Giles and the villagers, he crossed the park towards the approaching group, who came up apace, sweating, clearly having hurried some distance. Then he saw that Edward Birch was not among them. The first man, one of the torch-bearers, halted as the riders reined in.

'Sir Giles!' he cried out breathlessly. 'I fear to say it – yet I must. We have found a body!'

Sir Giles jerked the reins as if he had been struck. Beside him Ridley let out a choking sound, half gasp, half oath.

Without waiting for their instruction the man who had spoken turned and prepared to lead the way back towards the village.

Less than a quarter of an hour later the little group of riders gathered in the failing light about another figure holding a torch, who was waiting for them beside the road that led from East to West Everley. Thomas was among those who had got themselves quickly mounted – he was lucky to have Cob to ride – and followed Sir Giles at a gallop. As he drew close to the standing figure, he saw that it was Edward Birch. When Sir Giles drew rein he stepped forward, looking ill at ease.

'We thought it best to wait for you, sir,' Birch said in a subdued voice. 'No one has touched the . . .' He gestured away from the road. All eyes turned to see a shapeless bulk, partly covered with dried grass.

Sir Giles dismounted, his face haggard in the torchlight. Ridley dismounted too, then stood as if unwilling to be first to approach the body. Nobody, in fact, seemed to relish the task. Sir Giles looked about and saw Richard Hawkes standing silently beside his own horse, with Thomas beyond him. At Sir Giles's gesture, Hawkes stepped forward.

'Your pardon, Master usher,' Sir Giles began, then caught his breath as if choking back a sob.

Hawkes nodded, then surprised Thomas by turning to beckon him forward. 'Will you hold the torch, falconer?' he asked.

Thomas took the torch from Birch, who looked warily at him for a second before lowering his gaze. Then he and Hawkes walked the few yards from the roadside towards the huddled shape. As Thomas held the light the other man stooped, steeled himself and began to clear the grass aside. Then he stopped, breathed in sharply and sat down on his haunches.

Thomas peered closer, then drew breath himself.

The prone figure was naked – and unmistakeably male.

Within the hour Thomas found himself included in the small

48

party that followed Sir Giles silently through the gathering gloom, back across the hare warrens he had traversed that afternoon, towards Haxton and beyond, to the Avon valley. Here, with little more than the light of a half moon to guide them, they forded the river at the tiny hamlet of Enford, then turned abruptly down an unmade lane between beeches and oaks. The riders slowed to a walk, following Sir Giles. Thomas, in the rear, saw Richard Hawkes drop back apace, allowing him to catch up.

The discovery of the body, he sensed, had somehow broken the tension between himself and the usher, though they had done no more than share a brief moment of fear, followed by one of relief. When the truth was quickly made known, relief was indeed the prevailing emotion among the group. A quick examination of the body had revealed little, though the cause of death seemed plain enough: the man had a broken neck. But whoever he was – and nobody, it transpired, had ever set eyes on him before – he had been stripped of all clothing and possessions, which suggested that this was no accident. Some reasoned that he may have fallen from his horse, and merely been robbed by someone who chanced upon the body – for it was cold, and had clearly lain near the road for some time. Odd then, others reasoned, that no horse was found; and that no one had noticed a horseman, with all the harvesting going on. But then Edward Birch – for it was he who had found the body – told how it had been covered with a mound of grass, as if someone had made a hasty attempt at concealment. And that, for the time being, seemed to put an end to the speculation.

Sir Giles, overcome with relief at the realization that the body was not that of his daughter, had ridden some distance away, seemingly to compose himself. Hawkes it was, rather than Ridley, who had then taken charge, instructing someone to ride over to Everley Manor and inform Henry Sadler, who was also the magistrate, of the discovery. Birch, once again, would remain with the body until help arrived. And word would be sent back to Chilbourne that Sir Giles intended to keep to his original intent – to ride to Cracked Oak in search of Lady Jane.

Now the usher rode in silence beside Thomas for some moments before speaking. When he did, it was in a voice low enough for only Thomas to hear.

'You have a good pair of eyes, I am told,' he said, keeping his eyes on the path ahead. 'But for Sir Giles's sake I would ask you to keep them hooded here, as if they were your falcon's.'

Thomas frowned to himself.

'My master rarely visits this house,' Hawkes went on. 'Though its owner, the Lady Euphemia, is his kins-woman . . .' He seemed uncharacteristically hesitant. To his surprise, Thomas sensed that the man was highly embar-rassed. 'Lady Jane used to visit her – I should say, still visits her,' the usher added quickly. 'She is a kindly girl, and has been a good companion to . . .' Again he strug-gled for the right words. 'To one who is, I may say, of uncertain temperament.'

Thomas thought then of John Cardmaker's remark back in the stable yard. But before he could phrase a question, the usher raised a gloved hand and pointed off to the right. Thomas saw the bulk of a large, dead tree, whose broken and blackened branches seemed to reach menacingly above their heads.

'The house is named for yon cracked oak that was split asunder by lightning,' Hawkes told him. 'Some folk here-abouts deemed it an ill omen.' He was silent for a moment before adding: 'I hear that in happier times, as a child, Lady Euphemia would play hide-and-seek in it. That was, of course, before she went to Court.'

Thomas blinked. 'Our Queen's Court?'

'She was a lady-in-waiting to the Queen, albeit for short duration,' Hawkes nodded. His glance strayed as lights sprang up ahead. The silhouette of a large, steep-gabled house showed in the moonlight. 'I have said all I may,' he resumed. 'Remember what I asked you.' Then he touched heels to his horse, and rode ahead to rejoin Sir Giles.

Thomas followed the other riders through a gateway into an overgrown courtyard, aware now of a sound that came from somewhere in the house. Peering upwards, he saw an

50

open, lighted window, and realized what it was: a pair of virginals, played with some gusto, if not complete abandon.

From the very first, it was obvious that matters were somewhat out of joint at Cracked Oak.

As the visitors dismounted in the courtyard, the main door opened to reveal a very old attendant, something between butler, steward and servingman – indeed, Thomas would learn, he filled all these functions and more – holding a lantern and peering at them. Then he stepped forward on to the wide step, and made a slow, painful bow. Those close by could almost hear his bones creak.

'Sir Giles!' the old man cried. 'An honour, sir . . .'

'Master Byres,' Sir Giles answered. 'Your mistress is still awake, I believe?' He gestured to the lighted window above, whence the music continued without interruption.

'Indeed, sir. My lady is seldom abed before dawn,' the steward answered, and coughed. He wore a dusty black doublet and breeches that had been the fashion more than twenty years ago. There was a short silence, then the old man stood aside and gestured towards the doorway. 'Will you and your friends please to enter, sir?'

Sir Giles walked inside. Ridley, his nose wrinkled with distaste, followed while Hawkes and Thomas brought up the rear.

The entrance chamber was a shock. Old furniture, some of it damaged or mildewed or both, stood around the walls, covered with a layer of dust. There were hangings that had once been rather grand, except that they were now so moth-eaten and faded that their subjects were indiscernible. A door to the left was ajar, but the passage beyond was unlit. At the far end a wide staircase rose into the impenetrable gloom above.

Sir Giles, clearly uncomfortable, faced the elderly steward. 'I am in some haste, Master Byres. Will you conduct me to Lady Euphemia at once?'

The old man bowed again, raised his lantern and led the way to the stairs. Ridley and Hawkes followed and, since everyone seemed to have forgotten his presence, Thomas did likewise.

The stairs creaked alarmingly. At the top, a wide landing lined with more rotted hangings led past closed doors to a lighted chamber, the door of which was half open. The virginal-player – who must, Thomas guessed, be Lady Hart herself – played on at some volume, and with considerable passion. Highly intrigued, Thomas followed the other men through the doorway into the room, which was surprisingly large. At once the music stopped, and a silence fell. Then came a cry that was closer to a screech and a figure leaped up from a stool near the far window.

'Sir James! Thank heaven – you've returned!'

Lady Euphemia Hart ran, or rather tripped like a young girl, across the floor. The room being lit by few candles, the effect was somewhat eerie. The lady, who wore a large farthingale, was at times in shadow and other times lit garishly as she approached. She halted, then peered at Sir Giles, and her face fell. A look of dismay crossed it, to be replaced by one of resignation. 'Sir Giles . . . Dear cousin . . .'

She made her curtsey, then straightened to be revealed in the flickering light of Byres's lantern. She was wearing a flame-red gown over an embroidered orange-and-yellow kirtle. The neck was cut low, half exposing her breasts, above which sat a chain of gold set with rubies and other stones. As his gaze wandered uneasily upwards, Thomas stared at a milk-white neck and face, heavily rouged about the cheek-bones, the lips painted cherry-red and the eyebrows black. Strands of grey hair straggled from beneath an orange periwig. Then he saw the eyes, the creases around which were filled with white lead paste, and took a breath. Sir Giles's cousin dressed like a young lady, but she was more than a decade his senior – fifty, or perhaps older.

'Euphemia . . .' Sir Giles gave a little cough before bowing, then stooped dutifully and planted a kiss on the proffered white cheek.

'Shame on you, Cousin!' Lady Euphemia cried, suddenly cheerful, and at once began ticking off the points on her beringed fingers. 'First, for not informing me you were coming. Second, for not visiting me for so long – and third, for not telling me you were bringing so many handsome companions . . .' Her gaze wandered from Hawkes, whom she seemed to recognize vaguely, to Thomas, whom she appraised with a rapacious gleam that struck fear into his very heart, and finally to Ridley. At sight of his face, rigid with displeasure, her eyes widened.

'I have not had the honour, sir,' she murmured.

Sir Giles presented his guest, whereupon an odd expression flitted across Lady Euphemia's face. But turning to her aged servant, who still stood nearby, she said: 'Wine and cake for our guests, Bartholomew – at once.'

Byres coughed. 'There's no cake at present, my lady . . .'

Lady Euphemia's mouth opened like a trapdoor, but at that instant there came a rustle from across the room. With the other men, Thomas turned to see another figure, whom nobody had noticed, rise from a seat and walk towards them.

'There's manchet bread and malmsey, my lady . . .'

Euphemia threw a vague look at the elderly woman, who was of somewhat less than Byres's years. 'Then we shall have that!' she cried. But Sir Giles, fidgeting rather obviously, hastened to intervene.

'Nay, Cousin, we shall not stay,' he murmured. 'We are on an errand of great import. It has been a night of tragedy . . .'

Lady Euphemia stared, then broke into a crooked smile. 'How exciting . . . tell me more!'

Since no seat was offered, Sir Giles was obliged to commence his explanations where he stood. 'My dear daughter, Jane . . .' he began, then stopped. Lady Euphemia's eyes gleamed in the light of the lantern.

'Gone?' she asked.

There was a stirring, and it was Ridley who stepped forward, clearly having used up all reserves of patience. 'What do you mean, gone, madam?' he growled. 'Was she here? If so, when?'

Lady Euphemia smiled sweetly at him, then turned to her woman-in-waiting – if that was what she was. Thomas saw that the woman was plainly dressed, tall and sturdy despite her sixty years or more, which she carried well.

'Shall we ponder awhile, Mary?' Lady Euphemia asked. 'See now – when did Lady Jane last visit us?'

'I don't rightly recall, madam,' her servant replied. 'Mayhap it was last month, just as the harvest started.'

Ridley bristled but Sir Giles, wearing a pained expression, hastened to intervene. 'I pray you, think on it, Cousin,' he muttered. 'Jane has been missing since this afternoon. We have searched high and low, and I am in fear for her life. Already we have received one terrible shock . . .' His hand began to rise of its own accord, in his customary all-explanatory gesture.

Lady Euphemia's expression changed in an instant. She now appeared ready to burst into tears. 'Oh, poor Cousin . . . You are worried—'

'Of course he's worried!' Ridley almost shouted, causing a ripple of alarm around the room. 'A young girl out alone after dark, in this wild country with Christ-knows-who abroad . . .' He broke off, struggling to master his anger.

Lady Euphemia gazed solemnly at him. 'You are naturally concerned for your betrothed, sir. A delicate young prize, of such refinement and beauty, for one of your years . . . She must be a heavy loss.'

Ridley froze, then, as if afraid of what he might say or do, turned and strode noisily from the room. Those that remained heard him cursing as he stumbled down the unlit staircase.

'Cousin, I pray you . . .' Sir Giles began, then hesitated as the change in Lady Euphemia's countenance caught even him unaware. She was smiling, like a young girl surrounded by admirers.

'Your pardon, dear Giles,' she said in a soothing tone. 'Now he's gone, we may speak freely, may we not?' She turned to her woman, who bobbed and disappeared through the door. With a bow and a wheeze, Bartholomew Byres turned to follow.

And, every inch the gracious hostess, Sir Giles's cousin led the way towards a table where sat two old-fashioned carved chairs, gesturing to him to join her.

With a glance at the others, he followed. Richard Hawkes and Thomas made their brief bows, turned at once and left him alone with the Lady Euphemia.

Five

The next day was Sunday, and the little church of East Everley was packed to the doors.

Since half the villagers had been up all night, let alone the staff of Chilbourne Manor, Thomas was not surprised at the sluggish condition of the sleepy-eyed folk who filed through the doorway at a little past seven o'clock. What did surprise him was the size of the congregation. Sir Giles and his family, along with their ward, Gervase, and the higher Chilbourne servants, were wedged into the Buckridge pews at the front, whose finely carved oak seats and panels served as a reminder of the grandeur the family had once commanded. Behind, villagers and farm folk crammed into the lesser pews, a shuffling, coughing, fidgeting crowd of all ages and both sexes that spilled out into the aisle, backing up to the ancient stone font at the rear. Thomas found himself standing beside the cook, James Clyffe, whose breath smelled strongly of alc. But as a drinking man, it soon became clear that Clyffe was a mere prentice compared to the rector, Dr Julius Parry.

No sooner had the single bell ceased its clamour, to general relief, than the vestry door flew back and a stout figure of middle height lurched through the opening, staggered across to the pulpit and gripped its base tightly, as if he might fall to his knees at any moment. Which, Thomas saw, was more than likely to happen, since the man was spectacularly drunk.

'Our Father!' Parry shouted, gazing out at the sea of faces with a defiant air. His face was clean-shaven and shiny, framed by locks of lank brown hair. He breathed fiercely for a few moments, then with a supreme effort forced himself to climb the two or three steps to the lectern, which he grabbed like a lifeline. 'Our Father!' he repeated, and at once the congregation took the hint and began mumbling their way through the Lord's Prayer. By the time it was over, Parry seemed somehow to have mastered himself. Once again, he glared at the assembled company. 'Psalm ninety-four!' he called out. 'O Lord God, to whom vengeance belongeth!'

Thomas glanced about him. Nobody, he gathered, seemed surprised at the rector's demeanour. As if to confirm his impression, Clyffe began muttering in his ear.

'Don't fret yourself, falconer. On a bad day he couldn't even climb the steps. Yet he'll get through the service and deliver a sermon that sets your teeth on edge.'

And, despite appearances, the cook's words proved to be true, for once into his stride, the rector of East Everley stormed through the morning's service at a cracking pace. For his first lesson he chose the Plagues from book seven of Exodus, sending a chill through the bones of every man, woman and child as he spoke of the horrors suffered by the victims. By the second lesson – the Rich Man and Lazarus, from Luke's gospel – Thomas sensed he was well warmed up. In quick succession there followed the Litany and responses, the Ten Commandments, an epistle and a reading – the Ten Virgins from Matthew's gospel, which Parry seemed to find particularly exciting. Then came the Nicene Creed, another psalm, and finally the sermon, for which clearly all were waiting. Within seconds a silence had fallen, so intense that Thomas could hear plovers calling, far away on the Downs. For Parry had chosen as his theme 'A Daughter's Duty to her Father', the significance of which was lost on nobody. Then, after more psalms and an impatient request from Parry as to whether any children were to be presented for baptism – thankfully none were – came the final business of the morning, which everyone had been expecting. Parry, perspiring visibly, stepped unsteadily down from his pulpit and nodded to a pale-faced Sir Giles Buckridge, who stood up and faced the congregation.

'My good friends,' Sir Giles began, and at once there was general shuffling of feet and an outbreak of coughing. The knight of Chilbourne, folk knew, was no orator, and would make a poor successor to their rector. Nevertheless, Thomas guessed that there was not a soul present who was unaware of the disappearance of Lady Jane, the fruitless searches of the previous night, and the grim discovery of a body. The visit to Cracked Oak and Sir Giles's private audience with Lady Euphemia had likewise, it appeared, proved futile. So, finally, all looked upon the taut face of Sir Giles and prepared to hear his words.

'You all know, I believe, that my eldest daughter, Lady Jane, is missing. Last night's search has revealed nothing. So I am here to ask – nay, to implore you . . .' He faltered, and some looked away in embarrassment – among them, Thomas noticed, Lady Katherine and her daughters.

'To implore you,' Sir Giles continued, 'to aid us in our hour of need. I know that, like the good people you are, you will not fail me or my family. We must search the Downs west of Chilbourne – indeed, south and north as well. To the Avon valley and beyond – up as far as Rushall, and down to Netheravon.' He paused. 'I . . . I will furnish horses and provisions where I may. Those who bring word of any sighting of my dear daughter, or indeed any news at all, I will reward in any way I can.'

There were sceptical expressions at that, and some whispers, while the younger children were becoming restless. Seeing there was little else to say, Sir Giles made his farewell to the congregation and stepped aside, then turned back in some agitation.

'The . . . body of the unfortunate soul who was found last night on the road west of here has been taken to Everley Manor. The honourable Master Sadler will conduct an inquest in due course. He has requested anyone who knows aught of that matter to come forward . . .' He hesitated, aware that a tense silence had fallen. 'I . . . That is all, I think. I know our good rector, Doctor Parry, will give his blessing to all those who embark on the search . . .' Raising his hand in the vague gesture that was familiar to all, Sir Giles nodded to his family, who had already risen, and led them swiftly out of the church.

Thomas followed Clyffe outside into the sunshine, glad

57

to breathe sweet air after the fetid smell inside, and joined a small group of Chilbourne men that included Richard Hawkes and Judd Chalkhill. Redmund Oakes, it seemed, was spared attending the service because of his infirmity. Looking round, Thomas saw knots of village men gathering, preparing to form search parties. Then, as he turned back towards Hawkes, he saw Sir Giles walking towards him. Beside him strode a tall, dark-bearded man, well dressed in a black doublet and riding boots.

'Master usher,' Sir Giles began, and as Hawkes made his brief bow, added: 'This man is the Crown Purveyor. He will be staying in the region hereabouts for some time. Or so it would appear . . .'

Hawkes looked up in surprise, as did the others. The tall man smiled at them, a flickering smile with little warmth.

'Edmund Warren, Purveyor to Her Glorious Majesty, Queen Elizabeth,' he said. 'I am ordered to survey the manor of Chilbourne and all its demesnes, including the lands of all copyholders and tenants, the farmsteads and cottages. I must make report of all livestock, for potential purchase. I will, of course, expect full co-operation from all servants of Sir Giles.'

There was a stunned silence. Thomas now saw the sickly look on Sir Giles's face; here was another, clearly unexpected blow to a man who was already distraught. Crown Purveyors, universally disliked if not feared, had the power to make compulsory purchase, at minimum prices, of animals as well as grain and other foodstuffs for the use of the monarch and her train. The man's arrival could hardly have come at a more inopportune moment.

'You find us utterly unprepared, Master Warren,' Sir Giles said at last. 'Had I some warning of your impending visit . . .'

But Warren was now wearing a reassuring smile. 'Nay, sir,' he murmured, 'I have no wish to cause distress at such a time. I have learned of the desperate straits you are in.' When a pained look crossed Sir Giles's features, he added: 'I have obtained lodging for myself and my servant nearby. I will commence an appraisal of the lands hereabout at once

– you need not concern yourself, for I shall ask nothing of you. Only that you leave me free to go where I will.'

The relief on Sir Giles's face was obvious. But, glancing round, Thomas saw an odd look on the face of Richard Hawkes.

'You are a stranger to the district, sir,' he said, fixing Warren with a hard look. 'Surely it is best that you have someone to guide you, while you poke about.'

His tone was not lost on Warren. Meeting Hawkes's expression with one of equal coolness, he answered, 'I have no need. I am provided with maps and a full list of all holdings hereabout. I need none to teach me my work.' He turned to Sir Giles. 'I know you have much to occupy yourself with, sir, and have no wish to intrude at such a time. If I may be of assistance . . .' He raised an eyebrow.

Sir Giles nodded. 'We will speak again I expect, Master . . .'

But the man was already turning to go. As he did so, Thomas caught a cold look in his eye that alarmed and surprised him: this man, Crown Purveyor or no, was as dangerous as any who had crossed his path.

But for now he had other matters on his mind – as did everyone else.

The search continued throughout Sunday, and into the evening. Thomas, well mounted on Cob, was asked to help Hawkes and others in crossing the Avon valley and combing its far side, as far upstream as the hamlet of Rushall. They stopped frequently, questioning harvesters and cottagers – everyone they encountered, in fact – but learned nothing. Lady Jane Buckridge, it seemed, had simply vanished.

In the afternoon the group split up, and Thomas was paired with John Cardmaker the hayward to search the little farmsteads downstream as far as Fittleton, which proved just as fruitless. Finally, as evening closed in, the two tired men forded the river again and turned back towards East Everley. Cardmaker, a man of the fields, looked out of place on horseback. Slowing his borrowed mount to a walk, he unstopped his leather costrel, such as Downland men always have at

59

their belts, took a long pull and offered it to Thomas. Gratefully Thomas accepted it, drained the last of the cider and handed it back.

'Best applejack I've tasted in years,' he said, then realized the other had halted. Two riders were ascending the shallow slope towards them. As they drew near Thomas saw, to his surprise, that one was Edmund Warren, the Crown Purveyor. The other was a squat, heavy man with what looked like very cropped black hair. But on closer inspection this proved to be a leather skullcap, which covered his head and ears and was tied beneath the chin.

Again Thomas felt his muscles tense as they had on meeting Warren that morning. He would have preferred merely to wave and pass by without stopping, but both the Purveyor and the other man had stopped and were waiting for the other two to approach. Cardmaker, who had learned of Warren's identity after church service that morning, drew rein and nodded. Warren nodded in reply, but the other – presumably his servant – merely stared.

'Are you at your work already, on the Sabbath?' Cardmaker asked in a sceptical tone. Warren, sitting astride his tall horse in a relaxed fashion, favoured him with a bleak smile.

'Merely getting to know the country,' he answered. 'And you, master hayward, are assisting Sir Giles in his hour of need, I see. A noble gesture.'

Cardmaker's eyes narrowed. 'I would aid any man whose child was lost,' he murmured.

Warren's gaze shifted towards Thomas. There was a moment's silence. 'I don't believe we were introduced,' he said.

'I don't believe we were,' Thomas agreed.

There followed another pause. Thomas was aware that Warren's sullen companion, who sat beside him on a smaller, far humbler horse, was eyeing him keenly.

'You are a servant to Sir Giles?' Warren asked, rather impatiently now.

'For the moment.' For some reason Thomas found himself unwilling to oblige the man with any information at all.

The silence grew uncomfortable. Cardmaker's tired horse

shifted restlessly beneath his portly frame. Leaning forward to pat the animal's neck, he muttered, 'We'd best be on our way. We must report to Sir Giles.'

'Then we shall not delay you any longer.' With a last, oddly suspicious look at Thomas, the Purveyor gave the rein a twitch and drew his horse aside so that he might watch the other two pass in front of him. As they did so, without comment, Thomas saw the surly expression on the face of Warren's servant, and understood suddenly the reason for the man's peculiar-looking headgear. When he and Cardmaker had ridden on for a while, he glanced back and saw the two men still watching him. Only then did they turn away and urge their mounts forward, towards the Avon valley.

Cardmaker's curiosity was aroused. 'Why'd they be going towards Enford at this time of night?' he wondered. 'And did you ever see anyone with a cap like that before?'

'Yes,' Thomas answered. 'And I believe I know why he wears it. His ears have been cropped.'

Cardmaker stared. 'D'you say so? Then he's a felon, done something wicked.'

'Coining, most likely,' Thomas told him. 'That or forgery. Save that he looks an unlikely forger to me.'

'To me too,' Cardmaker agreed. 'In fact, he do look more like a wrestler.'

Thomas turned to him. 'I believe you're right,' he said. 'That, or an inquisitor's right hand – the one that deals out the pain.'

Cardmaker shuddered. 'By Christ, what have we done to have folk like that inflicted on us? As if we bain't have enough troubles already.' He was falling into the complaining tone of the permanently put-upon that to Thomas was familiar. Though, as he had begun to like the hayward well enough, he paid it little mind. 'Least, I have,' Cardmaker continued. 'Like who's been shifting the boundary posts on East Field by night!'

Thomas stiffened but, keeping all expression from his face, asked innocently: 'How long's that been going on, then?'

'Too long!' Cardmaker spat. 'And when I find out who the blasted culprit is, I'll crop his ears myself!'

Thomas clicked his tongue and urged Cob into a trot.

That night there was a better supper for Thomas in the kitchen at Chilbourne, and, to his relief, a better atmosphere than the one he had encountered on his arrival. It seemed that his willingness to share the household's hardships – as well as the success of yesterday's falconing – had won him considerable respect, from the cook at least. Instead of pease and barley, there was a roasted plover, a few vegetables, fresh-baked bread and a dish of summer fruits, all washed down with a mug of Chilbourne's own ale. The higher servants, it seemed, were in the Great Chamber in confer-ence with Sir Giles and Lady Katherine, so Thomas was pleased to take his meal seated on a convenient chopping log outside the back door, in the balmy air of late evening.

When it was over he rose to look in at the falcons' mews, to feed and water Tamora. But when he arrived he found Ridley's fine hawk tethered outside the weathering. Beside it sat the little lanner falcon that the man had presented to Lady Jane Buckridge, and with which she had hunted only yesterday.

With a twinge of irritation, Thomas realized that Ridley was still at Chilbourne – perhaps intending to stay until Jane was found. He was musing on this when a movement caught his eye. He looked up to see John Steer trotting towards him, and was suddenly aware that in all the excitement he had almost forgotten about him. Then he caught the other's expression and waited.

'We are summoned to Sir Giles and my master,' the little falconer said without preamble.

'Is there news . . .' Thomas began, but the other was already turning to go. With a sigh, he started to follow. Tamora would have to wait for her supper.

As Thomas followed Steer through the door of the Great Chamber, he was aware at once of an air of high excitement, quite different from the one of gloom he expected after the day's search had brought no comfort. The remains of a supper were still upon the table, but Sir Giles was pacing about the hall. Redmund Oakes was seated, as were a red-faced Ridley and Lady Katherine. Richard Hawkes was on his feet, apparently remonstrating with Sir Giles. There was no sign of Margaret or Emma, or of Gervase. But Eliza Willett sat beside a pale faced Lady Kathcrinc, as if instructed to offer her what comfort she could. Her eyes skilfully avoided Thomas's.

As the two falconers approached and made their bows, Sir Giles looked up and gestured them forward impatiently. It was then that Thomas saw he held a paper in his hand.

'Falconer . . .' he began, though it was unclear which of the two he was addressing. 'An extraordinary thing has happened!'

They waited while Sir Giles turned in agitation to Hawkes, and thrust the document towards him. 'Master usher . . .'

Hawkes took it while Sir Giles, seemingly unable to keep still, strode to the table, sat down, then stood up again. Ridley, for his part, sat glowering at everyone.

Hawkes faced the two falconers and made his announcement.

'Lady Jane is safe!'

Six

There was a brief silence while Hawkes waited for the news to sink in.

'Safe and well,' he added. 'That is, if we are to believe this . . .' He held up the paper. 'And Sir Giles is convinced it is in his daughter's hand. In it, Lady Jane seeks to soothe her parents' fears, telling them she is mortally sorry for having frightened them, but that she is in good health and none need fear for her safety.'

The usher paused, then added: 'There is more that need not concern you . . .' he trailed off with a sideways glance at Sir Giles. 'Suffice it to say, the search will be called off. That is, as far as appearances go.'

Thomas sensed the same reaction in Steer, standing silently beside him, when Hawkes added: 'But you two men will continue it.'

Thomas blinked. Sir Giles, whose manner suggested a mixture of fear, relief and embarrassment, took a step towards them. 'Turn the matter about,' he said, 'and you will see that it is the best course. You men have sharp eyes, you can go where you will, exercising your birds – none will pay you any mind. You may search far and wide, without anyone knowing that you do so.' Looking away, he muttered: 'The people of Everley will learn that my daughter was taken ill while riding, and returned unseen to Chilbourne, where she retired to her chamber before anyone knew of it. She has since gone to stay with relatives in Salisbury, where she may receive physic and recover. The impending nuptials may have been a strain upon her . . .'

At that, Ridley stood up suddenly and banged his hand down on the table. Platters jumped in the air.

'By the good Christ, I'll not have that put about!' he cried. 'Let alone the fact that it sounds like a cock-and-bull tale, you seek still to lay the blame on me somehow, though I am as sorely wronged as you are – if not more so!'

There was consternation all round. Thomas and Steer lowered their eyes, aware that this was a continuation of an argument that had probably been raging all evening – one that they were not supposed to be privy to.

'Dear friend Stephen.' It was Lady Katherine who with her customary calm began to restore decorum. 'That is not a matter that concerns the falconers. I pray you will let my husband instruct them, before you fall to further rant.'

Ridley exhaled, then forced himself to incline his head towards Lady Katherine, and sat down.

Hawkes was looking at Sir Giles. 'Perhaps I might speak privately with the falconers, sir, and instruct them further.'

Sir Giles swallowed and nodded. 'If you please, Master usher.' When he faced Thomas and Steer, there was a look of humility, even pleading on his face.

'I ask your help, Thomas, and yours John Steer – though I know it is not your place, nor your calling. This message –' he indicated the letter again – 'was brought by a village boy, on foot, earlier this evening. He was out chasing rabbits on the Downs when a man on a horse, he said, rode up and gave him a penny to carry it to me. The boy had not seen the rider before, though he believed he was a servant, and not high-born. We do not know how far he had ridden, but . . .' he made his vague gesture, which conveyed all he thought necessary.

Hawkes turned to the door, signalling to the falconers to follow. A moment later they had made their bows to their masters and left the Chamber, with no small relief.

Night was falling as they walked outside, through the stable yard, until they were almost at the park gate. Only then did Hawkes stop and address them. He seemed tense, and his expression was not encouraging. 'It is a hard task to lay upon you, yet I know of no one here who may accomplish it better,' he began. 'You will both be mounted, and so you may roam far – further than the search has yet taken anyone.

65

Across the river, to Devizes if you must, or north to Savernake Forest.'

Thomas stared. 'Master Hawkes, this is likely impossible—'

'I know!' Hawkes cut him off abruptly. 'We must be seen to do all that we can – do you not understand that?' Then at once he seemed to regret his words, and turned towards Steer. But to his and Thomas's surprise, the little falconer wore a smile.

'Save your words, Master Hawkes,' he said. 'I know full well how the land lies.'

Hawkes frowned. 'Your loyalties are to your master, of course. Hence, no doubt you will—'

'I will search as diligently as Master Finbow here,' Steer said. His face was a blank.

'That is all I ask,' Hawkes said after a moment. 'Do Sir Giles's bidding – look everywhere, even as far as Salisbury if you will. Yet, let such enquiry as you make be discreet.' He hesitated, then added: 'I trust you now not to repeat what I say. There is more in that letter than you were told. A part of it tells that in time Lady Jane's disappearance will have meaning, that she believed she had no choice, and that she hopes to be restored to her father and mother with no harm done to anyone.'

He glanced at Steer, who was staring at the ground. From a nearby hillock, a nightjar called. After a moment he lifted his eyes and met Hawkes's gaze.

'To *anyone*?' he enquired.

'No harm done,' Hawkes repeated.

And Thomas too understood, for it seemed plain that while no real hurt would be done to Steer's irascible master, there may well be a severe disappointment – which gave Thomas no small pleasure. For in his heart he knew that whoever Lady Jane intended to marry, it would not be Stephen Ridley.

Later that night, after the two falconers had spoken briefly and resolved to meet at first light, Thomas decided to go for a walk before going to his bed. He knew he would not sleep easily: events had flooded in thick and fast these past few days, and he needed to think.

The night was clear, with the chill that may come in late summer after a hot day. The heavens, scattered with a myriad stars, arced above him as he strode through the open gates and out towards the hayfields. A stack of newly cut hay sat near the paddock fence – Sir Giles's share of the common crop which, he recalled with wry amusement, was likely somewhat less than he was entitled to. Though the answer to that mystery – the small matter of who was moving the boundary posts – was known to him, he thought it best to remain neutral. He had a feeling that in time he might need Edward Birch as an ally more than he needed John Cardmaker. And besides, he had never been one to inform on his fellows.

He glanced up and saw the unmistakeable silhouette of a nightjar, large as a barn owl and as soundless in flight, crossing the sky away to his left. There was no sound, save the distant bark of a dog-fox. He lowered his eyes, falling into the easy gait of the Downland man, and trudged along the path between fields of stubble. Two things nagged at him: the manner of Lady Jane's disappearance, and the conversation he had had with Gervase Lambert, not far from where he now walked. He had the distinct feeling that the young man would know something of the matter – though when he was likely to see him again he did not know, for the falconry lessons had seemingly been forgotten. That at least was something to smile about; as was the timely disappearance of the ramage hawk . . . it was almost as if the Fates were trying to make life easier for him – until now. The thought of searching half of Wiltshire for the missing Lady Jane afforded him no pleasure at all.

He walked the empty land for an hour, turning matters over without coming to any conclusion. Then he turned back towards Chilbourne, guided by moonlight. As he descended the slope, the dark shape of the manor and outbuildings came into view. Horses snorted in the paddock. He gained the stable yard, then wondered if he was likely to disturb Judd and Nan. They probably thought he was in his bed in the loft . . . He stopped, unsure whether to call out. As he did so he saw a flicker of something pale, over by the rear door of the house.

He stared. All within the house was dark. But as he stepped softly on the weed-choked cobbles he saw it again, and this time there was no doubt: someone was standing beside the outbuilding nearest the kitchen door. Then he recalled that this was the wash-house – Nan's domain – and relaxed. Whatever business she was about, it was none of his concern, and he could go straight to his bed. Hence his surprise, as he turned away, when the figure raised a hand and gestured to him.

He stared, and his heart thudded. It wasn't Nan.

He walked forward, quickening his pace. As he drew close he saw the woman signal him to be silent. She wore a pale gown and hood, which she threw back. He stopped.

'I have little time,' Eliza Willett said softly, and reached out a hand. He took it and pulled her gently towards him, in a movement that seemed expected, and quite natural to them both. At once she lifted her face, kissed him, then drew back.

'Not now,' she whispered. 'And not here . . . There is my chamber – look above.'

He looked and saw a high window, on the corner of the upper storey, about which ivy clustered. He also saw that it was possible to climb on to the wash-house roof, and so gain a foothold. Then he turned back to her, feeling suddenly ridiculous.

'I'm not a youth who may climb in through windows . . .' he began, then caught his breath for she was smiling at him. Her dark eyes glittered in the half-light.

'If you were such a youth, I would not take the trouble I have taken to prepare the way for you,' she said.

He breathed in deeply, aware how much he desired her. A man like him, he thought suddenly, should take what chances life offers and be glad of them. He leaned down and kissed her. She did not pull away from him, nor did she resist when his hand moved inside her gown and found her breast.

'We could go to my pallet in the stable loft,' he whispered. 'Though it's not a fair bed—'

68

Eliza pulled back. 'Listen,' she said in a tone that put him on his guard. 'Matters here are not as you think . . . You are being used.'

He frowned. 'Do you mean the search for Lady Jane?'

'Perhaps . . .' She peered up at him, her face tense in the moonlight. And though he longed to lay her down, peel her clothes off and feast upon her body, he waited. 'I cannot say much,' she said, with a little frown of her own. 'My own place here is precarious . . . It is not Ridley, but the young people here. They are the ones you must watch.'

When he shook his head, not understanding, she put her hand to his face again. 'We will talk, my sweet, after we have lain together – but not on your pallet in the dark. I wish to see you clearly when you uncase, as you will see me.'

He caught his breath, pulling her towards him, pressing her close so that she felt his body through their clothing.

'Yes, yes,' she murmured. 'Wait a little longer and I will cleave to you, and you may do what you will . . .' She gripped his arms, pulling back. 'Let it be tomorrow night.'

He nodded, taking her hand and kissing it, his other still pressing the back of her shoulder. 'After dark, when it's quiet, I'll climb up.' He wanted to laugh. 'I hope yon ivy is strong enough!'

'It must be,' she answered, and pointed with her chin towards the high window. 'The casement will be open, and a chest placed below it for you to step on to.'

'Tomorrow, then.'

'Tomorrow.' She kissed him quickly and pulled away. He watched her slip silently through the rear door, which he now saw was ajar. Then it closed and she was gone.

The morning dawned, dull and misty. Swallows darted about the gabled roofs of Chilbourne. In the distance, harvesters could be seen heading for the fields to do battle with what remained of the corn crop. And anyone who cared to look would have seen the falconers, Thomas Finbow and John Steer, riding out, each with a hawk on the wrist; as natural a sight as any on the Downs.

They had no grand plan, other than to retrace the route Thomas and Richard Hawkes had taken the previous day, then to continue westwards beyond the Avon valley. The journey would take them close by Cracked Oak, whose occupants had made a considerable impression on Thomas. He mentioned them to Steer, who had not spoken since they passed through the gates of Chilbourne an hour ago.

'My master likes her not,' he said finally, without looking at Thomas. 'I mean the Lady Euphemia.'

'I believe the feeling was mutual,' Thomas told him, recalling the brief exchange in the candlelit parlour. 'Nor did Lady Euphemia appear to like the notion of your master's betrothal to Lady Jane.'

Steer grimaced. 'Who does?'

'Sir Giles, for one,' Thomas replied.

'He is a fool,' Steer said suddenly, causing Thomas to turn in some surprise.

'Mayhap he is, but he is in such straits that he has little choice but to do your master's bidding.'

'You have heard of the Queen's loan,' Steer said with a nod. 'Yet that was merely the last straw – the man has failed at many enterprises, and was in debt before even that.' When Thomas frowned, he added: 'But I speak not of those things. I speak of his not knowing what goes on under his own roof.'

Thomas made no reply, for it sat well enough with his own impression. And since last night's hurried, passionate encounter with Eliza, he had begun to wonder what really was afoot at Chilbourne.

'For one thing,' Steer continued, still not looking at Thomas, 'I believe I know who freed that ramage hawk.'

'Mayhap you think I did it,' Thomas said with a wry look. 'I'll confess I was glad enough to see it gone.'

Steer shook his head. 'Nay, I would say such a deed were beyond you. You are too honest.'

'It sounds like a fault, to hear you say it thus,' Thomas answered mildly. Turning, he saw that Steer was smiling – a rare enough occurrence.

'One of the daughters did it,' he said. 'The youngest, most

like – she's full of mischief. Though I deem it was at Lady Jane's bidding.'

Thomas stared. 'How can you know?'

'I suspect it,' Steer said, and turned to look directly at him. 'For she would see it as a conceit – to echo her own bid for freedom. Do you not mark that?' When Thomas raised an eyebrow, he added: 'I have studied logic, Master Thomas, among other things. I was not always a falconer.'

Thomas nodded, aware that somehow he had already divined there was more to this little rake of a man than met the eye.

'I was a sizar at Cambridge,' Steer told him. 'A scholarship boy, whose parents had not the means to pay for my studies, so that I must work my way through. A knowledge of hawks helped.'

Thomas gazed long at him. 'Why then did you leave your studies?'

Steer shook his head. 'Ridley,' he muttered.

And as if to make it clear that that were all he was prepared to say, he tugged the hood from the mighty Callisto, who had sat patiently on his gauntlet all the while, raised his arm and allowed the bird to soar. Thomas watched it, then followed suit with Tamora.

Within the hour they had crossed the river at Enford and were passing the lane leading to Cracked Oak, the hawks now hooded and back on their gauntlets. The cloud was lifting, the sun beginning to warm their backs. In daylight, Thomas saw that the Lady Euphemia's house was clearly visible down the short lane, as was the crabbed shape of the dead oak tree, to which two horses were tethered.

He drew rein, noting that one was a fine tall gelding, the other a smaller, poorer workhorse – whose owners were, respectively, Edmund Warren and his servant.

Steer pulled his own mount to a halt and glanced at Thomas.

'What are your thoughts?' he asked.

'I'm not sure,' Thomas replied. He pointed to the horses and gave Steer a short account of his meeting with the Purveyor and his man the day before.

71

'You wish to ride up to the house?' Steer asked sceptically. Thomas shrugged, aware that such a course was imprudent, if not foolhardy. What explanation could they give for their presence?

He was on the point of leaving the matter and riding on when there came a shout – sharp and decidedly unfriendly. Both men turned to see that Warren himself had appeared, seemingly from the corner of the house, and was walking towards them.

'What do you men want here?' he called out, then stood before them as if intending to bar their way.

Neither of the falconers replied at first. A thought passed through Thomas's mind: while the Purveyor's authority was indisputable, his tone was far too belligerent, as if he had something to hide . . . Which, Thomas realized with almost a jolt, was certainly the case. Because behind the anger in the man's dark eyes, Thomas sensed unease.

'I might ask the same of you, master,' Thomas answered finally. 'Is the Lady Euphemia's house to be assessed for purchase, too?'

Warren bristled. 'It's no business of yours what I do here,' he said. 'I'd advise you to take your hawks, and yourselves, elsewhere.'

Before Thomas could reply, Steer spoke up. 'But we are ordered to pay our masters' respects to the Lady Euphemia,' he said in the mildest of tones. 'We have a brace of partridges for her supper.'

Thomas smiled inwardly at Steer's ingenuity. The falcons had indeed brought down several birds that morning.

Warren glared, stepped forward and held out his hand. 'Then give them to me, and I will see that she gets them.'

Thomas felt a surge of his inbred Downland stubbornness. Leaning forward to pat Cob's neck – and no one with any knowledge of horses could fail to note that his mount was as fine as the one Warren rode – he gazed down at the man.

'We were instructed to place them in the hands of Master Byres, Lady Euphemia's steward.'

Warren's impatience was growing. 'What does it matter?'

he countered. 'I will tell him you brought them, and you may ride on.'

'Now I think on it,' Thomas went on, 'I recall the Lady Euphemia retires at dawn, and sleeps until the afternoon. I wonder that you should be here so early in the day.'

Warren's eyes blazed, though outwardly he remained calm.

'You're an insolent cove, for a falconer,' he said in a low voice. 'Mayhap you need to be shown your place.'

Thomas returned his gaze. But at that moment there came a sound, and Warren's thickset servant with the black skullcap materialized, seemingly from nowhere. He padded up, round-shouldered and surprisingly light on his feet, and stood watching the two horsemen without expression.

Warren half turned to acknowledge his man's presence. 'Miles is in a poor humour today,' he said with a cold smile. 'He needs little provocation to fall to breaking heads.'

Neither of the falconers doubted the truth of that. Steer glanced at Thomas, no doubt wishing to convey the notion that on this occasion, discretion would be the best course. Sighing inwardly, Thomas lifted the rein and prepared to move off. But without warning Warren sprang forward, grabbed the bridle and held it. Cob snorted and shook his head.

'Haven't you forgotten something?' the Purveyor asked icily.

Thomas felt Tamora twitch under her hood and was forced to steady himself, as Warren added: 'The birds you were bringing Lady Euphemia? Or was that a lie?'

But Thomas brought his left arm up in a half circle, as if to release the falcon, forcing Warren to let go of the bridle and step back. A look of alarm crossed his face briefly before he mastered himself.

'Now I think on it,' Thomas said, 'the Chilbourne cook wanted all our catch. Yet we may return again soon, with a delicacy for Lady Euphemia.'

With that he touched boot heels to Cob's flanks and urged him forward. Steer followed quickly, without looking back. In a very few minutes the house with its small cluster of trees was far behind, and they were cantering easily up a gentle slope with the vast expanse of Salisbury Plain before them.

After they had ridden for a while, Steer – who seemed to be unaffected by the ill-tempered confrontation – wondered aloud at the men's presence at Cracked Oak at such an hour. And where were the servants?

But Thomas was preoccupied. Something, he knew, was wrong; yet precisely what it was remained dark to him.

As far as the search went, the day was a failure. After completing a wide sweep across the Plain, then circling northwards by Wilsford Down and Woodborough, the two men crossed the upper reaches of the Avon at Manningford Abbas and returned to Chilbourne from the north as evening drew in. They had searched hamlets and villages, isolated farms and shepherds' huts, occasionally making roundabout enquiries, yet everywhere the response had been the same: no one knew anything of a young woman answering Lady Jane's description. So at last, weary from the long day's ride, they were content to feed and settle their birds for the night, then take supper in the kitchen and go to their beds – Steer to the cramped chamber he was sharing with most of the house servants, Thomas to his stable loft.

He slept for two or three hours, then woke in utter darkness, dimly aware that there was something he must do. Then he remembered with a start his tryst with Eliza, and sat up, stretching his long limbs and frowning to himself. *I am in no fit state for playing at peacock*, he thought. Then a picture of Eliza's upturned face, lips parted, sprang to his mind, along with the memory of the warmth of her body, and in seconds he had pulled on his clothes and was descending the ladder to the stable below.

From a distant corner came the sound of snoring and, peering through the gloom, Thomas believed he saw the bulk of Judd Chalkhill on a bed of straw – alone. He moved softly through the door into the yard, hearing only nightbirds calling in the distance. Soon he had reached the wash-house, clambered on to an upturned tub and was moving gingerly along the tiled roof towards the rear wall of the house, which towered above. The dark mass of ivy shone, its leaves reflecting little patches of moonlight. Without allowing himself to dwell on the foolhardiness of his enterprise, he grasped the nearest fronds of thick ivy, and tested them with his weight: they were firm. The next moment he had swung himself from the roof and was working his way towards his goal: the half-open casement above.

A sound made him freeze. He peered upwards, to be rewarded by the sight of Eliza's head poking out of the window.

Involuntarily he almost laughed aloud, then stifled it. He realized then how tense he was, and that a thought had been at the back of his mind all day that it was a dream – or worse, that she had been toying with him. Now he relaxed. It would be all right. Breathing steadily, he raised himself the last few feet until his head was level with the window sill.

He found that he was grinning, and berated himself for a lovesick fool. Yet it was real – here she was, in her shift, dark hair loose about her shoulders, leaning towards him and planting a wet kiss upon his mouth.

'Quickly,' she said, and swung the window wide. And in seconds he had clambered through, found the chest below and was stepping into the dark room. As he tried to accustom his eyes to the indoors a light blazed suddenly. He blinked and saw Eliza had struck a tinderbox and was putting the flame to a small candle. She placed it on a beam over the empty fireplace and turned to him with a smile.

He caught his breath, then took a step towards her.

There was a narrow bed, and that was enough, but she did not lead him to it – not yet. Instead she raised her arms, lifted the long, white, ruched shift over her head and put it aside. In the warm, butter-yellow glow of the candle, he saw her body for the first time, and swallowed. *So like Mary's*, he thought vaguely, then put the old memory aside and began to loosen his shirt.

Seven

She was by turns a doe and a vixen, a maiden and a scold. One moment she cleaved to him like a lover, kissing his body and murmuring soft words of encouragement, taking him inside her with a deep sigh of pleasure. But later, after they had both slept awhile, she turned fiercely upon him and tore at his chest and shoulders, laughing at his wide-eyed stare, then sat astride him, commanding and impatient.

'I will be Phyllis,' she said. 'She was the wife of Aristotle, who rode him round the room like a beast, naked and bridled.' She took hold of his manhood and, when he gasped, smiled broadly. 'Or shall I be Joan of Arc – La Pucelle? I've a dash of Huguenot blood, so I'm told, as well as speaking passable French. See: *Veux-tu m'entrer?*'

He stared, then looked away, aware suddenly of the yawning chasm between his class and hers. Once, four years ago, he had spent a secret night with his master's wife, Lady Margaret, at her bidding in a house in London. The experience had been unlike those he had known with women of his own station. Neither of them had spoken of it again; it was as if it had never been. Eliza, he saw – younger and fiercer, if not insatiable – had used men like him before, perhaps more often than he cared to dwell on.

'Am I then your toy?' he asked. 'A puppet, to play what part you will?'

She said nothing, but her smile faded. 'You're my foil,' she said sharply. 'If you were a swordsman I would fain see your *mandritta*, and your *imbroccada*.' Then just as abruptly the smile returned and it was warm and loving, as she had been when they stood in the yard the night before. 'Nay, Master Thomas,' she murmured. 'You are no woman's puppet

76

'. . . Or man's either. Else I would not let you into my bed, let alone my heart.'

She let out a sigh and let him go, swinging her thigh across his body, then lying back beside him.

'I never knew a woman change her moods so fast,' he said.

She turned and nestled against him, now like a young girl. 'Tell me things I have not heard before,' she asked him.

Thinking there was small likelihood that anything he knew would interest her much, he murmured: 'I thought there were things you would tell me.'

She was silent for a moment, then said: 'Mayhap I could. Like how I was bought by Sir Giles – just another of his bad bargains.'

He turned to look at her, and waited.

'I am his ward,' she said. 'When I was sixteen he bought my wardship from Sir John Hunt, thinking I would inherit a small fortune, only to find the estate is worthless. Do you wonder that he is laughed at in every corner of the county?'

'And what age are you now?' Thomas asked, realizing with some alarm that she was younger than he had thought.

'I am nineteen,' she told him. 'They keep me as woman-in-waiting to Lady Katherine in the hope that by the time I am of age their fortunes may have changed. Else, with no dowry, I am likely to end an old maid, like the daughters.' She spoke without self-pity and when he searched her face, he saw no sign of tears.

'I thought you were some years older,' he said at last, feeling a twinge of embarrassment. He was almost twenty years her senior.

'People do,' Eliza said simply. She put out a hand and rubbed the sparse reddish hair on his chest. 'No matter, my swain. I know what I am, and what I do.'

'I believe it,' he said, and took her hand. 'I also think you know much of what goes on at Chilbourne . . . Even, mayhap, things you are not meant to know.'

A smile spread slowly across her face. 'So,' she murmured, 'this is why you came to my bed. You are hunting for clues.'

He met her eyes. 'It was you who said I was being used.'

She hesitated. 'Are you not dismayed,' she asked, 'at being engaged to instruct Gervase, who is no more suited to hawking than a huntsman is to composing madrigals?'

'The young man and I have already spoken of it,' Thomas told her. 'He will keep up the lessons to please Sir Giles – though they will be short, as well as infrequent . . .'

'So he may go where he will.' Eliza nodded. 'Have you wondered where he goes?' Thomas was about to answer, but instead shook his head slightly and waited. 'Have you seen him of late?' Eliza enquired.

'Not of late,' he admitted with a feeling of unease. He looked into her eyes and saw a trace of amusement. 'Is he involved in Lady Jane's disappearance?' he ventured.

Eliza laughed softly. 'They planned it together, my sweet.'

Thomas took a breath involuntarily. 'How . . .?'

'See now,' Eliza said and, passing her hand across his chest and stomach, began stroking him as if he were her pet. 'I will tell you what I can, so long as you never say it came from my lips.'

He gave a brief nod, trying to focus on her words, not on the effect her grooming was having upon him.

'When I say you are being used, I mean in two ways. On the one hand, you must be seen to search the county for Jane, to satisfy Sir Giles and Ridley. If you found her, I have little doubt the wedding would go ahead, for Sir Giles is in desperate straits and resolved to see it through. His hope is that Ridley, wed to a healthy young bride, will not live long . . .'

She broke off with a half-smile. Thomas saw then the shape of Sir Giles's plans, and felt a degree of contempt for him.

'The Lady Katherine . . .' he began, but Eliza put a hand on his lips.

'She hates the arrangement,' she said quietly. 'Yet she will not disobey her husband. She fears for the future if they fall deeper into debt.' When Thomas said nothing, she went on: 'Now I will tell you the other way in which you are being used: by Gervase, and by Jane herself.'

He started. 'What do you mean?'

'They are pledged that Jane shall never marry that monstrous old man. The sisters have made a bond – not Margaret, for she is too young, and they have not told her all. But Emma and Jane . . .' She hesitated. 'I will not tell you all, for I too wish to help.'

But he was agitated now, and she sensed it. 'Do not judge them harshly, Thomas,' she begged. 'They saw no other course, for Jane's happiness, than the one they have taken.'

'At least tell me that letter was not false,' he said at last. 'That she is safe—'

'She is safe, and unharmed,' Eliza murmured. 'And when the time is right she will come back and face the consequences.' She paused, then added: 'You should not be deceived by her manner; Jane is cleverer than she looks.'

He frowned. 'Who was it that released the ramage hawk?'

She smiled. 'I suppose one of your calling finds that a hard blow. It was Emma who freed the bird – as Jane asked her to. It was a sign of her own escape. Her mother understood – only her father is too thickheaded to see it.'

He sighed. Suddenly he was the repository of more secrets than he wanted. 'And how,' he asked after a moment, 'did she make her escape?'

Eliza ceased her grooming and, putting a hand to his chin, began tugging at his beard instead. She was like an overgrown child, he thought, who must play all the while.

'You were close by, were you not?' she enquired. 'Saw you not where she went?'

He stared. 'On the open Downs, with not a tree in sight . . .' He caught the twinkle in her eye and stopped. 'Nay, I did not see – nor did anyone.'

'Then all went as planned,' Eliza said. But sensing his discomfort, she added: 'You and Master Hawkes should have dug deeper at Cracked Oak. Instead you stood aside while the Lady Euphemia pulled the wool over her cousin's eyes, as she has always done. She is not so simple-minded as people believe.'

At that he raised his head, rested on his elbow and stared at her. 'So John Steer and I are to wander the county till Doomsday on a fruitless errand,' he said, sounding

more angry than he expected to. 'While half the household laughs up their sleeves at us. Know you not what a
fool it makes me? I have a daughter, and a place back at
my master's manor in Berkshire, where I am needed—'
He broke off, for she lifted her face, and kissed him firmly
on the mouth.

'I know, my handsome falconer,' she said softly. 'Yet I
am not to blame.'

He let out a sigh. 'No.'

'And I would help you if I could,' she went on. 'Only I
have no powers here.'

He nodded slightly, then saw a sly look steal across her
features. The next moment she slid her hand downwards,
and smiled broadly when he shivered from head to toe.

'Save one,' she finished.

In the chill hour before dawn, Thomas left Eliza's chamber
by the way he had entered it, managing to get himself down
to the stable yard without making any noise. On the cobbles,
he pulled on his boots, stood up and moved quietly towards
the stable. But as he reached the entrance the unmistakeable
sound of hoof-beats stopped him in his tracks.

He turned quickly, peering through the gloom, and thought
he made out a horseman slowing to a walk beside the paddock.
As he watched, the figure dismounted, led his mount through
the gate and quickly began unsaddling it. Within a few
moments he had the trappings in his hands, had shut the gate
and was walking rapidly towards the stable.

Instinctively Thomas flattened himself against the wall
behind the open stable door. He heard the man approach,
heard his soft footfalls on the cobbles. He passed within a
yard of Thomas and entered the stable. Thomas waited, and
heard – as no doubt the other man heard – the unmistakeable drone of Judd Chalkhill's snoring from the far end. A
moment later the man reappeared empty-handed, whereupon
Thomas stepped away from the wall and blocked his path.
There was a sudden intake of breath.

'In God's name, what . . .' Gervase Lambert stood before
him.

'Were you taking an early ride, sir?' Thomas enquired.

Gervase stared, clearly lost for words. Seizing his advantage, Thomas pressed it home. 'Perhaps you have been visiting Lady Jane . . .'

The young man's face was pale and gaunt in the half-light. This time he wore no satin doublet, only plain riding clothes. After a moment he said: 'I believe we had an understanding, Thomas.'

Thomas raised an eyebrow. 'That was before I knew you were party to your sister's disappearance.'

'Who told you that?' Gervase demanded.

'Forgive my impudence, sir,' Thomas replied, 'but I don't feel inclined to answer questions. Mayhap you will answer some of mine?'

The reversal of their situations, by virtue of the power of the knowledge that Thomas held, was not lost on the young man. He swallowed, then appeared to choose the line of least resistance.

'I will answer some of them – if I can,' he said.

Thomas fixed him with a hard look. 'Where is Lady Jane hiding?'

Gervase blinked, then shook his head. 'No. Do what you will, but I will not tell you that.'

Thomas sensed a resolve there that would not bend, and his estimation of Sir Giles's young ward went up a notch.

'Will you tell me how long she intends to remain away from her father's house?'

Gervase hesitated, then answered: 'Until her plans are brought to fruition.'

'What plans?' Thomas asked, but the other was already shaking his head.

'You will learn in time, as will everyone else. And you will rejoice for her.'

Something fell into place then. With a start, Thomas realized the answer to this riddle was so simple that he had failed to see it before him – as, it appeared, had everyone else.

'Because she will be married,' he said, and almost laughed. What better way for the girl to put herself beyond the reach of her unpleasant suitor? Those whom God had joined, not even Ridley and all his wealth could put asunder . . .

But Gervase, very agitated now, stepped close to him so that they were almost touching. His voice was low and urgent. 'I implore you, Thomas – if you care about her happiness, as well as mine, you will forget what you have just said, and not speak of it to anyone.'

As well as mine . . . It was Thomas's turn to stare. 'You! You are marrying her – the one you spoke of as your own sister!'

Gervase gave a short laugh. 'But she is not my sister! We have loved each other since we were children . . . We always swore we would marry . . .' He broke off and looked away unhappily. 'Only Sir Giles stood in our way – him and his consummate skill at losing money.'

Thomas took a gulp of night air and breathed out, shaking his head. Now what was he to do?

Gervase faced him again. 'I see what a bind we have placed you in,' he muttered. 'But I believe you are a true friend, and would not ruin our happiness.'

Now that the matter was laid bare, Thomas began to turn it about. 'But how?' he began. 'She cannot marry without her father's consent . . .'

'If the banns have been read three times, and a man of God performs the proper rites, he cannot undo it,' Gervase countered. 'No one can!'

'Man of God?' Thomas echoed. 'That drunken parson—'

'Not Parry!' Gervase's tone was scornful. 'He is the last one I would trust.' He glanced suddenly at the sky; dawn was nearly upon them.

'Let me say this, Thomas,' he said. 'You may search, and you may find her before the time we need has elapsed. But what pleasure will it afford you? To see her brought back, weeping – for she has wept long and pitifully for the hurt she did her mother and father – to submit to being joined in wedlock with that . . .' He stopped and looked Thomas in the eye. 'She would rather die.'

Thomas said nothing. Invisible mules tugged him in opposite directions. He served Sir Robert, who had placed him in Sir Giles's service, and Sir Giles had all but begged him to find his daughter. Yet the girl was safe, and biding her time until she could marry Gervase – which was clearly her desire. And nobody who had seen the girl could wish her anything but joy . . .

Gervase was peering at him in the gloom. 'Well, what will you do?'

Thomas frowned, feeling the young man's anxiety about him like a cloud. There was one course open to him, but he had small liking for it. 'I will do nothing,' he said. 'For now.'

Gervase sighed and his mouth began to widen into a smile, until something in Thomas's manner stayed him.

'For now,' he repeated. 'If you will give me your word that you will tell Sir Giles what you do.'

Gervase gaped. 'I cannot . . .'

'You must,' Thomas told him. 'You owe him the duty of a son – even if you end up as his son-in-law . . .' He trailed off, steeling himself to disregard the look of helplessness on Gervase's face. 'Think what harm you may do – to your future, let alone that of Lady Jane.'

'Harm?' Gervase repeated after a moment. 'What of the harm that will be done to her if she marries that harsh old man who cares for naught but his own interests?' He grew suddenly heated. 'You have seen, I guess, how he treats his falconer. Would you care to know how he treats his women servants?'

Thomas frowned. 'I can imagine it.'

'I doubt that,' Gervase told him, then mastered himself with an effort. 'Yet I will not say more.'

He took a step, then turned back to Thomas. 'I love her from the depths of my heart, falconer,' he said quietly. 'And I too would die rather than see her marry Ridley.'

Thomas sighed. 'You must tell Sir Giles,' he said, 'and face the consequences. It is best coming from you, surely?'

Gervase hesitated, then without a word turned and walked away towards the house.

From the depths of the stables, Judd Chalkhill's snoring continued unabated.

*   *   *

An hour later John Steer rounded the yard wall and trotted up towards the weathering, to find Thomas already tending the falcons.

Sharp-witted as usual, the little man sensed that he was not in the humour for conversation, and busied himself about his work in silence. Below them, they heard the morning stirrings of the household coming to life. A cock crowed in the coop, and horses snickered in the paddock.

A short while later, the two men walked steadily away from Chilbourne, uphill towards the Downs. There was low cloud this morning, which did not look as if it would lift. A light breeze blew across from the Plain, lifting the plumage of the hooded birds on their wrists.

They walked for a quarter of an hour before releasing the falcons and letting them soar. After a moment, Thomas turned to see his companion watching him without expression. Then for the first time he noticed the dark bruise on Steer's left cheek.

'What have you been about, John?' he asked. 'Getting yourself into mischief?'

Steer shook his head, and Thomas saw the look on his face, and drew breath sharply. 'He did that. Your master?'

Steer gave the tiniest of shrugs, then, peering closely at Thomas, narrowed his eyes.

Thomas was angry – angrier than he had been for a long time, and for reasons he did not fully understand. Taking deep breaths of the damp morning air, he gazed upwards towards the towering falcons, then back to Steer.

'What in God's name are we doing here?' he asked suddenly.

Steer raised his eyebrows. 'Where would you rather be?'

In Eliza's bed, Thomas thought, then turned his mind to the present. 'Our search is pointless,' he said. 'I have no stomach left for it.'

Steer watched him.

'I have a proposition for you,' Thomas told him. 'We ride across the river again and find an inn where the ale is good and nobody cares who we are. And there we sit, and tell each other our troubles.'

Steer returned his gaze. Then, to Thomas's relief, he gave a quick smile of agreement.

The inn was at Upavon, a village little more than two miles upriver from the Enford crossing. After turning the horses over to an ostler, who for another penny agreed to keep his eyes on the hawks, hooded and tethered to a rail, Thomas and his diminutive friend walked into the taproom. There they found a bench near the chimney corner and, each with a mug in his fist, they talked.

They talked not of their work or their craft, for that needed no elaboration. They talked instead of their families: Thomas with a lightening of his heart as he spoke of Eleanor, now fifteen and a much-treasured maid to Lady Margaret Vicary. Steer spoke of his son and Thomas fell silent, letting the man finish his tale. For John Steer's son, after an unpromising start in life, had fallen foul of the law and taken a grim path, ever downward and ever darker.

'My master paid his debts at first,' Steer said haltingly, seemingly unused to telling the tale. 'I owe him much, though it hurts me to say so.' He drank long and deep from his mug and stared into the fireplace, where logs were piled but unlit. 'I left my studies,' he admitted, in the saddest voice Thomas had yet heard him use. 'Because I got a woman with child.'

Thomas's silence seemed to encourage him, for he went on, 'She was one of Ridley's servants. When she died giving birth to the boy, Ridley said he would take him away, or sell him, he cared not. I had been helping his falconers – I had the way with hawks, even Ridley could see it. So after I had gone down on my knee to him, he gave me a place, provided I worked for low wages and looked to the child myself. It has been hard.'

The drawer appeared and Thomas signalled to him to bring each of them another mug.

'Serving a harsh master is always hard, but bringing up a child alone is harder. It surprised no one when Kit – my son – ran wild and took to brawling, as he took to dicing and gaming, and finally to the road. I could never master him – he was bigger than me by the time he was twelve years old.'

Steer broke off, shaking his head. 'Small wonder after the life he has led that he would end up a wanted man. He's for the gallows if ever he is caught. A high lawyer, who waylays folk and robs them. I hear his favourite haunt is a place called Hounslow Heath.'

Seeing the helpless look on the little falconer's face, Thomas placed a hand on his shoulder. Steer looked up. 'Nay, I ask not for your pity, Thomas,' he said softly.

'Will you not take my friendship?' Thomas asked. A thought had occurred to him. The drawer appeared with two full mugs then, and each of them took a drink.

'I have needed another falconer to help me at Petbury for years,' Thomas said, wiping his mouth. 'My master is kindly enough – if I spoke with him . . .'

But Steer shook his head. 'Ridley would never release me from his service,' he said. 'He told me once that if I tried to leave he would call in all the debts he has paid on my son's behalf. If I failed to pay them – as he knows I cannot – he would issue a suit against me, and have me clapped up in the debtors' gaol.'

Thomas let out a sigh. 'He's a man who enjoys having folk in his power.'

'That he does,' Steer agreed. 'And he always gets his way.'

Thomas frowned at the floor. 'Maybe not in everything,' he said at last.

Steer glanced at him. There was a warmth between them that owed little to the drink, though it had helped. 'Tell me now, what is on your mind,' Steer said. 'I know something troubles you.'

And so Thomas told him at last of the plot hatched by Gervase Lambert and Lady Jane Buckridge to marry in secret and return to Chilbourne as man and wife.

Steer gasped aloud. 'Good Christ – my master will throw a fit!' Then he gave a little nervous laugh. 'Would that I might see his face . . .' His smile faded. 'He would not brook such an insult. He will have Lambert killed.'

Thomas's eyes narrowed. 'He would not dare. The young man is Sir Giles's ward – and Sir Giles, for all his faults and his poor reputation, is a knight of the shire, and not without influence.'

'True.' Steer was thinking hard. He took another pull from his mug to help him. Thomas took one too.

'What a coil we are in, Thomas,' the other said after a moment. 'We know more than is good for us.'

'We do,' Thomas said, and laughed suddenly. Steer looked at him and broke out into a smile. Then he was laughing too. The two of them, now the dam had burst, laughed longer and louder, causing the few drinkers in the inn to glance round and grin in sympathy. Whatever the joke, it must be a good one.

And, draining their mugs, the two falconers called for more strong ale, and fell to laughing again – at their predicament, at the folly of their betters, and at the whole world in general, which seemed more and more ridiculous the longer they dwelled upon it, and the more they drank. Until, in the middle of the afternoon, they staggered out into the street and remembered they had left their mounts and hawks in the stable. Then it was, struggling to clear his fuddled mind, Thomas lurched to a nearby horse trough and ducked his head under the cool water. Steer saw and decided to duck his head too. The two of them drank a little, then sat on the ground, gasping, until the village began to swirl a little less about them, and their senses began to function a little better. Then it was that a thought sprang up unbidden from Thomas's recent memory. *You and master Hawkes should have dug deeper at Cracked Oak*, Eliza had said. And he knew then what they should do next.

'Will you ride with me over to the Lady Euphemia's house once more?' he asked. 'And help me poke around a little?'

Steer peered at him, trying to focus. 'What for?'

'Just to say we have been searching, as we were ordered to do,' Thomas told him, smiling broadly.

Steer's smile was even broader. 'Gladly,' he said. 'Only I've a better reason: if that whoreson Purveyor fellow is there again, I'll knock the smirk off his face!'

Thomas stared, sobering up more rapidly now. But before he could make reply the little man was on his feet, dusting off his breeches. Then he walked away towards the stable.

Thomas got to his feet and followed.

Eight

B y the time they had ridden some miles downriver and found Cracked Oak amid its copse of beeches, they were sober enough to begin regretting their decision.

Evening was drawing in, and the hawks were edgy and wanted feeding. Besides, as Thomas and John Steer rode up the short lane, they found no horses tethered to the fabled oak tree – nor, for that matter, to anything else. They halted, sitting their mounts and staring at the old house, basking in the haze of late afternoon. An air of tranquillity, even timelessness, hung over Cracked Oak, which, on closer inspection revealed telltale symptoms of neglect and decay: peeling paint, cracked stonework and a sagging roof. Martins darted in and out of their nests under the eaves. Glancing up, Thomas saw that some of the first-floor casements were open, but there was no sound of the Lady Euphemia at her virginals. In fact, there seemed no sign of anyone . . .

Unaccountably, Thomas felt a prickling at the back of his neck. Glancing at Steer, he saw that he too was uneasy. A minute passed, and no servant appeared in the doorway. The only sound was the cooing of ringdoves in the trees behind them.

'Is anyone at home?' Thomas called out, but there was only silence. Then, as both men were dismounting, they heard a muffled shout from somewhere in the house. It was followed by another – a different voice.

Quickly they found a suitable branch and tethered the hooded falcons. Then Thomas strode to the front door and banged on it with his fist. As Steer came up beside him, they heard another cry, and this time there seemed little doubt: someone was calling for help.

The door was locked. Thomas put his shoulder to it, but the heavy old timbers held. 'I'll find a window,' Steer said, and trotted off round the side of the house. Thomas thumped the door again, and was answered by what seemed like a chorus of voices from within. Whoever it was, they seemed to be on the ground floor – yet for some reason were unable to come to the door.

A shout brought him running around the rear of the house, where there was an overgrown kitchen garden, in time to see Steer's legs disappearing through an open casement. A moment later he heard the groan of old bolts being drawn, and a back door creaked open. Thomas walked inside to join Steer, both of them blinking in the gloomy interior.

The shouts came again, with redoubled vigour, from some-where ahead and to their left: women's voices, and the feeble cry of an old man. But it was then, as his eyes grew accus-tomed to the unlit passage in which they stood, that Thomas saw the devastation.

The floorboards had been ripped from their ground-frame, the interior walls laid open as if with an axe. To the right was the doorway to a storeroom, which had been ransacked. It seemed that everything had been thrown down from the shelves, which had then been torn from the walls. The lath-and-plaster partitions had likewise been pulled apart, the floorboards lifted. Dust and debris lay everywhere. Cracked Oak looked as though it was undergoing the first stages of demolition.

Ahead and to the left was another door, and now there was no mistake: the shouting came from within. Thomas picked his way across the ruined floor, gripped the latch and lifted it, but the door did not move. He glanced down and saw a heavy lock, but there was no key in it.

'We'll have to force it,' Steer murmured, coming up behind him. He too looked amazed by the state of the house.

'I'm the heavier,' Thomas said. He stepped back, then shoulder-charged the door. At first it held, but on the third attempt it gave with a splintering crash, so that he fell forward and almost toppled over a broken stool that lay in his path. On every side was more destruction: boards lifted and thrown aside, an oaken chest forced open . . . But what pulled him up short was the sight of the Lady Euphemia, flanked by her two ageing servants, sitting on the floor by the far wall, the three of them tied up and bound together with twine, and shouting with a mixture of anguish and relief.

It was dark by the time Sir Giles arrived at Cracked Oak, accompanied by Richard Hawkes and John Steer, leading extra horses. Thomas had agreed to stay with the Lady Euphemia, after she and her two servants had been freed and helped to the best chamber on the upper floor to recover a little. Though this room, like every other in the house, had been taken apart with a systematic determination, even fury, that defied description.

It was the ageing Bartholomew Byres who gave most cause for concern, the reason for which was not hard to see. He was not only weak from the treatment he had received – he had been beaten about the head. And it was the Lady Euphemia herself, after Mary Henshaw had brought cloths and a basin of water, who bathed the old man's cuts and bruises while maintaining a stream of invective that allowed Thomas not a moment to interrupt.

'You were right, my dear, and I was a fool – a foolish old maid to trust them, let alone allow them into my house . . . Letters patent notwithstanding. Indeed I'm a fool twice over to believe such a knave to be a servant of Her Majesty, God save her. One look at that ape he keeps for a servant should have sufficed . . . Oh, look at your poor ear . . .' She broke off suddenly, sniffed loudly, pulled a soiled kerchief from her sleeve and wiped her nose.

Thomas had quickly thrown a few floorboards down and found chairs enough for them all to sit while he hunted about the house for strong liquor to revive them. This proved difficult: the kitchen was a mass of broken shelves, smashed crocks and jars. Forcing his way through a doorway to the still room, he saw even worse destruction. Sacks of grain and herbs lay slashed open, pits had been dug in the earthen floor, shutters were ripped from the window frames . . . Seizing a half-empty flagon of sack, which had somehow escaped the carnage, he had hurried back to the upper floor to offer some succour to his charges.

Their story emerged piecemeal, and it was chilling enough. Warren the Purveyor – who was clearly nothing of the kind – had arrived on Sunday afternoon, and had charmed his way into Lady Euphemia's presence. Once inside, his manner had changed alarmingly. He had summoned his servant, who had laid hold of both Mary and Bartholomew and forced them to remain in the upper chamber with their mistress, while to Lady Euphemia's horror the two men began to take the house apart. Not only were they deaf to all questions, let alone protests, they had spent the next two days ransacking each room in turn, while their prisoners were moved forcibly from one part of the house to another and kept under lock and key. They had been allowed a little food and drink, but nothing more. Finally, that same morning, the two men had bound them, locked them in the downstairs room and ridden away without a word.

'Which means they were in the midst of their knavery when John Steer and I came by here yesterday, sir,' Thomas muttered some time later to Sir Giles. He frowned. 'And we rode away and left them to it . . .'

The little party stood outside the front door of the house. Steer was readying the horses. The exhausted Lady Euphemia and her servants were to move to Chilbourne for the time being, while she and Sir Giles decided what was to be done.

'But in God's name, if the man isn't a Crown Purveyor, then who is he?' Sir Giles asked in exasperation. 'And what the devil was he looking for?'

There came a cough, and both men turned to Bartholomew Byres, tired and bruised, who was standing close by. The old man bowed. 'With your pardon, sir, there is something that might throw a little light on the matter.'

Richard Hawkes came up then, at his most officious, carrying a flaming rush torch, to report that they were ready to leave. Sir Giles nodded impatiently and held up a hand.

'In a moment. First, Byres has something to tell us.'

The old man coughed again, then turned and led the way around the side of the house. Sir Giles signalled Hawkes to

92

bring the torch while he and Thomas followed. Presently the four men stood in the kitchen garden beside a tumbledown hut.

'They – Warren and his man – brought me out here last night,' Byres began. 'They left my lady and Mary locked inside. They wanted to know of Master Tyrrell's visit . . .'

Sir Giles frowned at the old man. 'Tyrrell – not Agnes Tyrrell's boy?'

'Indeed, sir,' Byres answered. 'The Lady Euphemia's nephew, Master John. She was always fond of him – though he has not been here for some years. He left the University . . . Indeed he is believed to have left England, and gone to sea.'

'What did they do here?' Hawkes asked impatiently. Byres turned to him with a bleak look.

'They hurt me sorely, sir,' he replied. 'Or rather, the servant did – Miles, he is called. I heard the name . . .' He hesitated, then collected himself. 'They said if I knew where it was I should tell them, and they would spare me and leave us in peace. I told them I knew not what they meant, whereupon they grew angry, and . . .' His rheumy eyes dropped and he touched the bruises on his cheek.

'Go on.' Sir Giles's voice was harsh in the semi-darkness. Thomas glanced at him, then at Hawkes. Even he seemed held by the old man's tale.

'I could not help them, and in the end they believed me. They were taking me back inside the house when Warren stopped and said he had a task for me. He sent his servant off and he brought a bundle of clothes – or so it seemed to be. And he said I was to burn it, and leave no trace. If I did not do so he would have Miles break my arms.'

There were low exclamations from the men standing close, their faces garish in the sputtering torchlight. But Thomas saw the look in Byres's eyes and spoke up.

'You did not burn it, did you?'

A trace of a smile appeared on Byres's lips. 'I did not, Master Thomas. I made a fire, here in the garden, and burned twigs and rags – anything that came to hand. The bundle I hid, for I have faith in my Maker, and I believed He wanted me to live, to tell my story.'

Sir Giles let out a gasp. 'You have done well! Where is this bundle?'

Byres was already pulling open the door of the hut. While Hawkes held the light, he stooped and rummaged among a muddle of old garden tools and sacks. Finally he pulled out a dark roll of woollen cloth, surprisingly bulky and tied with a piece of frayed rope.

The men's curiosity had got the better of them, and in their eagerness they had almost forgotten the Lady Euphemia. Sitting unsteadily on a horse beside the ruined oak tree, she called out as they reappeared: 'Cousin, if I do not find myself in a comfortable chamber soon, with a posset beside me, I shall die!'

'Of course, my dear.' Sir Giles, reverting to his normal condition of agitation, gave the order for all to mount up and ride for Chilbourne. But first he beckoned Thomas forward.

'Tomorrow morning,' he said in a low voice, 'bring it to the little chamber on the south side of the house, before dinner. Until then keep it safe, and speak of it to no one.'

Thomas nodded, took the mysterious bundle and walked over to a nearby tree, where Tamora was still sitting patiently under her hood.

The next morning, events moved quicker than Thomas expected. When he and John Steer, having exercised their birds, walked into the kitchens in the hope of finding a breakfast, Redmund Oakes rose from a seat near the fire to greet them.

'I have Sir Giles's instruction,' he said, looking at Thomas. 'You are to retrieve the object he entrusted you with last night, and bring it at once to the Great Chamber.'

Thomas nodded and went out. It seemed Steer would be breaking his fast without him.

A few minutes later, carrying the bundle, he followed the slow-moving Oakes through the house and into the Great Chamber where, to his surprise, several men were already gathered about the table. As Thomas made his bow and approached, he saw there was one he did not recognize: a tall, good-looking man of perhaps forty years, well-dressed

94

in a richly faced gown. The others he knew well enough. Sir Giles, Richard Hawkes, Bartholomew Byres – and Stephen Ridley, seated apart, wearing the glare that seemed to have become his customary expression.

'Falconer.' Sir Giles beckoned him forward. 'This is Henry Sadler, the heir of Everley Manor, and the magistrate. I have asked him to be present to help us investigate our . . .' As usual, he searched for the right words. But Sadler, with an authority that came as naturally to him as it sat so uneasily upon Sir Giles, raised a hand.

'In good time,' he said. 'For I have matters to air before you first.' He glanced around, taking in the gentleman servants – Hawkes and Redmund Oakes – as well as the others. Sir Giles, after a moment of uncertainty, spoke up.

'Only the most trusted are here, including the falconer. He is loaned by Sir Robert Vicary – you may speak freely.'

'Then I will.' Sadler nodded. 'But first let us examine the clothing you spoke of.'

At a nod from Sir Giles, Thomas brought the bundle and placed it on the table. Everyone leaned forward – even Ridley, his curiosity overriding his ill humour. Hawkes, at Sir Giles's request, brought out a knife and cut the rope, then spread the contents out. A suit of clothing it was, of good-quality black fustian, together with a short cloak. There was also a set of points, three shirts, some stockings and handkerchiefs and a spare set of buttons.

There was something else, wrapped in another shirt, which by its soiled condition seemed to have been worn recently. When Hawkes unwrapped the object, it proved to be an embroidered leather purse, now empty. He held it up and read out the initials, which were visible to all. E.W.'

'Edmund Warren.' It was Henry Sadler who now spoke. 'The inquest on the body of the man found by the roadside on Saturday, over which I presided, has concluded that he died of a broken neck, supposedly from a fall. But there were other injuries that suggest the death was no accident.' Glancing around he added, 'It is my belief he was waylaid, pulled from his horse and brutally murdered. The assailant – or assailants – then stripped the body to remove all identifying items, and concealed it. They also took his horse. These belongings, I am certain, are those of Edmund Warren, the Crown Purveyor, whose body it was.'

There was a silence. 'Then the man who took his place . . .' Sir Giles trailed off, but every man's mind was moving in the same direction.

'The man who took his place no doubt thought himself very fortunate,' Sadler went on dryly. 'He had found the perfect excuse to enable him to go where he would, looking for . . .' He shrugged. 'Whatever it was he was looking for.'

He turned to Byres. 'I understand that neither you nor your mistress have any idea what it was the man and his servant were seeking.'

Byres shook his head very deliberately. 'I know not, sir.'

Sadler looked at Thomas. 'I hear it was your timely arrival at Cracked Oak that saved the Lady Euphemia,' he said. When Thomas confirmed that it was so, he asked: 'Will you tell us why you went there, at that particular time?'

Thomas hesitated. He had hoped that Gervase Lambert might be present, for it seemed clear that Sir Giles was still in ignorance of his daughter's plan. Matters were becoming somewhat tangled. But, unwittingly, Sir Giles himself came to his rescue.

'Thomas has my leave to go where he will, as does Master Ridley's falconer,' he said. 'They are searching for my daughter—'

'And small progress have they to show for it!' It was Ridley, of course. There were muted sighs from the Chilbourne men.

'What more would you have me do, friend Stephen?' Sir Giles asked with a helpless look. But Sadler was still watching Thomas, who realized that it would be difficult to keep secrets from this man. He tried to remain impassive, even when the magistrate repeated his question.

'With your indulgence, sirs, I asked the falconer why he and his fellow chose to go to Cracked Oak at that time.'

Thomas took a breath and answered. 'Something I was told, sir, gave me cause to seek for clues to the whereabouts of Lady Jane Buckridge.'

Ridley half rose from his chair. 'You mean you have news,' he began icily, 'and you have not seen fit to impart it to us?'

Thomas sought for some reply, but help came from an unexpected quarter: Bartholomew Byres.

'With your pardon, sir,' he murmured, then coughed as all eyes swung in his direction. 'Master Thomas is correct. Lady Jane did spend one night under the Lady Euphemia's roof.'

There was consternation. Sir Giles, his brow wrinkling in the familiar furrow, turned upon the old man. 'Which night?'

Byres coughed. 'Last Saturday night, as I recall . . .'

'But why have you not spoken of this before?'

'I . . . I beg that you ask the Lady Euphemia, sir,' Byres answered, and put a hand to his brow. He looked shaken and tired. Frowning, Sir Giles turned to Hawkes.

'Pray find Mary Henshaw and tell her we crave the Lady Euphemia's presence – now.'

Hawkes hesitated. 'I fear the lady is still abed, sir . . .'

'Now!' Sir Giles repeated.

Hawkes turned sharply and left the room, whereupon Henry Sadler addressed his host. 'It would appear, Sir Giles, that those men did not find what they sought. I think, therefore, that they are still in the area, in hiding somewhere.'

Sir Giles sat down heavily. 'Very likely,' he replied vaguely, though it was clear his thoughts were now fixed upon his daughter.

'I propose to inform the High Sheriff of Wiltshire,' Sadler went on in a firm tone. 'Officers should be brought in to search the county. We are seeking a pair of murderers.'

Sir Giles swallowed. 'My daughter too is in hiding, some-where . . .' He looked up, as if the gravity of the situation had suddenly struck home. 'By the Good Lord, she may be in great danger!'

'Aye – she may indeed!' It was Ridley again, glaring at Sir Giles. 'Had you mounted a proper search, instead of entrusting it to falconers, she might now be safe within these walls – or, better still, within mine . . .' He broke off and turned away.

Thomas kept his eyes on the floor. Somehow, he thought,

this must be remedied; he would not keep Sir Giles in the dark any longer. Wherever Lady Jane was, she could well be in danger.

He looked up as the door opened and a solitary figure entered: Gervase Lambert. The other men watched as he walked the full length of the Great Chamber and bowed low to Sir Giles. Then relief swept over Thomas as the young man made his announcement.

'Sir, I have something to confess to you. And it will not wait.'

They listened, some in disbelief, some in growing anger, as Sir Giles's ward – without, to Thomas's relief, glancing in his direction – told his story. When it was done, an apoplectic Sir Giles, who had been pacing the floor, strode up to Gervase as if to strike him. The watching men stiffened, Sadler taking a step forward as if to stay Sir Giles, but the latter somehow mastered himself.

'You have done me the most cruel injury!' he cried. 'You who were like a son to me . . .' He broke off, close to tears. 'You have betrayed me – betrayed us all!'

'Indeed he has. And he shall pay!'

Thomas felt his hackles rise at the menace in Ridley's voice. To his surprise, the man had sat in silence throughout Gervase's confession. Now he rose, his face a hard mask.

'Were I a younger man I would strike you, as is the old custom, and name the time and place for our duel,' Ridley said, fixing Gervase with his cold eye. 'But a man of my years has a different kind of reputation to uphold. One for steadfastness, and determination.' He looked at Sir Giles.

'We have an agreement, sir,' he stated. 'And I will hold you to it. If you fail to meet your obligation, I will issue a suit for breach of promise – not to mention damages.'

There was alarm, not least on the face of the aged Redmund Oakes. Henry Sadler stepped forward. 'Gentlemen, let us not act in the heat of the moment—'

'There is no heat, sir,' Ridley answered. 'My anger I will contain, and keep contained until such time as I receive redress – one way or another.' He faced Sir Giles. 'You are a fool who has let opportunity slip through his grasp on numerous occasions,' he sneered. 'This time, you will see, it shall be your ruin. In the meantime, I will no longer remain under your tumbledown roof.' And, turning on his heel, he strode out of the chamber, slamming the door behind him.

Sir Giles sank into his chair as if the door's slam were the Crack of Doom.

Redmund Oakes was the first to move. Dragging his feeble frame to the table, he picked up a flagon, poured wine into a goblet and held it out to Sir Giles. After a moment the knight took it with a little smile of gratitude, and drank.

'Sir Giles.' All eyes turned to Henry Sadler, relieved that someone seemed ready to take command of the situation. 'With your permission . . .' He inclined his head towards Gervase, who still stood before them, tight-lipped and pale, like a penitent. Sir Giles gave a shrug as if lost for words, whereupon Sadler turned quickly to the young man.

'Where is Lady Jane hiding?' he asked abruptly.

Gervase swallowed and stood his ground. 'I cannot say, sir.'

'You must.' Sadler's face wore no expression.

'Sir, I have sworn to her that I love that I will let no man come between us,' Gervase replied.

'You mistake your position,' Sadler answered coolly. 'You have no rights in this matter, and you owe a duty to your guardian, Sir Giles. You shall tell us where Lady Jane is, so that she may be brought home to her father's house.'

Gervase said nothing.

'I will repeat it once, and once only,' Sadler told him. 'Either you reveal the whereabouts of Lady Jane, or . . .'

'Or what, my dearest Henry?'

The voice was familiar to all, and it came from the far end of the Great Chamber, where the Lady Euphemia, resplendent in a sea-green gown chased with silver thread, stood, attended by an embarrassed-looking Richard Hawkes.

Sir Giles rose from the table, summoning a sickly smile.

Nine

Lady Euphemia Hart, revelling in the attention of a group composed entirely of men, sat in an upholstered chair beside Sir Giles.

'There was romance in your heart, once, dear Cousin,' she murmured. 'Where it has fled to, I know not. How you could sanction the betrothal of such a dear, sweet creature as Jane to that dried-up merchant with an abacus for a soul . . .' She broke off, seemingly unaware of the impatience of her listeners. 'Love, sirs – love is everything! When I was at Court, betrothed to Sir James Warr, I would have died for love! I still would . . .'

Absently, she fingered the chain about her neck. Her thoughts were straying. Thomas, standing on the edge of the group, saw it as clearly as the other men.

'Euphemia, my dear . . .' Sir Giles struggled to keep his temper. 'Know you not what harm you have done? You have deceived me—'

'For Jane's sake!' Lady Euphemia retorted. She had clearly been in some haste to ready herself, for the ceruse paste on her face was somewhat thicker than usual, while the patches of vermilion had spread alarmingly towards her ears. 'How could I stand by and see the poor girl's life ruined?'

She cast an eye around the assembled men, settling on Henry Sadler. 'You, sir – a man who has married for love! As did your dear father, rest his soul . . . Could you permit your own fair daughter to throw aside her happiness for the sake of a dowry?'

But even Sadler, it seemed, was lost for words. And it was to unspoken relief all round when Bartholomew Byres gave his usual cough and stepped forward.

'My lady, there are other matters to consider . . .'

'Oh, boil your ears!' Lady Euphemia snapped. 'If you speak of the ruffians who held us prisoner, that has naught to do with it . . .' She caught her breath and looked about, suddenly less sure of herself. 'Can it have aught to do with it?'

'I think not, Lady Euphemia.' Henry Sadler managed an indulgent smile. 'Robbery is what drove them. Do you have any valuables secreted in the house?'

Lady Euphemia gave a little snort. 'You are too kind, sir. The whole county knows I'm as poor as a church mouse.'

Sir Giles, his forehead furrowing, got to his feet again. 'Euphemia, might we return to the other matter that has caused us such distress? Will you please tell me where Lady Jane went after she spent the night at Cracked Oak?'

'That I cannot,' Lady Euphemia replied, 'for I did not ask her, and she did not tell me. When she left my house early on Sunday morning, we agreed that the smaller the number of people who knew her destination, the better.' She smiled vaguely at Gervase Lambert. 'You must ask her betrothed.'

'He is not her betrothed!' Sir Giles exploded and turned furiously upon Gervase. 'You still refuse to tell me where she is?'

Gervase looked even paler now. 'She is safe and well, sir. That is all I will say.'

'Very well . . . You leave me no choice.' Sir Giles summoned the last shreds of his authority and announced: 'You will be confined to your chamber, under lock and key, until such time as you agree to speak. Your meals will be brought to you, and you will not be allowed visitors.' He paused. 'Even you can see that there may be no wedding without a bridegroom!'

Looking round, he gestured to Richard Hawkes, the only man suited to such a task. Embarrassed, Hawkes stepped forward and placed a hand on Gervase's shoulder. Without a word, the young man turned and allowed himself to be led away.

There was a silence, broken only by Bartholomew Byres's cough. Then the Lady Euphemia rose majestically, gathering the folds of her gown about her.

'I'm ashamed of you, Cousin!' she cried, and swept out.

Thomas, who had had enough excitement for the present, made bold to speak up. 'May I return to my duties, sir?' he asked.

Sir Giles, who had sunk back into his chair, looked up as if he had forgotten who Thomas was. 'Yes, yes,' he muttered, then frowned suddenly. 'Ah . . . the falconry lessons. I fear they will have to cease, for the time being . . .'

Thomas bowed gravely and went out.

He found John Steer at the weathering, fastening the straps on a wicker cage. Callisto, Ridley's beautiful falcon, sat perched inside, hooded and docile.

As Thomas walked up, the little man straightened and faced him. A look of understanding passed between the two of them.

'Remember what we talked of,' Thomas said. 'If you came to Petbury, I would speak to my master—'

'I know you would.' Steer held out his hand, then dropped it unexpectedly and stepped forward. It was a clumsy embrace, Thomas being a head taller than his friend, but it was enough.

Then Steer picked up the cage, gave his quick half smile and trotted away towards the stable yard, where Judd Chalkhill was readying his master's horse. He did not look back.

Thomas took Tamora on his wrist and walked off towards the Downs.

It was a sombre day. An air of gloom hung over Chilbourne, so Thomas stayed outdoors, busying himself cleaning out the weathering and tending to the two hawks – Tamora and the little lanner falcon Ridley had presented to Lady Jane, which had been left behind, unclaimed and seemingly unwanted. In the afternoon he took the bird out and exercised her, letting her go where she would. By evening she had brought down a few game birds, which he bagged up and took back to the kitchens. In the fields, the harvesters toiled at the last of the corn crop. Tomorrow was Lammas

102

Day, and the festivities would burst forth. But what cause for rejoicing would there be at Chilbourne?

Thomas took his supper alone, sitting on the slope above the house, looking out to the distant Plain. What purpose was there now in his being here? He resolved to confront Sir Giles in the morning and ask to be released from his service so that he might return to Berkshire. Sir Robert would understand when he told him what had happened. The affairs of the Buckridge family were not his concern.

His glance strayed to the house, and to a certain upstairs casement above the wash-house roof.

That night Thomas lay on his pallet in the stable loft and waited until he heard Judd Chalkhill's snoring from below. He reflected that Nan had not shared Judd's bed for some nights – not since he had startled them on the evening of his arrival, almost a week since. Perhaps it was not such a frequent arrangement as he had thought.

He slept a little then woke abruptly, judging that the hour was right. Within minutes he had dressed, crossed the stable yard and, without invitation this time, was climbing the thick ivy to Eliza's chamber. There was no light within, and the window was shut. Struggling to maintain his grip, he tapped on the glass. To his relief, after a moment the casement was opened and Eliza's head appeared.

She was half asleep, her hair untidy, but she smiled, and the cares of the day fell from Thomas's shoulders as he squeezed his tall frame into the room and wrapped her in his arms.

It was different this time; she took him quickly, without words or frills, thrusting her body against his as if to hasten his consummation. *The little death.* When it was over, sooner than he wished, and he had lifted himself breathlessly from her, she lay beside him in silence without nestling against his shoulder. Finally she spoke, her voice coming out of the darkness as if far away.

'Now I am not Phyllis, but the Whore of Babylon.'

He started. 'Nay – I wished to see you, whether you would bed me or no, for I may be leaving here tomorrow.'

She did not react.

'You told me I was no woman's puppet,' he went on. 'Likewise are you no man's whore . . .'

'I need not your words of comfort,' she told him. 'I have coupled with men of every station – even falconers.'

If she strove to hurt him, she was surprised when he lifted his head and kissed her tenderly on the lips.

'Then they were the luckiest of falconers,' he said. 'I hope they knew it.'

But she turned away and was quiet for a while – until he heard her muffled sob, and sat up at once.

'Forgive me,' he said quietly. 'If I have used you ill—'

'No!' She turned suddenly and threw herself against him, weeping like a child. He held her, stroking her back, waiting for the sobbing to subside. Finally she drew back her face, wet with tears.

'This is a house of lamentation,' she said. 'I would wager every woman weeps in her bed tonight. Emma, Lady Katherine, Margaret too . . . and one young man, locked up like a felon.' She shook her head helplessly. 'What a pass we have come to.'

He sighed. 'There is naught you nor I can do . . .'

She wiped her eyes, recovering quickly. 'Would that our places were different, and you could take me away from here.'

He hesitated, rejecting responses that he knew were empty. Then he saw her looking fixedly at him.

'You would not do so, even if you could,' she said at last, nodding slowly to herself. 'For there is someone else in your heart.' Before he could reply she added: 'I would guess that someone shares your bed at home.'

He nodded. Nell shared his bed sometimes, it was true, but . . .

'Nay!' she exclaimed, looking wide-eyed at him now. 'She isn't the one either – there is another!'

He swallowed. 'Are you a witch?' he muttered at last.

At that she smiled, and she was again the Eliza he had known two nights since, who had sat astride him and told him who she was. 'What is her name?' she asked slyly.

He looked away. He never spoke of Moll, the innkeeper he had known back in the year of the Armada, who would spend what days remained to them with her lover, an Italian who was dying of the stonemason's sickness . . . He could not be with her, so Moll was locked away, along with her sweet singing voice, in one of those chambers of his mind that he tried not to visit. Like the memory of war, long ago in the Low Countries . . .

'Moll,' he said finally, forcing the word out.

'Yes,' she murmured. 'It is she you think of when you lie with me.'

He shook his head slightly. 'I swear it isn't so.'

She slapped him then, hard across the cheek. He blinked.

'You ever lie to me again, I shall denounce you as a violator who forced his way into my bed,' she said.

He stared. 'I believe you would do so.'

'Oh, yes, my handsome hawksman, twice my age though you may be. I would do so, and watch you hang too.'

He had no words left. After a moment she placed a hand on his cheek where it smarted from the blow. 'Leave tomorrow if you must. I will not weep.'

But when he rose from her bed, she stayed him.

'Only think of me at times, when you share your pallet at home, instead of your Moll.'

He dressed in silence and climbed out into the cool night, a breeze from the Downs rippling the ivy as he descended. But the night was not over.

In the yard, Thomas pulled on his boots, then made his way softly back to the stable. As he slipped through the half-open door, he realized something was amiss. It was a moment before he realized that there was no snoring. Indeed, when he peered through the gloom, he saw that Judd was not there.

Tired and heavy of heart, he dismissed the matter and made his way to the ladder. But he had barely begun to climb when a cry rang out that stopped him dead. He listened until it was followed by another: a man's voice, raised in anger – or was it terror? Judd's voice. Judd was outside, howling in the night . . .

Thomas hurried from the stable and looked about. There

came another cry – from beyond the paddock, close to a small tree. Squinting, he made out a figure, bending, or perhaps kneeling. As he ran towards it, he realized it was Judd. But it was not the Judd he knew – the slaughterman and wrestler, the indomitable ox. As Thomas approached, he turned and stared with a face deformed by anguish. His hair hung like rat-tails about his cheeks, down which ran real tears. Then he turned away, his broad shoulders trembling, and Thomas looked and saw the prone figure in the grass beside which Judd kneeled, cradling her limp head in his huge hand.

'Nan!' he roared, as if he could revive her by the sheer power of his lungs. 'Nan!'

But Nan could not answer, because she was dead.

She was placed in the wash-house among the buck-tubs and heaps of laundry over which she had presided. Richard Hawkes took charge, instructing Thomas to take care of Judd, who was now seated in the stable, silent and withdrawn. It was dawn, and Sir Giles would have to be told. But first the usher came into the stable yard and called Thomas out to him.

'I will need your help,' he said, seemingly not liking the notion. 'Find out what you can from Judd.'

'He would not harm her,' Thomas began, but the other man shook his head quickly.

'I know that – everyone here knows that.' He lowered his voice, as if there were anyone to overhear. 'She has been raped and strangled – I'm certain of it.'

Thomas stared. 'How can you know?'

'Because I have seen it before,' Hawkes answered. Facing Thomas in the half-light, he added: 'I was not always in service here, falconer.'

He offered no further elaboration, and Thomas did not press him. With a nod, he turned and went back into the stable.

Judd stood before him, staring down at the floor. 'She had a tryst with someone,' he said. 'I know not who 'twas.' He looked up and his voice rose. 'I'll find 'ee, and I'll rend 'ee . . .'

106

'Not now,' Thomas told him. 'Rest now—'

'I won't!' Judd cried. 'I'll not rest till I take his dirty neck in my hands like 'e took Nan's . . .' He broke off, blinking, his arms raised, gazing helplessly through his tears.

Thomas looked kindly at him. 'I know.'

Judd allowed himself to be led to his straw bed in the far corner like a lamb. There he lay until mid-morning, when he was summoned to tell his tale to Sir Giles.

The parley was a tense but businesslike affair, Thomas learned later, for he was not called to give his account until dinnertime. Henry Sadler arrived with Sir Henry Willoughby, the Sheriff of Wiltshire and, along with Redmund Oakes and Richard Hawkes, were closeted in private audience with Sir Giles. Food was sent in and finally Thomas, who had finished his tasks and had waited for some hours, was summoned.

The men sat in a small chamber on the south side of the house, the remains of a hasty meal to one side. When Thomas entered and made his bow, Sir Giles spoke up at once.

'Falconer – I need your eyes and ears.'

Thomas waited, with the sinking realization that he was not going to be able to leave Chilbourne after all.

'The search for my daughter will continue,' Sir Giles told him. 'I ask you to be one of the party I have charged with the task, under the leadership of our usher, Master Hawkes.'

Thomas glanced at Hawkes, who was standing to one side. He did not meet his eye.

'In view of what has happened here, I intend to take no chances, even though I am assured my daughter is housed safely somewhere . . .' He broke off, somewhat distraught.

Sir Henry Willoughby, a bluff, grey-bearded man in an old-fashioned fur-trimmed gown, spoke up impatiently. 'Sir Giles, for the last time – would it not be simplest to merely make your young ward talk, and put an end to the matter?'

Sir Giles turned. 'What would you have me do, Master Sheriff? Put him to the rack?' When Willoughby snorted, he added absently: 'Gervase has shown courage I did not know he possessed – the boldness of a man in love. I do not doubt that much.' He looked at Hawkes. 'I have drawn up a list of places Jane might go to – friends, distant relatives . . . I want them all visited.' Hawkes inclined his head.

Sir Giles now gave way to Willoughby, who addressed the room in general. 'While that search proceeds apace I will instigate my own, for the murderers of Edmund Warren, the Crown Purveyor, and the washerwoman, Nan Greenwood.' He looked hard at Thomas. 'The slaughterman I have interrogated. Now, falconer, you will tell us what you know.'

Thomas nodded and began to give his evidence.

The search party, well mounted, left Chilbourne less than an hour later. This time Thomas carried no falcon, and there was no pretence of any other purpose than the one in hand. Hawkes, grim-faced and clearly not relishing the task, nevertheless led the group with the air of one determined to see it through. Behind him came Thomas, riding Cob, and two others: John Cardmaker the hayward, and a young village man he had brought with him, named Will Tapp. What payment Sir Giles had promised them, Thomas could not imagine. Perhaps he was relying on Cardmaker's innate sense of justice.

For his part, Thomas was not sorry to leave Chilbourne behind and gallop out on to the open Downs. The atmosphere in the house was oppressive. Servants went about their tasks sullenly. Lady Euphemia seldom left her chamber, and Lady Katherine spent her time shut away with her daughters, leaving her husband to pace about the Great Chamber in agitation – or worse, to wander about the manor, indoors and out, poking into everyone's business. Most had become adept at avoiding him.

Their first stop, for reasons Thomas did not understand, was Cracked Oak. But as the little group turned into the familiar lane, he almost gasped at the sight that greeted them, for the searchers had been back.

The chief sign of activity was a series of holes, or rather small pits, that had been dug in various places about the garden, especially near the split oak tree itself. Looking to the house, the riders, sitting their mounts in consternation, saw that it too had come in for further attention, not least because the front door stood wide open.

With a muttered curse, Hawkes dismounted. In the absence of any instruction, the other men followed suit, picking their way through the ruined forecourt to peer through the doorway. This time, Thomas saw, light showed through the roof. Seemingly the attic had now been torn apart, along with the rest of the house.

'Whatever they're looking for, it must mean a lot to 'em,' Cardmaker muttered.

No one spoke. The destruction of Cracked Oak, and the reason for the Lady Euphemia's removal to Chilbourne, were now common knowledge back in East Everley, if not further afield.

Hawkes, who had been looking through the doorway, turned away and walked briskly towards Thomas. 'Well, falconer,' he asked, 'is there aught here to provide us with a clue?'

Thomas raised an eyebrow. 'If you mean, what were they looking for—'

'Of course I don't mean that!' Hawkes snapped. 'What has happened here is not our affair. I mean, if you were young Gervase, and you and Lady Jane had planned your escape starting from here early on Sunday morning, which way would you go?'

Thomas was nonplussed. 'I know not, Master usher. I do not know the country, nor what friends or relatives the Lady Jane has, to whom . . .'

Hawkes was glaring at him, as hostile as he had been a week ago, when Thomas first encountered him in the kitchen at Chilbourne. 'I know that! I ask you to put your imagination to work, that we may descry which route she took.'

Thomas remained calm. 'I know not.'

Meeting Hawkes's eye, and seeing the anger in it, a thought came to him. There was more to this, and it concerned him alone. Though what was the substance of it, he could not fathom.

Hawkes shifted his gaze to the hayward. 'You at least know the country, John Cardmaker. Will you not help us?'

Cardmaker, shorter than Hawkes by several inches, puffed out his pigeon chest and responded in his officious tone. 'I cannot, Master Hawkes. Nor is it my place to speculate on the doings of my betters. I was asked to aid you in your search. Which direction it takes be up to you.'

Young Will Tapp, who had been standing nearby and clearly not liking the usher's manner one bit, muttered: 'That's told him, John.'

Hawkes span round. 'What did you say?'

'Nothing – just clearing my pipes,' Tapp answered and, as if to confirm the fact, coughed loudly and spat into the nearest of the freshly dug pits.

Hawkes bridled, glancing from one man to the other. There was a silence before John Cardmaker decided to be charitable.

'One thing I might do,' he began, 'seeing as what the ... what young Master Gervase and the Lady was about, is go to church.' When Hawkes frowned at him, he added: 'Can't have a wedding without banns being read – three times, at that ...'

Thomas nodded. 'Well reasoned, Master hayward.'

Hawkes considered the matter. 'Three times ... If the first time was last Sunday, she would need a further two weeks.'

'Unless they been read in secret,' Cardmaker interjected in a phlegmatic tone. 'It do happen, so I hear.'

Hawkes's frown had cleared. 'It is a start,' he said. 'We will visit every church within a day's ride. The Lady Jane could not, I reason, have gone further off than that.'

Cardmaker's jaw dropped. 'By the good Christ, that could mean Salisbury, or Marlborough, or Devizes, even! They all be within a day's ride, if you'm well mounted.'

Hawkes's official face was back. 'You agreed to help Sir Giles in his distress. Do you have a better plan?' He glanced at the others. 'Do any of you?'

Thomas eyed him. 'The list of people Sir Giles drew up – those Lady Jane might have gone to ...'

'There are too many,' Hawkes replied irritably. 'Lady Jane had – has – many friends.' He looked away, the weight of his responsibility sitting heavily upon him.

'Parson Parry be one that don't scruple to marry folk without proper banns,' Will Tapp mused.

110

Hawkes stared at him. 'So close to Chilbourne? Surely not.'

Then it was that Thomas, in one of his very rare lapses of concentration, made the mistake of answering. 'Nay, Master Gervase told me he would never trust Parry.'

Then he realized what he had said, as Hawkes's head snapped round in his direction.

'He told you that? When?'

Thomas clamped his mouth shut, but too late.

'When?' Hawkes almost shouted.

Thomas faced him. 'When I last spoke with him.'

'When was that? And where was it?'

With a sigh, Thomas answered. 'In the stable yard at Chilbourne, three nights ago.'

The silence was intense. From the trees behind Cracked Oak, ringdoves were calling.

To Thomas's surprise, and no small relief, Hawkes turned away then and walked towards his horse. After a moment the others followed. But as he placed his boot in the stirrup, the usher fixed Thomas with a hard look 'You and I will speak further of this. And I warn you, there will be a reckoning between us.'

He swung himself into the saddle. In silence, Thomas followed suit. Try as he might, he could not fathom the reason for the depth of hostility that Hawkes displayed towards him. But one thing he did not doubt: there would be a reckoning. It was no empty promise.

Putting boot heels to Cob's flanks, he followed the usher out of the ruined gardens of Cracked Oak and along the river towards Upavon.

Ten

That day they searched the Avon villages, as Thomas and Cardmaker had already done the previous Sunday. But this time they stopped at every church, talking with villagers and churchwardens. St Mary the Virgin at Upavon, St Matthew's at Rushall – even the little church at Fittleton, which had no incumbent priest of its own. Nowhere had banns been read in respect of the wedding of Lady Jane Buckridge and Gervase Lambert. It was the same story all along the valley. Finally, tired and hungry, the four men recrossed the river at Enford and made their way back via West Everley towards home.

It was evening, and a mood of excitement gripped the little village of West Everley, which was hung with green boughs for the Harvest Home festivities. Lanterns blazed from the trees, and folk called out to those they recognized – John Cardmaker and Will Tapp – to step down and join the celebrations. But Cardmaker, an East Everley man through and through, told them he was headed for the White Hound and the wrestling.

'Will you come too, falconer?' he asked Thomas as they walked the exhausted horses the last mile, passing revellers on the road where the body of the Crown Purveyor had been found only days before. That unpleasant business, it seemed, had almost been forgotten. It was Lammas Day, the harvest was in, and everyone's mind was turned towards merry-making.

'I would delight in it,' Thomas answered with a glance towards Hawkes, who was riding sullenly at the head of the party. Overhearing them, the usher turned in the saddle.

'Go where you will,' he said in a tired voice. 'There's

naught more we can do tonight. You have earned the right to drink yourself senseless, if that is your desire.'

Thomas turned to Cardmaker and Will Tapp, who broke into a grin.

So it was that an hour later, having stabled Cob and tended the hawks, Thomas walked the short mile into East Everley. Drinkers spilled from the well-lit interior of the White Hound, through the open door to the green outside, where a pitch had been prepared for the wrestling match. And the first person Thomas recognized as he drew near was Edward Birch.

Wearing only a pair of knee-length nether-hose and light shoes, Birch was seated on a stool, surrounded by admirers. Some were the worse for drink; others were busy placing wagers – an important bout was clearly in the offing. Thomas looked round for Birch's opponent and thought suddenly of Judd, who had boasted to him of his prowess in the wrestling field. He remembered how the slaughterman had looked that morning, after the shock of Nan's death. More likely, he thought, Judd was still lying distraught on his bed of straw.

A voice at his elbow made Thomas turn. It was John Cardmaker, in a clean shirt and neatly tied jerkin, looking more cheerful than when he had said his farewell a short time earlier.

'If you intend to keep your word, you may buy me that mug you promised a week or so back,' he said.

'Gladly.' Thomas smiled. 'But we should make haste – I wouldn't want to miss the bout.'

Cardmaker snorted. 'Plenty of time. Not that it'll be much of a bout: Clyffe's inside, getting enough ale down him to sink a galleon.'

'Clyffe – the cook?'

'If there be another of that name round here, I've not heard it,' Cardmaker told him, and led the way towards the inn door. With a glance at Birch, now on his feet and limbering up, Thomas was inclined to agree: the bulky Chilbourne cook would hardly be a match for the man who had clamped his hand like a carpenter's vice that morning, and smiled easily while he did it.

Will Tapp was standing just inside the inn door, paying close attention to a young village girl. He hailed Thomas as though he were a long-lost friend. 'You are right welcome,' he cried, slapping him on the back. 'See how East Everley folk do mark our harvest!'

'I will,' Thomas answered, and looked around for the drawer. The place was roaring already; no doubt the whole village was here – and the whole of West Everley on its way too.

He saw James Clyffe standing in a corner with one or two supporters, a mug in his large fist. He too wore wrestling clothes, with a jerkin over his shoulders.

'His way of training,' Cardmaker remarked in a disapproving tone. 'It'll all be over in less than a minute.'

Thomas forced his way through the throng to the taproom and called for three mugs of the house's best. The sweating drawer, working the spigot furiously, signalled that he would oblige as soon as he could. Thomas turned to go, then saw Judd Chalkhill.

He was sitting alone in a corner, staring at the floor. Men eyed him warily and kept their distance. The news of Nan's death had no doubt spread, though to see the merrymaking, it was clearly not going to be allowed to overshadow the evening. As Thomas walked over to him, Judd looked up.

'See the harvest doll, out on the green?' he muttered.

Thomas shook his head. It was customary for the last sheaf of corn that was harvested to be made into a doll, soaked with water as a rain charm, and saved for next spring's planting.

'Nan and me did 'ave a jest about it,' Judd went on. ''Er said if I proved fertile and us 'ad a harvest of our own, we'd have to marry. And I said 'er hair was like straw anyways . . .' He raised his mug to his mouth, then saw that it was empty.

'Come out and watch the wrestling,' Thomas urged. 'If you don't fancy a bout yourself, watch Clyffe get beaten.'

Judd sniffed. ''Tain't that. If I did have a bout, I'd likely forget who I was wrestling . . .' He gritted his teeth and looked Thomas in the eye. 'I keep seeing Nan . . .'

114

The drawer appeared then and thrust three brimming mugs towards Thomas. He took them with a sigh, and left Judd to his reverie.

Outside, James Clyffe was now on the green, surrounded by a group of well-wishers, though few were risking hard-earned money by betting on him. Rather, Thomas saw by their private smiles, they had wagered on him to lose.

The umpire Thomas recognized as one of the harvesters he had spoken with when he had first arrived. Stepping between the two opponents, he called the crowd to order. There was a surge of excitement; folk were pouring out of the White Hound and forming a great throng about the pitch.

When his name was called, Birch turned about, grinning, to receive a roar of acclaim. He worked his huge arms and did a couple of knee bends, then smiled broadly at his opponent. Clyffe, somewhat red-faced from the drink he had taken, glared in reply and flexed his own biceps. But though he carried at least an extra stone in weight, there was little doubt that most of it hung around his middle and spilled over his breeches.

'The bout be over when a wrestler fail to get back on his feet, or signal his desire to yield,' the umpire shouted. 'If neither opponent do yield, the tally of falls be made. If I call a hitch, 'tis no fall – both hips and a shoulder, or both shoulders and a hip, must touch the ground to make a fall!'

'Let 'em go to it!' someone called, prompting a chorus of agreement. Thomas, having handed Cardmaker and Will Tapp their mugs, smiled and took a long pull of tepid ale, glad to forget his troubles for the evening.

A roar went up and the bout began. The two wrestlers faced each other, then locked arms, grunting and straining. Birch, clearly the stronger, grasped Clyffe's left wrist with his right hand, and his upper arm with the left, then turned his back swiftly and pulled the arm across his shoulder. There was a gasp from several hundred throats, as Clyffe's feet left the ground. The next moment he had shot forward over Birch's head, and landed in the trampled grass with a thud.

Rather than go for a fall, Birch remained on his feet and

raised his arms, acknowledging the cheers. But some saw, as Thomas did, that the man's carelessness could be his downfall, for Clyffe, puffing like a prize bull, scrambled to his knees, reached forward and yanked Birch's legs from under him. The roar that rang out as he fell flat was mixed with laughter and a few jeers.

But Birch was no slouch, nor did he intend to spend too long in winning. He was on his feet in an instant, fighting for control of Clyffe's body as Clyffe was of his, each seeking to pin the other by his hips or shoulder to secure the first fall. But each time Birch almost succeeded, Clyffe managed to turn his huge body so that he landed on his chest or his side, forcing a hitch.

The crowd seethed and swayed, threatening on several occasions to engulf the wrestlers. Time and again the umpire thrust men back, shouting to them to make way. Once Clyffe, thrown for the fourth or fifth time, landed among a knot of spectators who were too slow to move. There was more laughter, but most eyes remained on the wrestlers, both breathing quickly now, sweating in the warm summer air. Dusk was falling and lanterns had been lit, some held up on poles, others stuck on nearby trees, reflecting patches of light from the heaving bodies of the wrestlers.

Thomas's mug was empty. He glanced round, debating whether to try forcing his way through to the inn. John Cardmaker was some distance away, and he was struck by the change in the portly little hayward. His cares seemed to have fallen away like chaff, and here he was bellowing for Birch, along with the rest of his village.

Thomas smiled and was turning back to the match when his eye fell upon a figure he vaguely recognized near the edge of the crowd. The man wore a cloak tied at the neck, and at first Thomas could not place him – then he remembered. It was the rector, Doctor Parry. And a vision came to his mind, of last Sunday's extraordinary sermon, with a drunken though eloquent Parry gripping the lectern to stop himself from falling down.

But Parry was not alone: standing at his shoulder, considerably taller, was a dark-bearded man, also cloaked, wearing a high-crowned hat. Thomas froze, for the man caught his eye briefly, then quickly looked away – but not before Thomas had recognized him as the one who claimed to be the Crown Purveyor, the man who had threatened him at Cracked Oak – who had held the Lady Euphemia prisoner while he ransacked her house . . .

Thomas started forward but the crowd was too thick, and none would give way. A sea of animated faces, mouths wide, bawling for Birch, stood between him and Parry. Using his height, peering above heads, Thomas caught a glimpse of a tall hat disappearing into the gloom beyond the lantern light. Looking towards Cardmaker, he opened his mouth to shout, but then realized it was useless. When he looked back the man had gone, and Parry too.

A minute later the bout ended as predicted. The only surprise was that Clyffe had lasted as long as he did, and there were shouts of sympathy, even admiration, as the sweat-soaked cook, bruised and exhausted, signalled his submission from a prone position by feebly flapping a hand. While Birch, also breathless but less bruised, acknowledged the cheers, Clyffe was helped up by two men who, judging by the expressions on their faces, were considerably richer than they had been fifteen minutes earlier, and were prepared to be charitable.

The umpire had raised his hands, and people were calling for quiet. 'Is there any man here who wishes to fight the winner?' he shouted. 'Else we will have our second bout, betwixt the chosen Harvest Home champions of East and West Everley!'

There was more cheering and Thomas saw two younger wrestlers, not so heavy as Birch, had come forward. Birch himself was pulling on a jerkin, clearly believing he had finished for the evening. But at that moment a thickset figure detached itself from the crowd and stepped softly into the wrestling field. Thomas stiffened, his hackles rising. Glancing aside, he saw that this time Cardmaker, too, had seen and recognized the man, for he was unmistakeable. He had stripped to a rough thigh-length shirt and breeches, but on his head was a black leather cap, tied over his ears. It was Miles, the tall man's servant.

117

A hush had fallen, for no one seemed to know the man. There was something unsettling about him as he spoke in an undertone to the umpire, who hesitated, then nodded. Gradually a hum arose, every man and woman questioning their neighbours. Who was he? Where had he sprung from?

The umpire raised his hand. 'A newcomer – a visitor, who says he hails from Devizes – will fight any man who dares, for a prize of twenty crowns!'

There was a gasp. Thomas, staring fixedly at the man, doubted whether the whole population of East Everley could raise that sum. This was a village affair: there were no town gallants here, no professional gamesters, no rich men who could pluck gold angels from their purses with scarcely a thought. He marvelled, too, at the man's boldness. If he and his master were the murderers of Edmund Warren – for they were without doubt the housebreakers of Cracked Oak – did he assume none knew it? Or did he not care? Even now, the Sheriff's men were searching for him.

But the crowd, save Cardmaker, who was staring in dumb silence, knew him not, and they were eager for more wrestling. When no one came forward with the offer of twenty crowns, the umpire turned and spoke with Miles again, who shrugged.

'Ten crowns, then!' the umpire shouted. 'Ten crowns, to hold our own against the townsman!'

There was muttering, and a few voices raised with offers of a groat here, a sixpence there. Then it was that Thomas saw John Cardmaker, wearing his official face, pushing his way through the crowd with difficulty. What will he do? Thomas wondered and, scarcely knowing that he did so, began pushing forward himself.

But events were moving fast, and in a different direction. A wide-brimmed hat had appeared, and coins were being thrown into it. Excitement had clearly spread to the revellers in the White Hound, which now seemed to have emptied. Men elbowed their way forward to throw money. Meanwhile Edward Birch stood silently, without expression.

The hat had passed Thomas, who ignored it, still trying to work his way forward. Now it reached the umpire again, and he, along with another man, began counting the contents. He raised his hands, and the hubbub lessened.

'Eight pounds, eleven shillings and five pence halfpenny!' he cried. The crowd shouted in amazement. Eight pounds was a year's living wage for an unskilled working man – some brought up their families on half that.

The umpire spoke to Miles who, if he was aware of his growing unpopularity, showed no sign of it. He merely nodded and looked towards Edward Birch, upon whom all eyes now turned.

At a sign from the umpire, Birch nodded and stepped forward until he was close to his opponent. Thomas stared at the drama that was unfolding: Cardmaker pulling himself free of the crowd, strutting up to the umpire only to be thrust back into the throng; watchers frantically placing bets; the two opponents face to face, eyeing each other unflinchingly.

'The bout will take place!' The umpire called – and a roar of approval went up. Birch was their man; he would not let them down. This time, almost everyone had put money on him.

Cardmaker was looking round for Thomas. Catching his eye, Thomas signalled that he would move close. After the bout they might be able to act, especially if they called on the umpire to announce that this man was a wanted felon. But for now they were helpless, for the crowd was at fever pitch, and to try and thwart them would have been folly. Pressing close on every side, villagers of East and West Everley put aside their traditional rivalry and united against a common enemy: an outsider, and a rogue too by the look of him, who was interested only in the money – their money, too. Even James Clyffe had appeared, to urge on the man who had trounced him but a short while ago.

Birch had got his wind back, which was just as well. Having eyeballed his opponent, he walked a few paces back to what had become his corner – though it was merely that part of the crowd where his supporters were thickest. There he stood, taking deep breaths, working his glistening body for what promised to be a far greater trial than the one he had just had. Someone offered him a mug, but instead of

119

drinking from it he poured the ale over his head and shook himself like a dog.

His opponent, Miles – if that was his true name, Thomas thought as he watched helplessly, pressed in on all sides – stood motionless, ignoring the taunts and jibes of young men and those who had imbibed too freely. Never for a moment had he taken his eyes off Edward Birch, save to look briefly at the hatfull of coins. A hush fell then as he took a pace forward. Birch took one too and it was as though an invisible spark shot between the two men, and cracked in the air. Without waiting for the umpire's signal – indeed, they seemed to have forgotten his presence – the two men leaped forward and cannoned into one another with an audible thud. And the crowd yelled in sheer, animal delight.

It was not a wrestling contest but a fight to the finish, in which such rules as existed counted for nothing. Instinctively, like ripples in a pool, the crowd widened their circle about the two heaving, grunting figures, who proceeded to do battle royal. And Thomas found himself muttering Birch's name, then calling it aloud, and finally shouting for the struggling man who had once debated with him in a hayfield about the rights of poor folk to take a little extra from their masters.

Miles was the first to fall, but it was no wrestling hold that felled him, rather Birch's sheer strength making him lose his balance. But as he went down, he caught the Everley champion by the neck, yanking him forward on to his knees. The next moment people cried out, for Miles had his hands about Birch's throat.

Birch, realizing the danger, managed to force the man's hands apart, then stepped back and aimed a kick into his side. The crowd groaned, hearing the thud, but Miles, though hurt, managed to roll aside and grasp Birch's foot. In a second he was on his knees, twisting the foot with all his strength. Then there came a nauseating sound: the crack of a bone being wrenched out of place.

Birch gave a little cry and, lurching forward from a sitting position, brought his fist back and rammed it into Miles's face. The crowd howled as Miles stepped back, blood spurting from his nose. Birch struggled to his feet, arms flailing, managing to catch Miles by the wrist. But the classic throw he had used so successfully on James Clyffe would not serve now, for the moment he put his weight on his shattered ankle, the pain told, and he winced and staggered. Miles, his face showing merciless anger now as the blood ran down his mouth and chin, seized his chance. His fists slammed into Birch's ribs and stomach, then, as Birch doubled over, he drew his foot back and aimed a kick at the damaged ankle. Birch cried out in pain, making a futile grab at the other's leg and missing it – which gave Miles another opportunity to kick him, this time in the solar plexus, and then as Birch dropped to his knees, at his chest, face and neck . . .

There was dismay. Some cried out to stop the fight, but others shouted them down. Thomas, heart in mouth, glanced at the umpire, who had come forward. Then, to his and the crowd's horror, Miles straightened up, saw the umpire, and promptly fisted him in the face.

The umpire dropped like a stone and the crowd fell silent. For Miles, panting and dripping blood, was looking deliberately around at them all, eyeing every man in open challenge. And there was not one who didn't step back, for they had looked into his eyes and seen their certain death, had they dared face up to him.

Birch, dazed and groaning, was struggling to raise himself, but Miles, with a half smile, turned to the crowd, shrugged, and kicked him again, this time in the head.

There came a sound like a sigh. Tense as a bow string, Thomas looked about, seeing that women had fallen away to the edges of the crowd, some clearly distressed. Only the younger and bolder village men stayed near the centre.

'Give way!' one called to Miles. 'He's finished – you have your purse!'

Miles took a pace towards the man, who blinked and fell silent. Thomas saw Birch, still conscious, struggling once more to rise. Blood ran down the side of his head, and from a gash on his cheek. Huge red weals, on top of the ones Clyffe had managed to inflict, showed on his body.

Miles looked round, saw him struggling, and stepped in for the kill. As the crowd watched in horror, he picked up his enfeebled opponent as if he were a doll and stood him on his feet. Birch swayed, tried to raise a fist, then cried out as the pain from the ankle shot through his body again. But Miles ignored him: he merely cracked him on the jaw, then, grabbing him by the hair before he could fall down, he butted him with his cannonball head, hard on the bridge of his nose. Birch crumpled like a dead animal, all his joints suddenly loose, and fell silently on to the red-spattered grass. There he lay on his back, eyes closed, blood running from his nose, face calm as if asleep.

The silence now was one of disbelief. Nobody moved when Miles straightened himself slowly, regaining his wind and wiping the blood from his face with the edge of his tattered shirt. But only now did the true reason for the dumb looks on the faces of every man there dawn on him. For Miles put a hand to his head and caught the dangling end of the leather thong that had tied his cap and which had been pulled away. At once he understood, and gave an animal snarl, whipping his head round, daring anyone to speak. None dared: they merely gazed at the terrible, scarred patches of tissue on either side of his head where his ears should have been.

And still they watched as he stepped over the still figure of the umpire lying nearby, caught up the hat containing the prize money and tipped the coins into his big, swollen hand. He found his jerkin and a short woollen cape, which no one had noticed him discard. Then he turned and stared fixedly at a point in the crowd until, like the parting of waves, a little path opened up for him.

He walked through it and away from the green, without looking back, until he reached the crossroads. And people watched silently as he disappeared into the night.

Thomas, scanning the crowd, then caught sight of a huge figure standing motionless beside the door of the inn. Judd Chalkhill had watched Miles depart, without expression. How long he had been there was anyone's guess.

They carried Birch and the umpire into the White Hound and summoned a healing woman. Now that the stranger had gone, excited talk broke out on every side, though some seemed scarcely able to believe what they had witnessed.

Cardmaker, furious at being ignored, was all bustle. Seeing Will Tapp standing dumbly to one side, he shouted at him to run to Everley Manor and tell Magistrate Sadler what had happened.

'And tell him the man who's just walked off with our money is one of the whoreson varlets they've been seeking!'

Men looked askance at him in his anger. The umpire, who turned out aptly enough to be named Benjamin Down, was conscious now. Sitting on a stool near the taproom door, he called out. 'What d'ye mean, John?'

'What do I mean?' Cardmaker echoed. 'I mean you've stood by like a lot of sheep and let him escape – a house-breaker, and mayhap a murderer too!'

There was muttering on all sides. Nursing a swollen jaw, the umpire waved Cardmaker over and urged him to explain. And so, with not a little pride at being the repository of important information, the hayward told everyone within earshot about the events at Cracked Oak, and the hunt for Miles and his cold-eyed master, who were very likely the killers of the man found by the roadside – the real Crown Purveyor.

The umpire exploded. 'I knew it! He'm no Devizes man! Not with that manner of speech . . .'

By now the inn was packed to bursting point. Folk gaped at the news and urged Cardmaker on, pressing him for details. East Everley, it seemed, had never known so much excitement. But Thomas, growing tired of the whole business, left them and pushed his way into the taproom where a small group was clustered round the bloodied figure of Edward Birch.

The healing woman was near to sixty years, sunburned and spare from a lifetime in the fields. She had cleaned Birch's wounds and dabbed ointment on them, and stopped the bleeding from his nose. But the ankle was beyond her skills.

'Ye'd best find a barber-surgeon, Edward,' she murmured. 'One who'll set the bone fair and bind 'ee. 'Twill be many days before ye can walk on it, and ye'll be a crutched man for weeks – mayhap for longer.'

Birch, pale-faced and drawn, lay on a board that had been placed across a couple of barrels, bearing his pain in silence. Looking at the concerned faces about him, his gaze fell upon Thomas and his eyes narrowed in recognition.

'Falconer . . . We did not finish our discourse, as I recall.'

Thomas gave him a wry smile. 'It was a brave fight you made, Master Birch.'

'Who was the man?' Birch asked, looking around. But at that moment there came a chorus of angry shouts from the big room.

'Now what's afoot?' the healing woman asked in a tired voice. 'Bain't they had enough blood for one night?'

Thomas cocked an ear to the hubbub and turned back with a frown. 'They're raising a hue and cry,' he said, and shook his head. 'It should be a matter for the Sheriff . . .'

At that moment a fair-haired woman in a hat and home-spun cloak pushed her way into the room. Seeing Birch, she gave a little cry and knelt quickly at his side.

'You great fool!' she cried. 'Now what have you broke?'

Birch grimaced. 'I'll be well enough by and by,' he muttered, and threw Thomas an embarrassed look. 'My wife, Frances . . .' When Frances glanced up at the tall falconer, Birch explained: 'He helped carry me in.'

Frances threw Thomas a sharp look. 'Why? Had he a wager on you losing?'

Thomas shook his head, but the woman turned quickly back to her husband as he gave a little grunt of pain. She looked anxiously to the healing woman, who told her the news.

'By the heavens!' Frances Birch cried. 'And where am I to find a surgeon?'

'One at Pewsey died last spring,' the woman answered. 'There be one at Marlborough . . .' She looked round, for there was more noise from the other room. Glancing through the doorway, they saw men surging outside, some plucking lanterns from the trees by the green.

Thomas sighed, wondering whether the mob – for such it seemed to have become – was driven by the righteous desire to apprehend a felon, or by the notion that he had walked off with their money.

He turned and bent low beside Birch and his kneeling spouse. 'I will take you to Marlborough,' he offered. 'If you know where we may find the surgeon.'

Birch blinked. 'You would do that for me?'

Thomas shrugged slightly. 'I can't think of anything better to do,' he said.

Eleven

The next day, Thomas recalled, was Friday the thirteenth and, though he had never been a highly superstitious man, he soon found that his travelling companions were of a different mind.

It was a grim-faced Judd Chalkhill who drove the rickety cart with Thomas seated on the wagon bed beside the propped-up figure of Edward Birch. And as they left East Everley, reached the crossroads and turned north towards Marlborough, the matter soon came to light.

'Nan 'ad a lucky green stone that a swadder gave 'er once,' Judd said morosely. 'I ought to 'ave found 'ee and took 'ee with us, to ward off evil.' He gazed beyond the ears of the plodding horse to the dusty road ahead. 'I never asked what she did, for 'ee to give it.'

Thomas sat facing backwards, watching the village rooftops diminish behind them. Last night's spontaneous search of the neighbourhood by lantern-light had proved fruitless, as he expected. Most went to their beds afterwards, and no doubt many nursed sore heads in the morning, while mourning their empty pockets.

It was a good ten miles to Marlborough, by the straight road that ran through Savernake Forest. The sun was already up; he estimated it would be a four or five-hour journey – a journey, in fact, that had almost not taken place. For when he had presented himself at Chilbourne the previous night and told of the events in the village, he had found few sympathetic ears. Sir Giles, alarmed at the continued presence in the area of the bogus Crown Purveyor and his savage servant, had at once sent word to Sir Henry Willoughby. It seemed a watch had now been set at Cracked Oak, but there had been no further sign of the two men. Sir Giles ordered a bad-tempered Richard Hawkes to assist by mounting a further search in the morning. Hawkes it was who had objected strongly to Thomas's request to borrow a cart and take the injured Edward Birch to Marlborough, saying the man should look to his own family. But to Thomas's surprise, Redmund Oakes, the butler, in a rare use of his authority, overruled him, saying that the manor of Chilbourne owed much to the villagers of East Everley, and it would be wrong to deny one of the harvesters succour, especially in view of the circumstances. Sir Giles had finally agreed that the slaughterman could drive the cart, which would relieve them of his long face for a day, at least. The death of Nan Greenwood, it seemed, was of rapidly diminishing importance in view of the continued absence of Lady Jane – save for the fact that someone else would have to be hired to attend to the growing mountain of Chilbourne laundry.

Birch sat in silence as the little square tower of East Everley church disappeared in the morning haze. He half turned to Thomas. 'We've a long way to go, falconer,' he said. 'Shall we tell each other fanciful tales, like the pilgrims of old? Or talk of matters closer to hand?'

Thomas considered this, feeling the warm sun on his face. If he could not yet go home, at least this little excursion would take him away from the Buckridge family for a while. Since John Steer had gone, the notion of another mind to turn things over with cheered him, for he had already deemed Birch to be a shrewd man, if a somewhat sly one.

'I would talk of matters at hand,' he answered. 'I am tired of combing the Downs . . . I have been pressed into Sir Giles's service, and made privy to more of his family secrets than I like. I would that the matter were closed one way or another, so that I may return to my home and my work.'

Birch found his costrel, unstopped it and took a drink. Then he offered it to Thomas. To his surprise it was not cider he tasted, but watered sack.

'Strong drink for a journey, is it not?' he remarked, handing the bottle back.

Birch took it and smiled broadly. 'Don't ask where it came

from,' he murmured. When Thomas raised an eyebrow, he added, "Tis a holiday for me – and for you. Do we not deserve a little of the good things in life, to sugar our day?'

When Thomas shrugged, he went on: 'It seems to me there is much that preys on your mind. Mayhap that comes from having a livery . . .' He smiled. 'I have naught but my cottage and my family, and what I earn with my hands, and my wits.'

Thomas glanced at him. 'Apart from skulking about in hayfields, I never learned what work it is you do,' he mused.

'I don't recall I ever told you,' Birch replied.

Thomas said nothing.

'If you are debating whether to trust me or no,' Birch said after a moment, 'I would caution against it.'

Thomas glanced over his shoulder. Judd Chalkhill was muttering to himself, lost in some private reverie. He turned back to Birch. 'I will remember,' he said.

'But still, I am obliged to you,' Birch told him. 'For helping me, but mostly for not betraying me to the hayward, or to Sir Giles.'

Thomas gave a shrug. 'I've had other matters to think upon.'

'I heard.' Birch nodded. 'All the village knows how young Lambert spirited Lady Jane Buckridge off to be his bride, and set you and that whoreson Hawkes to search for her. And that she spent a night at Cracked Oak before she disappeared – and since last night, they know what happened there. Like they know of Nan Greenwood's murder, and how the Sheriff's hunting for two men – one of whom, it now seems, near wrenched my foot off.' He lowered his eyes. 'If I'd have known what manner of man I was fighting, I'd have done things different.'

'I tried to get close,' Thomas told him. 'So did Cardmaker.'

Birch grimaced. 'I've known some wicked men,' he said. 'But few that take pleasure in giving pain like he did . . . You saw how his ears were cropped?'

'I did,' Thomas agreed. 'And I know what kind of man he is, for I have faced him myself.' And when Birch looked sharply at him, Thomas told how he and Cardmaker had met the man and his master on the Downs, and how he had encountered him again at Cracked Oak, with John Steer. And how he had seen the man's master last night, on the edge of the crowd, standing close by Doctor Parry.

Birch started. 'Parry! He was with him?'

'It looked that way,' Thomas answered.

A thoughtful look had come over Birch's face. 'Why did you not tell this before?'

'I told Sir Giles last night,' Thomas answered.

Birch shook his head. 'He hasn't the wit to put matters together . . .' He broke off. 'Parry could be the link you are seeking.'

'Link?' Thomas frowned at him.

'Ask any man hereabouts, and he will tell you what manner of man is our divine rector,' Birch said with an edge to his voice. ''Tis not just the drink he succumbs to.'

With some difficulty he turned, as if to discover whether Judd was listening. He winced as his swollen ankle, roughly bandaged, pained him. Then he spoke again, lowering his voice.

'He uses whores worse than others use their dogs. I'm surprised you never ran into him of a night, sneaking about Chilbourne . . .'

Thomas started. 'You don't mean—'

'Nay!' Birch whispered, and jerked his head meaningfully over his shoulder, urging quiet. 'He was an old customer of Nan's . . . why would he throttle her? Parry's a rogue, but he's no killer,' Birch went on quietly. 'Nor do we have such here, east of the Plain . . .' He gazed at the stubble fields as they passed, empty of harvesters now, then looked hard at Thomas. 'I'd be looking for a stranger. A devil – nay, an animal – who takes what he will, and uses folk as an animal do.'

Thomas stared back at him. Miles. But then a dozen questions arose. Why did he come boldly into the wrestling field and offer to fight for money? Why were he and his master still close by? Then he thought of Cracked Oak, and the second visit they had paid – the pits dug all over the garden. They were short of money. Whatever they were seeking, they had not yet found it – and they intended to stay until they had.

There came an oath from the driver's seat, and he looked round sharply. Judd was pointing.

'D'ye see?' he cried. 'A hare with a black rump did fly across our path – what's that if it bain't an omen?'

He turned to the other two. 'I told 'ee I should have took that lucky green stone!'

Thomas met Birch's eye, then stared at the road behind.

Marlborough simmered in the noonday heat as, dusty and sore from the bone-wrenching ride, they pulled into the town square and halted. Along the shallow River Kennett the bustling market town lay, a mass of steep-roofed timber-frame houses and shops filled with the cries of sellers and the noise of animals. At either end of the main square sat a church. On the east was the ancient chapel of St Mary the Virgin, where almost a century before Henry VIII's famous chancellor, Thomas Wolsey, had been ordained. On the west was the church of St Peter. And it was here that Thomas made the first of his discoveries that would turn events around. As he and Judd, having asked directions to the house of the barber-surgeon, supported a limping Edward Birch between them, they passed the doorway of St Peter's, seeking a little street on the western edge of the town. And there, in plain letters on a paper stuck to the door, were pasted the wedding banns. At the bottom of the list of names were those of Gervase Lambert and Jane Buckridge.

Thomas stopped dead, which caused Judd to lurch forward, almost dropping Birch. Birch yelped as he was forced to steady himself by putting weight on his bad ankle.

'Your pardon,' Thomas muttered, peering at the church door. He read the words again as if unsure of what he had seen, but they were plain enough.

'Jesu, Thomas, what be about?' Judd demanded. Thomas could only point to the letters – which meant nothing to the other men. Quickly, he explained.

'She'm in Marlingborough?' Judd's mouth dropped open. 'Who do she know here?'

130

Birch, grunting with pain, butted in. 'Would you oblige me by getting me to the surgeon?' he cried. 'Then you can do what you please!'

Thomas turned with a smile, which quickly faded when he remembered something else. Surely Stephen Ridley's home was in Marlborough. Could he have learned of this?

Then he reasoned the matter out, and it seemed simple: the man had not thought of looking for the girl under his own nose. He assumed she was closer to home – to Chilbourne, and the Downs, and the vast empty Plain. A clever girl, was Jane. Eliza had told him as much.

He took Birch's arm again and, indifferent to the curious stares of townsfolk, headed for the barber-surgeon's street.

The barber-surgeon, somewhat prim in his skullcap, neat ruff and black gown, looked disapprovingly at the three men who stumbled into his parlour. His first concern was whether they had money to pay for the treatment. Upon being satisfied on that score, he bade Thomas and Judd leave and return in an hour. So, with no small relief, they said farewell to Edward Birch and went looking for somewhere to eat.

There was a large inn called the White Hart on one side of the square. Seated by a window, Thomas sipped his beer and watched the folk pass by, musing on his discovery. Now that he had located Jane – for she must be somewhere in the town – what should he do?

He watched Judd licking his platter clean, still hungry after his third helping. The ordinary had been good enough: loin of hare, cabbage and pease with hard bread. For some reason he thought of John Steer, no doubt tending Ridley's hawks at his grand house somewhere on the outskirts of the town. Had he too passed by the church and seen the banns posted? Who else might have done so?

He tipped his mug and took a pull, then saw Judd eyeing him.

'What'll 'ee do, 'bout they banns?' he asked.

Thomas shrugged. 'Sir Giles will have to be told.'

Judd picked up his own mug, swirling the contents as he gazed into it. 'Didn't never seem right, splicing her to that

131

old man,' he muttered. 'But then Chilbourne folk – high-born and low – don't have much in the way of choice these days.'

Thomas sighed. 'If you're done, we'd best look to our friend.'

Judd sniffed. 'Reckon his wrestling days be over,' he grunted. ''Tis pity, for I did sorely want to fight him again.' He glanced at Thomas, then looked away with a wry grin. 'You been lookin' for housebreakers, when you spent all morning sittin' in a wagon with one,' he chuckled.

Thomas frowned. Birch?

'He'd not scruple to a bit of thieving, that one,' Judd told him. His smile faded. 'Only he don't leave no sign, like they done at Cracked Oak. And he wouldn't tie folk up, neither – especially old women.'

Thomas was short with him. 'So why touch on the matter?'

'All right, hawksman,' Judd retorted. ''Ee don't have to fly into a fit.'

Thomas drained his mug. 'If you're ready . . .'

He stood up to leave. Judd had saved a wedge of pippin pie, which he stuffed inside his shirt, for Birch's dinner. Then, as they made their way to the door, Thomas caught sight of a tall woman, grey-haired but fit and erect, walking purposefully towards the square. With her was a man he had not seen before – a servant by the look of him, in plain drugget, carrying a covered basket.

Thomas froze, struggling to put a name to the face that was familiar. Behind, Judd muttered an oath as he almost crashed into him. 'Now what be ye about?'

And then the name came to Thomas at once: Mary Henshaw, the Lady Euphemia's servant.

Birch was waiting for them, pale-faced, on a bench outside the barber-surgeon's front door. His ankle was bound with oak splints on either side, and wrapped tightly with a linen bandage. As Thomas and Judd approached, he picked up a crutch and waved it at them.

'Least I can get about,' he said, though there was no mirth in his smile. 'Yon doctor wants payment for this, too.'

132

Thomas went inside and settled the account from the money Sir Robert had given him. Sir Giles, the night before, had been unable to put his hands on his purse at short notice. By the time he had re-emerged to rejoin his companions, his mind was working fast.

Judd was seated on the bench beside Birch, taking in the sunshine, neither of them in any hurry to move.

'Your master expects us back by nightfall,' Thomas said.

Judd nodded in morose fashion. 'That he do.'

'All afternoon, rattling along that dusty road . . .' Thomas began.

The two men looked up sharply.

'Suppose that poor old Chilbourne nag lost a shoe and went lame, just as we got into Marlborough,' Thomas suggested.

Judd's eyes narrowed.

'We'd have to get him attended to. Likely the farrier would say he isn't fit to go ten miles today. He'd need to rest, wouldn't he?' He glanced at Birch.

'Mayhap he would,' Birch agreed.

'So we'd be forced to find lodgings for the night,' Thomas finished.

The other two stared. 'If we had money for 'ee,' Judd murmured.

'Of course,' Thomas answered, jingling his purse. 'And in the morning, we could all meet at the stable – I mean, the farrier's – and be on our way. Isn't that fair?'

Birch managed a smile. 'I would gladly find an inn where I might dull this pain with a flagon or two,' he said.

Thomas glanced at Judd. 'I could look after 'ee,' Judd offered. 'Fetch his drink and his supper, and such . . .'

Thomas counted out some coins and handed them over.

'Till the morning,' he said.

After leaving Judd and Birch to spend the rest of the day as they would, Thomas walked back to the town square and took up a position at a corner from where he could see almost everyone who entered it. It was not market day, but there was the usual Friday bustle. Fish days, decreed by law, forced housewives and maidservants into the town to buy what they could. Here, far from the sea, there was likely to be less choice than in London, but river fish – pike, bream, trout, even perch – would satisfy any man's table. Hence the covered baskets that most women carried.

He waited half an hour before his hopes were realized. He had begun to fret that he might have been mistaken; as far as he knew, Mary Henshaw attended her mistress at Chilbourne, and had not left it since their arrival. But to his relief he caught sight of her, still accompanied by her attendant, walking between the stalls of the fruit sellers. There was no doubt in his mind now. There was a quiet strength about the woman that he had noticed the first time he saw her, at Cracked Oak. Though what further qualities she possessed, to be entrusted with some private business here, he had yet to learn. One thing he did dismiss was the likelihood that her presence could be unconnected with the name of Lady Jane Buckridge, there on the door of St Peter's church. That seemed to Thomas to stretch coincidence a little too far.

He watched her make a final purchase of vegetables, which her companion – or was he her protector? – stowed in the basket. Then the two walked off towards the edge of the square.

He waited a few moments, then followed them past the White Hart, and on towards the north-west corner of the town. Past alleys and ginnels – and close by St Peter's church, though they followed a narrowing way north of the graveyard and then turned left. Thomas came up to the corner, stopped and quickly looked round in time to see both Mary Henshaw and the man disappear through the door of a narrow-fronted house, no different to any of the others along this quiet street.

Now he hesitated. For the first time it occurred to him that there might be an entirely innocent explanation for Mary's presence. Perhaps the Lady Euphemia had a town house here that he knew nothing about . . . He pictured her, as he had last seen her in the Great Chamber at Chilbourne, telling Henry Sadler that she was as poor as a church mouse.

Was that true? If so, why had the dark-bearded man who had stolen the Crown Purveyor's identity gone to so much trouble to search Cracked Oak, room by room – and the garden too?

He made a resolve to drop all pretext and go straight to the house. After all, he was here on legitimate business. If he had chanced to see Mistress Henshaw in the square, why should he not be curious? He had the feeling that she would be the one who needed to offer some explanation.

He walked up to the door and knocked; but nobody answered.

He waited and knocked again, louder this time. Still nothing. He knocked again, so loudly that heads appeared at the doorways on either side. Glancing round, he faced a ruddy-cheeked woman with an untidy mop of auburn hair poking out from under her hood, watching him with frank curiosity.

'D'ye wish to break the door?' she enquired.

'Your pardon, mistress,' he smiled. 'I cannot get an answer, though I know there are folk within.'

'Very like,' the woman agreed. 'Though you may knock until Doomsday, and still get none. The young lady is a deaf mute.'

He kept his face blank. 'Young lady?'

'I have said.'

He considered a moment. 'And her maidservant?'

'She has none,' came the reply. 'Her mother visits some-times . . .'

Her mother . . . He swallowed, then stepped back from the door and smiled at the tousle-haired woman.

'Then I shall call another day,' he said, and walked off back the way he had come. Once round the corner he stopped, leaning against a wall-post. His breathing had quickened, and he knew why – just as he knew that by sheer fortune he had stumbled upon the hiding place of Lady Jane Buckridge.

He found the narrow ginnel on to which the houses backed, a foul-smelling way with privies and dung-heaps at either

135

end. A dog yapped at his boots, then gave up when he ignored it. Counting the number of back entrances carefully, Thomas arrived at the one which he was certain belonged to the house where nobody wanted to answer the door, only to find there was no rear entry. But there was a paling, not very high . . . In seconds he had climbed over it and was stepping through a small back yard that contained nothing but a stack of firewood.

The back windows were shuttered, and he had little doubt that the door was locked. But when he reached it and lifted the latch, to his surprise it opened. After a second's hesitation he took a breath then thrust it inwards.

He was in a dark passageway with doors opening to left and right. There was no sound from any of the downstairs rooms. Then he heard it and stood still. Music.

From upstairs came the sweet sound of a cittern, skilfully played, along with the high voice of a young woman singing.

He was so surprised that he failed to hear the soft foot-fall from the doorway to his left until it was too late. Something cracked down upon the crown of his head, a stunning blow that took away all his strength. As he fell, it seemed that the music grew faster and louder until it was like bees buzzing in his ears . . . Then the stone-flagged floor tilted upwards, and everything went dark.

He opened his eyes, then wished he hadn't as pain shot through his head from front to back, and forwards again. He closed his eyes, for nausea threatened, which he managed to control, then opened them very slowly. He was seated on a bench in a front room of the house. Sunlight streamed in through the windows. He moved, and found that he was unfettered.

Then a voice startled him. 'I didn't mean to fell you so hard. I didn't know who you were.'

He turned his head slowly. A thin-faced fellow in plain drugget was on his feet, peering rather anxiously at Thomas. He looked familiar. Then Thomas remembered: the one with the basket – Mary Henshaw's servant.

'Mistress is angry with me,' the man went on rather

urgently. '''Twould oblige me much if you said you weren't too sorely hurt.'

Nervously he proffered a cup. After a moment Thomas took it and drank some of the weak ale. He handed it back and blinked, trying to ignore the pounding in his head. 'Why would I want to oblige you?' he muttered finally.

'No reason,' the other replied. 'Only I'm but a servant like you, and could lose my place.' He looked away, not liking the look in Thomas's eye. 'For all I knew you were from Ridley . . .'

Thomas flexed his shoulders, still tired from his long journey in the wagon-bed that morning. Events were slowly falling back into place.

'Ridley?' He began to understand. 'So she is here, hiding under his very nose . . .' He fixed the man with a hard look. 'I speak, of course, of Lady Jane Buckridge.'

The man looked frightened. 'I'm but a servant,' he repeated.

'Hired by whom?' Thomas enquired. 'Gervase Lambert, or the Lady Euphemia, or . . .'

The man swallowed. 'Nay,' he muttered. 'Ask me nothing – she will speak with you soon, and . . .' He trailed off, flicking his tongue out to moisten dry lips. 'I am only here to protect her,' he ended feebly.

Something tumbled out of Thomas's memory. 'Was it you, last weekend, who gave a boy on the Everley Downs a letter from your mistress, and charged him to take it to Sir Giles?'

The man gaped. 'Who told it was me?'

Thomas began to feel like one who was holding a winning hand, when he believed he had lost. 'And who attended Lady Jane when she left Cracked Oak last Sunday morning, and rode here to Marlborough?'

The fellow looked round suddenly, for there was a sound from above. Only now did Thomas notice that there came no music from upstairs. His voice, and that of the servant, had drawn attention.

'I can say naught,' the thin-faced man said quickly. 'You must ask mistress . . . Only say I did not break your head, for she seems to favour you.'

137

'Favour me?' Thomas frowned, even as two sets of foot-steps came down the stairs and voices grew louder. He looked past the nervous figure of the servant and rose instinctively, trying to ignore the dizziness that came upon him.

Suddenly it seemed as though the room was full of people; and he was managing a bow of sorts, because before him stood the slight but composed figure of Lady Jane Buckridge.

Twelve

There was a short silence. Mary Henshaw had come in behind Lady Jane, and now stood by the window. She wore no expression, but Lady Jane favoured Thomas with a slight smile.

'Guido thought you were an intruder,' she said quietly. 'Which, of course, you are.'

Thomas nodded slightly, wondering how to conduct himself. He did indeed feel as though he had no business here.

'I was ordered by your father to search for you, my lady,' he said finally. 'I saw Mistress Henshaw in the square ...' He glanced at Mary Henshaw, who returned his gaze unflinchingly.

'Well, falconer,' Jane Buckridge said, 'now you have found me, what will you do?'

There was the light of challenge in her eyes. It struck Thomas that she bore little resemblance to the shy young woman he had first seen sitting demurely at her father's table.

'I also saw the banns at the church near the square,' he said, feeling somewhat dizzy again.

Lady Jane gave a little sigh, then noticed his demeanour. An expression of concern flitted across her delicate features.

'Please sit down, falconer,' she said. 'We will all sit. Guido ...' She turned to the servant. 'Bring some wine – the claret.'

Guido bowed and went out, clearly with some relief. Gratefully, Thomas sat down, his head beginning to clear. Mary Henshaw took a straight-backed oak chair from the wall and placed it opposite, whereupon Jane sat facing him.

139

'Shall I leave you, my lady?' Mary enquired.

'No, please stay,' Jane told her, gesturing to another chair. Mary Henshaw sat down upon it, arranging her skirts with some difficulty. Lady Jane, though she wore a Spanish farthingale with a kirtle over it, seemed to have no difficulty making herself comfortable. *She is mighty calm*, thought Thomas, *for one who has been caught out . . .*

'I asked what you intend to do now,' Jane said.

'In truth, my lady, I know not,' Thomas answered.

Jane smiled and he lowered his eyes, so pretty was she. Again, he found himself thinking the same thoughts that had since been echoed by others: how could a man like Ridley be allowed to make her his own, and use her as he would?

'Poor falconer,' she said at last. 'What a quandary we have placed you in.'

He managed a smile. 'True enough, my lady.'

'Well, you have a simple choice before you. When you return to Chilbourne . . .' A thought struck her. 'I assume you intend to return there?'

'I must, my lady,' Thomas answered. 'I have left one of my master's best horses in the stable there.'

'So,' Jane nodded. 'You either tell my father you have found me, or you do not. Simple enough.' Then, before Thomas could reply, she added: 'Of course, by the time he learns of my whereabouts, I could have moved elsewhere.'

'I suppose so, my lady,' Thomas said. 'But if you intend to keep to your wedding plans, he need only set a watch upon the church.'

'I could find another church,' Jane retorted, a slight flush on her cheek now.

'Indeed.' Thomas nodded. 'But how would Master Gervase know where to find you?' Then he glanced at Mary Henshaw, and felt suddenly foolish. She, of course, was the go-between. She it was who had been aiding Jane all along . . .

He looked deliberately at her. 'Assuming, that is, he were able to get away from his present accommodation . . .'

Now he had upset Lady Jane. 'I would thank you not to speak of my – of Gervase in that manner,' she said sharply. 'It is none of your affair in any case.'

140

'My lady.' They both turned towards Mary Henshaw, whose composure had never wavered. 'There is small need to distress yourself. We may put the falconer's choices to him in a different fashion.'

Thomas narrowed his eyes. Meeting them calmly, the elderly servant continued: 'Master Finbow will find that he has few allies at Chilbourne if he chooses to disrupt your plans. It may be that he oversteps himself.' She paused, then added, 'He might even find himself accused of violating a lady of the household. Such a crime is punishable only by death.'

A chill silence fell. At that moment the thin-faced servant appeared, bowed and placed wine and cups on a small table. He was about to pour, but after a swift glance at the company, he turned and disappeared at once.

Thomas looked steadily at Mary Henshaw, but his thoughts were leaping like grasshoppers. *Eliza . . . How much did Mary know?* Then a terrible thought struck him – that he had been used by the very woman who had warned him, to obtain his silence if the need arose.

Jane had glanced at her servant, then back to Thomas. 'That would be a dreadful matter, if it were true,' she murmured.

Thomas took a deep breath. 'It is not true, my lady.'

'But whose word would the magistrate take?' Mary Henshaw fixed him with a bland stare. 'That of a lady of the household, or a falconer, loaned by his master to give hawking lessons – who, from what I hear, has been lax in his duties from the moment he arrived?'

Thomas kept his temper, but now he felt the granite-hard malice of this old woman, sharp and unyielding. Had he known what sort of adversary she could prove, he told himself, he would have been more circumspect.

'I have done naught but serve Sir Giles,' he said, though he felt as though the ground were slipping away beneath him.

'And you may continue to serve him,' Jane said. 'Indeed, I see no reason why he should not permit you to return home soon, with a purse for your troubles. You have clearly been caught up in matters that are outside your territory.'

But, almost before he knew it, Thomas was voicing the thought that had just occurred to him. 'Does Sir Giles know you are aiding his daughter?' he asked, looking directly at Mary Henshaw. 'Moreover, does he know how far the Lady Euphemia is caught up in the same matter?'

Both women remained calm, but the flush on Lady Jane's cheek deepened a little. 'The Lady Euphemia's business is none of your concern,' she replied.

'Might I be so bold as to ask whose house this is, my lady?' Thomas asked, on another impulse that had sprung from nowhere. Seemingly without knowing it his mind had been turning matters about, and allowing one or two interesting notions to rise to the surface.

Mary Henshaw was very still, but he caught a look in her eye, and knew that he had struck his mark. Though the woman concealed it well, she was afraid.

'Enough!' Lady Jane had risen to her feet. Instinctively Thomas stood up too.

'You may leave now, falconer,' she said. 'Guido will ensure that you do.' Thomas sensed that Guido, though he could not see him, was hovering in the passage outside. 'And on your journey back to Chilbourne – for whatever the reason that brought you here, it is naught to me – I would urge you to think hard upon what I have said. It would be no great difficulty to have you charged and brought swiftly back to Marlborough, to be clapped up in the gaol.'

Thomas was about to reply but thought better of it. He bowed, the pounding in his head having diminished somewhat now, and walked out of the room. To his left, sunlight fell on to the passageway from the front door, which was being held open by the attentive Guido.

Thomas walked to the door, then stopped, only inches from the servant's face. He blinked and stepped back.

'On your way,' he said brusquely. But Thomas saw the unease in his eyes, and decided to play his last card.

'I'm a stranger here,' he said under his breath, 'and could lose my way . . . That blow on the head you dealt me might have confused me a little. Will you walk me to the end of the street?'

'I will not,' Guido snapped.

'Then 'twould be pity if my friends and I were to return here tonight,' Thomas told him. 'They are like to have taken a great deal of drink . . . I would of course try to stay them, but they would make such a brabble as might draw attention to your mistress's house. . . I hear the neighbours believe she is a deaf mute.'

Guido put out a hand to thrust Thomas through the door, but Thomas caught his arm and held it.

'Two minutes, then I'll leave and not return,' he said.

The servant cast a swift glance at the door to the front chamber. Lady Jane and Mary had not emerged, seemingly being engaged in some private talk. Quickly he ushered Thomas out into the street and followed, pulling the door shut behind them. They walked only a few paces before he turned.

'What do you want?' he demanded.

'A few answers,' Thomas replied. 'And I'll say naught about what you do in that house when your mistress isn't there.'

Guido flicked his tongue out, moistening his thin lips. 'I know not what you mean,' he began, but Thomas had picked up enough clues by now to press his advantage home.

'I hear Marlborough has become mighty Puritan in recent years,' he said. 'How would those solid town fathers deal with a man of your persuasion, who brings other men to his bed . . .'

'Damn you!' Guido faced him, a flush upon his pale cheeks. 'Ask what you will, and leave me be!'

'Does the Lady Euphemia own that house?' Thomas asked.

Guido hesitated, then looked away. 'From what I see, you have guessed it already.'

'Who else knows—' Thomas went on, but the other interrupted him.

'It was her father's property – an inheritance. She keeps her ownership secret, for she will be assessed for taxes . . . She pays a stipend to one of the town fathers, who guards the knowledge.'

Thomas started. 'Who?'

143

Guido shook his head.

'And you look after the house? Who pays you?'

Guido was angry. 'I am charged to keep the house as if it were mine own – that is all the payment I receive!'

Thomas considered. 'So the Lady Euphemia has helped Lady Jane plan her every move . . .'

But Guido was watching him closely. He seemed suddenly less afraid. 'You know less than I thought,' he said finally. 'The Lady Euphemia is prone to fancies. She forgets the hour, even the day sometimes.' He moved away, breaking into a chill little smile. 'If you continue delving into matters that don't concern you, you may pay a heavy price. I have told you all I will – now go to your friends and drink yourself to a stupor!'

And he walked swiftly back to the house, and disappeared through the door.

Thomas threaded his way slowly towards the town square. His heart was heavy, for he now found himself in a serious dilemma: to tell Sir Giles that he had found his daughter, and take the consequences; or not to tell him, and face the consequences of that. Either way, it seemed, was folly.

He quickened his pace, heading for the White Hart.

It was a sorry-looking trio who took the south road out of Marlborough early the following morning. Edward Birch lay as he had arrived, on his back in the wagon bed, where he could sleep off the surfeit of strong ale he had taken last night. Beside him lay not Thomas, but Judd Chalkhill, snoring champion of east Wiltshire, his clothes still damp from the grass where he had spent the night, senseless on the green beside the church of St Peter.

Wishing heartily that he had never seen them at all, Thomas sat in the driver's seat urging the ageing Chilbourne nag forward, though he had not the heart to use the whip. It had soon become obvious that Judd was in no state to manage the cart this morning, since he could barely manage his legs. Birch had left him in the taproom last night – drinking, Judd said, to dull the pain of Nan's demise – and gone to his own shared bed in a crowded chamber. In the morning he and Thomas had found Judd on the green, dragged him to a trough and shoved his head under, before stumbling off to the stable to recover the cart.

Today thick cloud covered the land like a horse blanket, as if to mock the woolliness Thomas found within his own mind. Food, drink and even sleep, surprisingly untroubled at that, had done little to help him resolve his predicament – especially since both Judd and Birch also knew about the existence of the banns. How they had remained secret from Sir Giles all this time seemed a small mystery in itself.

Slowly – slower than the previous day – the miles went by until, judging they had covered roughly half the distance, Thomas hauled on the reins and pulled the wagon to a halt beside an open stubble field. He clambered down from the seat, found the pannier and gave the horse a drink.

Birch shuddered, shook himself and raised his head from the wagon bed. 'We're not home yet, are we?'

Thomas glanced up from his task and shook his head.

'By the Lord, I've cured the pain in my foot by giving myself a worse one in the head,' Birch groaned.

'Serves you right,' Thomas threw back, in no mood for pleasantries. Then an idea struck him. 'You did thank me yesterday, for keeping quiet about what I saw in the fields,' he said, eyeing Birch keenly. 'You recall, the markers . . .'

'I recall well enough,' Birch said. 'Why do you bring it up now?'

'Because I want a favour in return.' When Birch said nothing, Thomas added: 'I want you to tell no one about what we saw on the church door . . . those words I spelled out to you.'

Birch stared at him, then his face cleared. Leaning over the side of the wagon, he spat heavily. 'That all?' he muttered. 'Consider it done, for I can't read, remember?'

Thomas nodded.

Birch jerked a thumb towards his slumbering companion. 'What about him?'

The horse had drunk his fill, and Thomas lowered the

145

pannier, patting the animal's rough neck. 'Leave Judd to me,' he said.

Chilbourne sat peacefully enough in its park, a column of smoke rising vertically from the kitchen chimney in the windless afternoon as Thomas eased the cart downhill and pulled into the stable yard. They had left Birch at the crossroads, from where he was able to make his way home, working his new crutch nimbly enough. Judd, who had woken up an hour since, slid his huge frame off the wagon bed and lurched towards the dung-heap, fumbling with his breeches. The sound of hard pissing, accompanied by a cloud of rising steam, assailed Thomas as he unhitched the horse.

'That's all I'm going to do,' he told the slaughterman. 'You can feed and stable the horse – I've got birds to tend.' And without waiting for a reply he walked off towards the falcons' mews, stretching his tired limbs.

Tamora heard him arrive and sat staring from her perch with what he could swear was a look of reproach in her yellow-ringed eyes. Some distance away the pale lanner falcon eyed him disdainfully. How he wished John Steer was with him, so that both birds could be taken out at once.

He found the gauntlet and untied Tamora, then allowed her to hop on to his wrist. Then he hooded her and was on the point of setting off for the Downs when a shout made him turn. James Clyffe had rounded the stable wall and was walking towards him.

'You took your time in Marlborough,' he said. 'Master's not pleased.'

'I'm mighty sorry to hear that,' Thomas told him, looking markedly unconcerned.

Clyffe grunted. His face still bore bruises from the wrestling two days ago. 'Well, least you can do would be to bring in a few game birds for supper,' he snorted. 'Only that's not why I come.'

Thomas waited, allowing his impatience to show. Tamora shifted slightly under her hood.

'Master says the ladies will ride out this afternoon,' Clyffe announced. 'You're to furnish the hawks.'

146

Thomas frowned. 'The ladies?'

'All of 'em,' Clyffe nodded. 'Been stuck indoors too much, Lady Kat says. And she's got Master to let young Gervase out for the afternoon, too.'

Thoughts were crowding into Thomas's mind. *Would Eliza be there?* He berated himself. He should have gone directly to Sir Giles on his return. Though, he reasoned at once, what good would it have done? He could not speak of what he had stumbled upon in Marlborough; not until he saw how the land lay . . .

'I'll make ready,' he said, but Clyffe was already walking off. 'You never did find me a great bustard,' he said over his shoulder. 'Fine falconer you are!'

Thomas watched him go, stroking Tamora's wing-feathers with his forefinger, and resigned himself to what the afternoon would bring.

An hour later the cloud had dispersed and the party assembled in the sunshine before the house. Lady Katherine, Thomas saw, had indeed been the instigator of it. Her whole manner spoke of someone who was running out of patience with the master of Chilbourne, if she had not already done so. He was struck by Sir Giles's demeanour: it was not mere tiredness that seemed to dull his limbs as he stepped up on to the mounting block and climbed into his saddle; he looked like a beaten man.

Besides Lady Katherine, Emma was there and also Margaret, whom Thomas had not seen for days. And, there was Eliza.

He avoided her eyes as he handed Tamora up to Sir Giles, then placed the lanner falcon, also hooded, on Lady Katherine's embroidered gauntlet. But he soon found that he need not curb his behaviour in any way, for Eliza merely greeted him absently, as she would any of the outdoor servants, and maintained a conversation with Emma. Then there was a minor commotion from the doorway and he turned in some surprise to see not only Gervase emerging from the house, but the Lady Euphemia too.

Gervase was pale of face, as if indeed he were a prisoner

freed for the day. His eyes met Thomas's briefly before he looked away. Everyone else, it seemed, was studiously avoiding him – except Lady Euphemia.

'What a glorious afternoon!' she cried to the world in general. 'Poets should write of it . . . Katherine my dear, I heap shame upon you for suggesting I remain indoors.'

Judd Chalkhill appeared then, leading extra horses. It looked as though he had exhausted the Chilbourne stable to do so, for the Lady Euphemia was to ride the tired old dun-coloured horse that had pulled the cart to Marlborough and back.

'Not indoors, Euphemia,' Lady Katherine replied. 'You are always free to enjoy the park.' There was an impatient edge to her voice and as if to cover any embarrassment Emma and Margaret began chattering, quickly drawing Eliza into their discourse.

Gervase stood observing the little scene as if detached from it. He took the reins of a grey gelding from Judd and mounted up. The horse twitched nervously, unused to its rider, until with some difficulty Gervase brought it under control. In doing so he had ridden a few yards – at which point he looked to where Sir Giles was sitting, watching him with a wary expression.

'What is it troubles you, sir?' the young ward asked. 'Did you think I was about to put spurs to him and ride off?'

There was a brief, tense silence, before Sir Giles replied.

'Have no fear on that score,' he said. 'The falconer and I will keep a close eye on you.' He turned a cold eye upon Thomas. 'I trust you intend to mark your duties today, falconer. I fear you have been somewhat remiss of late.'

Thomas bowed, sighing inwardly, and went off to fetch Cob.

The group did not stray very far from Chilbourne, for reasons that were glaringly obvious to everyone. Thomas, who had attended more hawking parties than he cared to remember, had never known one where the air was so thick with suppressed anger and unease. The young women, without hawks to occupy them, soon formed a tight little knot and rode together, talking privately. Occasionally one or other of the daughters would throw a frosty look at their father, who rode ahead, following Tamora as she soared above, hunting as energetically as any bird that has been unleashed after many hours of idleness. Which description also fitted Gervase Lambert, who would have ridden alone were it not for the attentions of the ebullient Lady Euphemia. Indeed, in her clumsy fashion, she seemed determined to emphasize that the young man was still one of the family despite his present, disgraced status.

Thomas, bringing up the rear on Cob, had little to do except bag up the occasional kill. He had dismounted to collect a partridge brought down by the lanner falcon when hoof-beats made him look up. Eliza had separated herself from the others and was cantering easily towards him.

Their discourse was brief. Reining in, she looked away towards the Downs as she addressed him. 'I trust you enjoyed yourself in Marlborough.'

'It was a tedious journey, Lady Eliza,' Thomas answered in a formal tone.

'I myself had a poor night's sleep,' Eliza went on, as if she had not heard. 'I was hard-pressed to find remedies for it.'

Thomas said nothing. The memory of the interview with Lady Jane and Mary Henshaw the previous day lay heavily upon him. How could he ever trust her again? He recalled what she had said the last time they lay abed together, about watching him hang . . .

She was looking directly at him. 'You are troubled,' she murmured. 'I wonder why.'

He faced her. 'I have much to occupy me now, lady,' he said, aware of how lame it sounded. 'I fear I must look to—'

'If you are about to plead your tiresome duties,' Eliza interrupted, 'I will think you far less of a man than I know you are.'

He met her eye, and saw the familiar sly look in it.

'I thought you and I had no need for falseness,' she murmured. When he made no reply, she said: 'I believe my window will be unfastened tonight . . .'

149

'Nay,' Thomas said, struggling for an excuse she would accept. 'I dare not . . .'

Eliza stared. 'Something new lies between us,' she said finally. 'Or did I frighten you with my threats last time?'

'Indeed you did,' Thomas lied, but she saw through it at once.

'Surely you know you have naught to fear from me,' she said in a childlike tone.

Thomas considered, then asked suddenly: 'I have not seen Mary Henshaw of late – does she not attend her mistress?'

Eliza frowned slightly. 'I believe her sister in Rushall is sick of a fever,' she said. 'Lady Euphemia has given her leave to visit her.'

Thomas watched her closely, seeing no sign of mendacity. His heart began to lift a little. But Eliza looked round sharply, for Sir Giles was riding towards them.

'I would talk with you, as well as bed you,' she said in an undertone. 'Please say you will be there tonight.'

He hesitated, then nodded quickly. At once she shook the rein, then urged her horse away. As Sir Giles drew close, she called over her shoulder: 'Remember, we would have quail at supper as well as larks – do what you can.'

She rode off without even greeting Sir Giles, who reined in heavily and looked down at Thomas. 'Is there not something you wish to tell me, falconer?' he asked.

Thomas swallowed quickly. 'If you speak of the journey to Marlborough, sir, the horse lost a shoe and we were at pains to find a farrier—'

'Nay, not that.' Sir Giles's eyes were impatient, and he was tense about the mouth. 'I have heard Judd's tale already.'

Thomas waited, his heart in his mouth.

'I speak of your telling my servants that you are discontent with your service here, and wish to return to your master.'

Relief flooded over Thomas. 'I ask pardon, sir,' he said. 'I have sought to speak to you of the matter, but I had not the heart, in view of your present troubles.'

Sir Giles lowered his eyes, then raised them again. 'I cannot say I blame you,' he said at last. 'Yet I need you still, to aid Master Hawkes in the search for my daughter.'

Thomas allowed his glance to stray into the distance, where Gervase Lambert was sitting in silence, momentarily free from the attentions of Lady Euphemia, who had dismounted to ease her legs.

'Surely Master Gervase is the one should relieve you of that burden, sir,' he ventured. 'Is he so hard of heart that he will see you torn with worry?'

'He is in love.' The words took Thomas by surprise. Glancing upwards, he saw an expression of such sadness on the face of the other that he was struck silent.

'Surely a man of your years has known such torment,' Sir Giles said. 'Would you not do as he has done?'

'I cannot deny that I would, sir,' Thomas replied after a moment.

'Then ...' Sir Giles trailed off, embarrassed, and summoned some trace of his authority. 'No matter. I intended to speak with you after supper, but this will serve. I charge you to aid Master Hawkes, any way you can. I rely on him now – indeed,' he added with a bitter smile, 'there is no other on whom I may rely, though I know he curses me in his heart.'

He glanced away towards the ladies, who were sitting their horses, talking together, then turned back to Thomas.

'We are certain now that Nan Greenwood was violated,' he said in a low voice. 'Her body has been sent to her family in Enford for burial, though they have been spared the details. In view of what you told me on Lammas night, I urge you to pursue any enquiry that might help us find those fellows – you know of whom I speak.'

Thomas struggled to keep disappointment from his voice. 'Sir, ought we not to leave this to the High Sheriff—'

Then he fell silent, for Sir Giles appeared not to have heard, having already turned his horse to canter away.

Thirteen

That night at supper in the kitchen, Richard Hawkes was even more surly than usual. He sat on a stool by the open door, venting his spleen to anyone within earshot.

'Master Ridley has instructed his lawyers to issue a suit against Sir Giles for damages,' he snarled. 'We'll all be put out of service – mark ye that?'

Clyffe, who was leaning over his cluttered table, already half-drunk, raised his head. 'I care less and less by the day,' he announced. 'I can find a place anywhere – I can cook! What can you do, Master usher?'

Hawkes glared. 'I can keep sober, for one thing,' he began, then broke off as Redmund Oakes shifted his frame awkwardly in the chimney corner.

'Peace, Goodman Richard,' he murmured. 'We are not at such a pass yet . . .'

'Yet it will come,' Hawkes said, and turned a baleful eye upon Thomas. 'There's one who cares not a turd for it all – or for us,' he grunted. 'He can return to his place of comfort, and turn his back on Chilbourne folk when they come a-begging.'

Thomas, who was stiff and tired and in no mood for the usher's humour, shot him a warning look. 'I've never turned my back on any soul who was driven to such measures,' he said.

Hawkes gave a snort of derision. 'What does a falconer know of hardship?' he demanded. 'You who smile while you pass the hawk up to your mistress, murmuring pretty thoughts in her ear . . . Like the huntsman who bends his knee to offer her the fewmets of a fresh kill, simpering while he peeks up her skirts – and will climb up them too, given half a chance!'

Clyffe gave a dirty laugh. 'I've heard it do happen!'

Thomas took a breath. 'I'll thank you to keep your fancies to yourself,' he said, looking straight at Hawkes. 'Else any man here might think 'twas jealousy drives you.'

Hawkes stood up. 'You dare presume a man of my station would be jealous of one like you? I could have you flogged and sent home in disgrace.'

'That would be one way of avoiding settling the matter like an equal,' Thomas answered, no longer mindful of his words.

The tension in the room was now palpable. Redmund Oakes got to his feet and took a slow step forward.

'Goodman Richard,' he said with uncustomary sharpness, 'I will have no brawling in my master's house.' Turning to Thomas, he added: 'If you have supped, falconer, no doubt you have duties to attend to.'

Thomas inclined his head respectfully. 'You are right, Master Oakes,' he murmured. 'I find the heat oppressive here, in any case.'

Still angry, he turned to go with a glance at Hawkes. 'Had I encountered you elsewhere, and not known your station, I would not brook such words,' he said.

Hawkes was still on his feet. 'Let me set your mind at rest, falconer,' he replied. 'For you and I will ride out tomorrow to continue our search – then who knows what opportunity may present itself . . .'

Thomas returned the man's stare briefly, then walked out into the balmy air of evening and went to tend the falcons.

A barn owl flitted past him some hours later as he climbed the ivy at the rear of the house, startling him so that he almost lost his grip. Half a night's sleep had done little to ease his mind, and it was with a mixture of emotions – anxiety, uncertainty, and a residue of anger at the stand-off he had had with Richard Hawkes earlier – that he finally heaved himself over the sill and through the open casement.

A stub of a candle burned on the chimney shelf, and she was waiting, lying in bed with the sheet pulled up to her neck, watching his arrival without apparent emotion.

He stumbled as he got down from the oak chest, then stood facing her. There was a silence.

'Well,' he asked finally, 'who are you tonight? Phyllis, or the Whore of Babylon, or a poor penniless ward – or concubine to the Grand Mogul?'

She gave a sudden laugh, putting her hand to her mouth to stifle it. 'Better.' She smiled. 'I think I like you better tonight than I have ever done.'

With a grand gesture she turned back the sheet so that he could see her body.

Quickly, he started to undress. And watching his hurried movements as he pulled the shirt over his head and threw it away, she raised herself suddenly and sat on the edge of the narrow bed, eyes wide.

'I'll be who or what you will,' she said softly. 'Only waste no more time, for you are late enough.'

It was almost dawn before he awoke. Eliza slept soundly beside him, hair across her face, one arm thrown over his chest. He took the arm and moved it gently, then shifted his body, preparing to ease himself from the bed without waking her. With displeasure, he remembered that he was charged to ride out once again on a fruitless search, and in the company of a man who seemed to have become his enemy. Then he recalled that it was Sunday, and that the household would first go to worship. He looked down at Eliza and saw she was awake and observing him silently.

'I must leave before it grows light,' he murmured.

'Would that you could stay,' she answered, and put a hand to his face. 'You did touch my heart, last night. I seldom let any man do that.'

He smiled. 'You have touched mine too. If matters were different . . .'

'We never had time to talk,' Eliza said, and yawned.

'I fear it must wait,' Thomas said. 'I must present myself to Master Hawkes again, and waste another day . . .'

Eliza hesitated. 'It's he I would speak of,' she said quietly. When he looked puzzled, she added: 'He is in torment, over me.'

154

He stared at her, and then a cloud seemed to lift. Sir Giles's words of yesterday came to him: *Surely a man of your years has known such torment* . . . It fitted. Was Hawkes's poor temper merely the result of a yearning for something he could never have? He could almost have laughed, were it not such a sad tale.

'Yes,' he said at last. 'I see it now.' He frowned suddenly. 'Does he know of our being together? That would explain why he seems set on goading me . . .'

She shook her head. 'I think not. He has loved me from afar since he first came here – indeed, before that. As the years pass, he grows more bitter. Yet he never speaks to me, or tries to breach the bounds of our stations.' She wore a sad expression now. 'He is a fool, for I would . . .' She trailed off, biting her lip, but Thomas took her hand and held it.

'Why then have you not let him know it, as you did me?'

'Your stay here is temporary,' she sighed. 'Him, I have to see every day.' She gave an impatient click of her tongue. 'If only he was bolder – took risks, as you have done . . .'

He sighed. 'I must go.'

She watched in silence as he got up and dressed swiftly. A faint light was already coming in through the casement.

'Swear you will not speak of this to Master Hawkes,' she said. 'It would cause much sadness.'

Thomas stepped forward, leaned down and kissed her. 'I will do your bidding always,' he smiled. 'One who is temporary must be grateful for whatever delights come his way.'

She returned his kiss and got up to see him climb out, waiting until he was safely down.

Two hours later Thomas emerged from East Everley church having been entertained along with everyone else by another bizarre sermon from Doctor Julius Parry.

The rector appeared no more drunk than he had been last Sunday, but his appearance was just as wild, and his sermon had a lurid air to it. He had chosen the tale of the Sabine Women, which he recounted with relish. How Romulus, the founder of Rome, needing to provide wives for his men, tricked the Sabine menfolk by inviting them to a festival, whereupon his followers carried off their women and ravished them. Parry's eyes rolled as he described the eyes of the sex-starved Romans, red with lust – and those of their victims, white with terror . . .

'That's not in the Bible,' Thomas had muttered to a sour-smelling Judd Chalkhill, who stood beside him in the packed rear pews.

'Is 'ee not?' Judd had asked. 'Then, by the Christ, 'ee ought to be!'

Once outside, Thomas collared Judd and asked him to keep his silence about the banns they had seen in Marlborough. Judd frowned. 'I thought 'ee was going to tell Master . . .'

'I will, in time,' Thomas answered. 'Will you trust me in this? I am still charged with aiding the search . . .' He trailed off, but Judd's eyes peered into his.

'Ah . . . mayhap I'll leave it to 'ee,' he said. 'For I'm trying to forget such matters.' He turned and walked away sadly, joining the throng of village folk as they drifted from the church.

Sir Giles and his family had already departed. Thomas was about to return to the house to attend Richard Hawkes when he saw John Cardmaker walking towards him.

'Have you news of the Sheriff's search?' he asked stiffly. 'For no one sees fit to tell me aught – am I not churchwarden here?'

An idea occurring, Thomas made a suggestion. 'I am to ride with Master Hawkes again, seeking for any sign of Lady Jane. We would be glad of your company once more, if you could be at Chilbourne within the hour . . .'

Cardmaker brightened. 'As it happens, I bain't too busy . . . I believe I could lay hands on a horse.'

'Good.' Thomas was about to move off when a cloaked figure emerged from the rear door of the church and began walking northwards to the crossroads. Thomas's conversation in the wagon with Edward Birch two days ago came to his mind. Parry . . . Parry could be the link. He turned to Cardmaker.

'Better still,' he said, 'will you meet us here?'

*　　　*　　　*

Less than an hour later Thomas and Richard Hawkes rode to the crossroads and found Cardmaker sitting on his horse, waiting.

Hawkes had said barely a word to Thomas, even when Thomas reminded him of Parry's presence at the wrestling match, in the company of one of the men the Sheriff was still seeking. He had then added a trimmed-down version of his conversation with Birch. Expecting a curt dismissal of the matter, he was pleasantly surprised when Hawkes announced that they would call at the parsonage house in the course of their enquiries – it could do little harm. But fixing Thomas with a cold eye, he had urged caution.

'The man is rector here, appointed by the Diocese of Salisbury – he is not without influence. You must hold your tongue while I speak with him.'

The three of them now rode northwards a short way past Everley Manor, then turned down a lane leading north-east, out of sight of the village. A large timber-framed house came into view, fringed with beech and oak. Away to the left was a smaller house, with a barn and fields beyond.

'That's the smallholding, belongs to the parsonage house,' Cardmaker told Thomas. 'Rector has his own tenant farmer.'

'He does seem to live well,' Thomas murmured, seeing a pair of horses in the paddock – one a little grey mare, the other a good, tall Barbary.

Cardmaker frowned. 'The grey is the rector's . . . I don't recall seeing the other before.'

Hawkes, riding a few paces ahead, turned to them both. 'I ask you to say naught, but keep eyes and ears open,' he said, and urged his mount forward.

Thomas sighed. He and Cardmaker brought up the rear, drawing to a halt before the heavy oaken door of the house. Hawkes dismounted and knocked loudly upon it. There was no answer.

For some reason, Thomas found himself reminded of his first daytime visit to Cracked Oak. That, too, had seemed remarkably peaceful. From the rear of the house, songbirds called.

Hawkes was frowning. 'Where's his servant?' he asked. 'He's always kept one, to my knowledge.'

There came a sound from a little wicker gate in the fence that ran from one side of the house. All three men turned sharply to see the Reverend Parry, still in his surplice, peering at them.

'Your pardon, Doctor,' Hawkes said, moving towards him. 'We are servants to Sir Giles Buckridge, charged with—'

'I know who you are, Richard Hawkes,' Parry answered loudly. 'What business do you have with me?'

For once Hawkes seemed unsure of himself. 'You will be aware that Sir Henry Willoughby is searching for two men who are believed to have committed foul deeds in the environs of the village . . . I wonder if you have seen or heard aught?'

'If I had, I would have communicated it at once to the authorities,' Parry answered. He all but ignored Cardmaker, who had quickly dismounted, cap in hand, and lost all vestiges of his pompousness. Instead, his gaze settled on Thomas, who still sat astride Cob, looking about with an innocent air.

'You, fellow! Who are you?'

Thomas took his time dismounting, then gave his name and station. Parry snorted, then turned back to Hawkes.

'I have seen naught that would interest you,' he said. 'My life here is one of quiet contemplation, heeding the word of God, and tending my flock as any shepherd will.'

Thomas stared, aware of the familiar, faint prickling at the back of his neck. Something in the man's stance, something he could not put a name to, told him all was not right here. He took a step towards Hawkes.

'Might we beg the good doctor's permission to search his property?' he suggested mildly. 'For your own protection, sir,' he added, directing a polite smile towards Parry. 'These men are believed to have been hiding out, in or near the parish . . .'

Hawkes was irritated by Thomas's forwardness. 'I was about to ask that,' he snapped, then turned to the rector.

But Parry was scowling. *He has remembered where he*

saw me, at the wrestling, Thomas thought, *hence, he knows I saw who he was with* . . . He seized the moment. 'One of the men is tall, heavily bearded,' he said to Parry. 'The other caused a stir on Lammas night, for he is a big fellow, a wrestler—'

'Enough!' Parry's voice shook, and his hands fumbled with the edges of his robe. 'You dare to examine me as if I were some servant?'

Thomas looked surprised. 'Nay, sir, I merely wish to see these men caught before they commit more wicked acts . . .'

Parry swallowed, as if his mouth were dry. All three men saw then how much he craved a drink. Though that in itself was no surprise, they also sensed his nervousness. Even Hawkes, ignoring Thomas's presumption, was curious now.

'It would seem a wise course, Doctor,' he suggested. 'The men may have hidden in a barn, or an outhouse . . . Any trace of their movements would aid the Sheriff – and Master Sadler too, who is keen to remove the fear that stalks our parish.'

Nicely put, Thomas thought. Cardmaker too had managed to recover some of his dignity and was watching intently. The three men waited for Parry's reply.

'Very well,' he said at last.

Hawkes waited a moment then, seeing no further words were forthcoming, nodded his thanks. 'We will be as brief as we can, Doctor, and will disturb nothing—'

'Indeed you will not!' Parry shot back. 'And needless to say my house is sacrosanct, as is my garden. It is a place of tranquillity, where I prepare my sermons.'

Hawkes hesitated, then gave a short bow. They turned back to the horses, but the rector did not move. Thomas took hold of the saddle pommel then smiled once more at Parry. 'Might I ask whose horse that is in your paddock, sir?' he asked. 'He looks very fine.'

Parry bristled. 'I bought him at the fair in Devizes,' he answered. 'And I find you impertinent beyond belief. I will convey my displeasure to Sir Giles before the day is over.'

Thomas swung himself into the saddle. Close by he could

hear Hawkes muttering furiously under his breath. Then all three of them were riding away from the house. Risking a quick backward glance, Thomas saw that Parry was gone.

They had only a matter of a hundred yards to go before they reached the entrance to Parry's tenant farm. Once there Hawkes dismounted, but before John Cardmaker could do the same, he raised a hand to stay him.

'The falconer and I will search the farmyard and the barn,' he said. 'Would you oblige me by making a sweep of the wood beyond?'

Cardmaker paused, a puzzled expression on his face. 'Sheriff's men already combed all the woods within five mile,' he began, then stopped when he saw the look on Hawkes's face.

''Tis your party, master,' he said, and with a glance at Thomas, he rode off.

Thomas's pulse was racing. Not a word was said as he and Hawkes walked together, a few feet apart, across the deserted yard towards the little thatched barn. A couple of scrawny chickens flapped themselves out of the way, but Hawkes did not notice. He merely shoved open the door and walked inside.

Thomas followed. Hay was stacked at one end, sacks of grain at the other. He stood, blinking in the dim light.

'Will this serve?'

Hawkes was facing him. Without waiting for a reply he untied his belt and threw it down. His doublet followed. With a breath, Thomas took off his own belt, eyeing the small knife in its sheath wistfully. Then he had no more time to think, for the other man had launched himself at him with full force.

He let out a gasp as the air was knocked out of his lungs, then fell back on to the earth floor, Hawkes atop him. Then he was struggling, using all his strength to grip the man's wrist, while Hawkes's other fist pounded him in the stomach and sides.

He aimed his own fist at Hawkes's head, and felt the jarring blow as it connected. Hawkes grunted and cracked Thomas on the mouth. Tasting blood, Thomas brought his knee back suddenly and banged it into Hawkes's side. He gave a little cry of pain, then another as Thomas struck him hard on the chin.

Thomas was the taller, but they were well matched in strength, and he had not the inner rage that drove Hawkes. Even as Thomas managed to hook his leg around the man and topple him, Hawkes was flailing about with his free hand, catching Thomas on the chin and neck. Then, as he struggled to recover his balance, Thomas used an old trick from his boyhood. Feinting with his left hand, he caught Hawkes's arm with his right and bent it sharply. As Hawkes hissed with pain, Thomas scrambled to his feet and stood over him, gripping his arm with both hands. Twisting it little by little, he forced his opponent down, avoiding the legs that kicked out dangerously close to his. Finally it was over, and Hawkes lay on his face and stomach, heaving but helpless, for Thomas was standing astride him, putting as much tension on the man's arm as he dared without breaking it.

There was no sound now but the panting of both men in the dusty barn. Sunlight lanced through holes in the thatch, while from outside came the indignant clucking of hens.

'Do we stop now?' Thomas said between breaths. Blood ran from his mouth and dripped on the back of Hawkes's shirt.

'No!' the other cried, though his face was on the floor and his voice muffled. 'Do what you will, I'll not yield!'

'If I snapped your arm, would that put an end to it?' Thomas asked him.

Hawkes struggled, but Thomas twisted his arm by another fraction, causing him to cry out. Any further, they both knew, and the bone would give way.

'Break it and be damned!' Hawkes shouted, with a vain attempt to turn his head. He brought his left leg back, trying to catch Thomas where he stood. But Thomas avoided it easily, then stamped his boot firmly upon it. Hawkes drew breath sharply at this added source of pain.

'How about a leg as well?' Thomas breathed. 'Would that not inconvenience you a little too much?'

Hawkes struggled, but he was weakening, and the pain

was beginning to tell. 'Damn your long shanks, and your bold words, and everything else about you!' he cried, but this was mere bluster now, and he knew it. 'I should have torn your eyes from your head when I was able – what manner of falconer would you be then?'

'A blind one,' Thomas threw back, recovering his breath a little. 'As you are blind not to see what is before you every day . . .' He broke off, regretting his words; Eliza had begged him not to speak of it.

But Hawkes misunderstood, or was not listening. 'You'll not sermonize at me, you runagate rogue!' he panted, and groaned a little as the pain in his arm grew harsher. 'I used not my station, but fought you as one man does another, with no witnesses . . .' He broke off suddenly, almost spent.

'I will release you,' Thomas said. 'Only let us not fall to again, for I fear we will both regret it.'

Hawkes made no sound. Slowly Thomas released his arm and stepped away. Finally he let go. Walking stiffly, he moved to the wall and leaned against it, taking gulps of the dry air.

Hawkes rolled over and sat up, working his arm painfully. Blooded about the face and head, they eyed each other grimly.

'Has that pricked whatever boil was troubling you?' Thomas asked at last.

Hawkes wiped his mouth with the edge of his shirt, which was streaked with dirt. 'You know naught about me,' he muttered. Stiffly, he got to his feet.

Thomas ignored him. With a single movement he tore a strip from the edge of his shirt, balled it up and held it to his mouth. The bleeding had lessened slightly.

Hawkes bent over, breathing steadily. Then he raised himself and looked Thomas in the eye. 'What meant you, when you said I was blind not to see what's before me?'

Berating himself, Thomas sought for some words to ward off the man's curiosity. 'I minded not what I was saying,' he muttered.

But Hawkes was not satisfied. 'You are hiding something,' he said.

Thomas shook his head. 'Enough. Do we go outside and continue as we are ordered, or return to Chilbourne?'

162

Hawkes opened his mouth, and then both men turned suddenly towards the doorway, for there came footfalls hurrying across the yard. Chickens squawked furiously.

'Master Hawkes! Thomas! Where be ye?'

It was Cardmaker. With a glance at Thomas, Hawkes answered him. 'In here.'

The door swung open and Cardmaker appeared, somewhat out of breath himself. Then he saw the condition of both men and his mouth fell open.

'Well?' Hawkes demanded. 'What's ruffled your feathers now?'

Cardmaker gulped. 'You better come and look for yourself – for there's been some devilry here, or I'm not village hayward!'

Fourteen

They rode in silence behind Cardmaker, who had quickly realized that he was not required to pass comment on the frightful appearance of either man. Past the farmhouse, from whence came no sign of life, back along the lane by which they had entered, then down towards the field in which Parry's horses stood, idly flicking the flies off with their tails.

Cardmaker halted. 'Something troubled me about that animal, Master Hawkes,' he said quietly. 'Never known rector buy something he don't truly have need for – he's a parsimonious man with money.' He dismounted and pointed to the Barbary horse. 'So I did walk up and take a quick look at him, seeing as rector wasn't about.'

Hawkes, out of patience, glared at him. 'Just tell me what it is you found, and put an end to your tale,' he said.

'His bridle,' Cardmaker said, somewhat abashed. 'It's stamped with two initials . . . I don't read too well, but they bain't rector's.'

'What does that prove?' Hawkes demanded in exasperation. 'It may still bear the initials of the man he bought it from.'

Then he looked aside, for Thomas, ignoring him, had dismounted and was climbing over the fence. Calmly he approached the big, sleek horse, murmuring soft words. It did not flinch when he drew alongside, patting its neck, and examined the animal's bridle. Parry's grey mare watched him suspiciously from some yards away.

Thomas turned and walked back to Hawkes and Cardmaker. 'E.W.,' he said. 'Edmund Warren. I'll wager any sum you like this was the Crown Purveyor's horse.'

Hawkes swallowed, seemingly at a loss for what to do next. 'How can you be sure?' he muttered.

'We should tell Sir Giles,' was all Thomas said.

'I know that,' the other snapped.

Cardmaker, half satisfied with his discovery and half anxious, spoke up. 'Master Hawkes, that bain't all I found.' When both men turned, he went on: 'Will you follow me back to the farm?'

Thomas mounted Cob and all three then rode back to the farmyard. There were still no signs of life from the house. Cardmaker, Thomas realized, was savouring the moment, as if he had kept the best until last.

'Someone's been staying here,' he announced.

'What do you mean?' Hawkes asked. 'William Jenkin farms here – Parry's tenant.' He half turned to Thomas. 'The man's a widower, keeps to himself,' he said shortly.

'Look like he's gone,' Cardmaker said, and pointed to the little farmhouse. 'You'd best go inside.'

He led the way boldly to the door, which, they now noticed, stood ajar. They went in.

At first there seemed nothing amiss. The downstairs consisted of a single room with a floor of beaten earth, poorly furnished and none too clean. Farm tools stood against the walls, along with the sort of household clutter a single man might accumulate. There was no fire in the chimney, nor had anyone raked out the dead coals. But against the chimney wall was a makeshift pallet of sheepskins.

Hawkes startled the other two by shouting abruptly. 'Goodman Jenkin! Are you here?'

There was only silence. 'I told 'ee – he's gone,' Cardmaker said. 'And whoever else been here is gone too.'

Thomas walked to a home-made ladder in the corner and climbed it until his head emerged in a low-ceilinged sleeping loft. One look was all he needed: a pallet, empty bottles, some chicken bones and rinds of stale bread. He descended again. 'Have you been up there, Master Cardmaker?' he asked.

Then he saw the dark spots upon the floor near the ladder.

'I have,' Cardmaker nodded, 'as I have noted the stains.'

He pointed them out, and looked expectantly at Hawkes. 'You'd best take a look.'

Hawkes stepped to the foot of the ladder, climbed it stiffly, poked his head through the opening and peered about. Then he too descended again.

'Someone has indeed been using this house.' He looked down at the spots of dried blood.

Thomas was examining the rude pallet against the wall.

'There's more,' he said, and showed them a deep red-black stain upon one of the old sheepskins. All three men now became aware of an unpleasant stench. The scents were mingled and indistinct, but they were without doubt of human origin. Someone of none-too-clean habits had slept here recently.

Hawkes looked about uneasily. 'But then where is Jenkin?' He frowned. 'Surely Parry must know of this . . .' He looked up, saw the other two men eyeing him. 'We should not leap to hasty conclusion,' he said, moistening his dry lips. 'This could merely be animal blood . . .'

He was pointing to the stains. Silently, Thomas bent and examined them, then straightened himself. 'It might well be,' he said. 'Yet how many farmers do you know would slaughter a chicken in the house?'

Hawkes had no answer. But Cardmaker, who had been strutting about importantly, had more theories to share.

'I would swear the stain on the bedding is not chicken blood,' he said.

Thomas nodded. 'I am inclined to agree, Master hayward.'

Hawkes glanced around the room once more, his nose wrinkling with distaste. 'I will tell Sir Giles, and recommend he turn this matter over to Sir Henry Willoughby,' he announced. 'Now, if you've finished poking about . . .'

He walked outside, followed by the others. In a very short time they had mounted and ridden back towards the village, glad to put some distance between themselves and the Reverend Parry's property.

At dinnertime, having washed himself, cleaned his hurts and put on his last clean shirt, Thomas presented himself in the Great Chamber at Chilbourne as he had been ordered to do.

166

Hawkes – presumably after attending to his own appearance – had been swift to inform Sir Giles of their discoveries, and word had at once been sent to Henry Sadler. It would take longer to reach Sir Henry Willoughby.

The atmosphere in the house was even more gloomy than usual. Thomas grew aware of it the moment he entered the room and found Sir Giles seated at the high table, with Lady Katherine at one side and Redmund Oakes on the other. Richard Hawkes stood stiffly apart, ignoring Thomas as he came forward and made his bow.

'Falconer . . .' Sir Giles mumbled. 'I hear you and the usher have made a grim discovery.'

Thomas merely nodded, assuming Hawkes had made his report. Then remorse descended upon him as he looked at Sir Giles's face and saw a man who had not slept for days. At once he knew that, come what may, he would tell him of his daughter, and the banns outside the church at Marlborough. But before he could put his resolve into words, matters moved out of his control.

The door flew open, loud voices were heard, and the red-gowned, orange-peruked figure of the Lady Euphemia appeared, flanked by her two servants: Bartholomew Byres, protesting feebly, stumbling in her wake, and behind, the erect figure of Mary Henshaw.

So, she was back. Thomas waited, his heart thudding. Then he realized that he had little to fear, as he was immediately forgotten. For to state that the Lady Euphemia was weeping was an understatement – she was inconsolable.

'Giles – Cousin! You have not heard the news?' she cried.

There was consternation about the table. Sir Giles frowned at her. 'Euphemia, what on God's earth—'

'John . . . That dear sweet boy! I cannot bear it!'

Reaching the table she sank into a vacant chair, howling. Clumsily, Byres handed her a lace-trimmed handkerchief into which she sobbed loudly.

Even Lady Katherine seemed abashed. Swiftly she looked towards the two servants for some explanation. It was Mary Henshaw, composed as always, who came forwards, made her curtsey and delivered the news.

'We have received sad tidings from London, my lady. Master Tyrrell – Lady Euphemia's young nephew – is dead. He escaped from the debtors' prison in Wood Street, and was found by the watch yesterday in a house outside the walls. Killed in a brawl, they say.'

The men exchanged glances. Lady Katherine arose and walked round the table to where the Lady Euphemia sat. She raised a red, tear-stained face and sniffed loudly.

'He was all the close family I had!' she wailed. 'Save you. Such a delicate, sensitive boy . . . They said he played the Queen of Carthage so well at Cambridge that he drew tears not merely from the Fellows, but the Master himself!'

Lurching to her feet, she fell upon the shoulder of Lady Katherine who staggered at the sudden weight, but did her best to console her. Byres stood by, wringing his hands helplessly. Risking a glance at Mary Henshaw, Thomas was reminded sharply of the last time he had seen her. Once again the hard face showed no emotion. Remembering too what the fidgety Guido had told him, he realized something else – that it was Mary Henshaw who ran Cracked Oak; Mary who ordered her mistress's days and commanded poor Byres . . . What else might this woman be up to?

He started suddenly, and found Hawkes at his shoulder. Meeting the man's eye, he nodded curtly, made his bow and turned to go. Nobody noticed, for attention was still focused on the trembling figure of the Lady Euphemia. With relief, Thomas got himself through the door.

Outside, Hawkes paused. 'You had a lucky escape,' he said. 'Parry has already accused you of privy insults to a man of the cloth. And being in charge of the party, I too am blamed.'

Thomas met his eye. 'You know as well as I, there's something wrong at that parsonage house. Remember I saw Parry at the wrestling, with the tall fellow who—'

'So you have said,' Hawkes interrupted. 'Save that no one else seems to have placed them together.'

Thomas's eyes narrowed. 'Cardmaker saw them too . . .'

'What do I care if he did?' Hawkes snapped. 'What does anyone? A tiresome cottager with pretensions beyond his

168

station . . .' He looked away, then said: 'Do you not see? None of it matters. This manor is cursed in some way – and the family too. Everything goes amiss with them . . . I wish I had never set foot in the place!'

And with that he was gone, leaving Thomas to his own devices.

Thomas spent the rest of that gloomy Sunday in the open air, glad to exercise both Tamora and the lanner falcon on the Downs. In the evening he took his catch to the kitchens and dropped it on Clyffe's table without a word. Taking what meagre supper was offered, he carried it outside and sat on the slope above the park, watching big white clouds drifting in from the Plain. Crows flew overhead.

He had turned matters over throughout the afternoon as he followed the falcons. The only course that seemed to remain open to him was to beg an audience with Sir Giles and tell him everything he knew. Lady Jane's future, he reminded himself, was not his concern, any more than the ransacking of Cracked Oak, or the murders of a Crown Purveyor and a washerwoman. Nor were Sir Giles's troubles – legal, financial or whatever they may be. He was eager now to return home, and was not prepared to brook further delays.

As night fell, feeling rested and calm if a little sore from his tussle with Hawkes, he paid a last visit to the falcons' weathering and saw both birds were content. He would suggest to Sir Giles that if there was no one to look after the lanner, Sir Robert would no doubt take her off his hands. Tamora would be glad, as he would, to return to Petbury and the country she knew.

He turned away, towards the stable and a good night's sleep, from which he would not stir – Eliza, he had managed to avoid thinking about. She too was part of Chilbourne, and her future was beyond his ken.

His mind was elsewhere, he realized later – much later. Otherwise a man of his sharp senses would have heard the sound of boots thudding behind him, long before he did. As it was he turned far too slowly, and found his arms wrenched back with a painful, jarring movement, then pinned behind him in an iron grip. A second later a large dirty hand was clamped over his mouth, almost making him retch.

He struggled a little, before realizing the utter futility of it. The next moment a rag was pulled tightly over his eyes, leaving but a sliver of light above and below. Then he was being frogmarched with considerable force, stumbling, past the weathering, uphill towards the trees that marked the north boundary of Chilbourne, and off into the gathering night.

The journey was shorter than he expected for some reason – not that it mattered, for he could see absolutely nothing, being bound and blindfolded and face down over the back of a trotting horse. His arms and legs were tied together beneath its belly, preventing any chance of his sliding off. As far as he could tell they turned eastwards almost at once, the only direction from Chilbourne he had not yet travelled. But then the road wound from side to side and he could learn little, save that from the echoing of the hooves they were passing through a substantial forest. It could not be Savernake, for that was too far off. Chute Forest . . . Did that not stand to the east, straddling the Hampshire border?

The echoes also told him that there were three horses and two riders, one leading the mount to which he was tied like a sack. From such a position of helplessness he could do nothing but conserve his energies and endeavour not to think too hard upon his fate.

Then suddenly it was over; they had halted, and there were voices, indistinct but not entirely unfamiliar. Before he could allow himself the luxury of speculation, however, there was the rasp of cords being cut. The next instant he was gripped by the hair and tipped backwards off the horse, to fall heavily on his side. There he lay, trussed like a capon, until some moments later he was lifted under the arms by someone of enormous strength and dragged across the ground. His boots scraped on soft earth, then bumped over a threshold, and walls closed fast about him, deadening every sound.

At once he was thrown down, landing painfully on his back. Not daring to raise himself, he remained motionless, breathing heavily, until the same powerful arms lifted him again and sat him up. He felt rough walls behind his shoulders and sank back, realizing he was in a corner and grateful for even this small comfort. There was movement further off, and the scrape of a tinderbox. Vaguely he was aware of a lantern being lit, and once again there came muttered, halting conversation. Then the blindfold was torn from his eyes, and he could finally see. Which, he realized quickly, was no blessing, for standing over him was the man called Miles, the savage wrestler who had beaten Edward Birch and smashed his foot. The man who had frightened an entire village into silence and walked away with their money. Miles in his leather skullcap, the servant of the tall, dark-bearded fellow who sat further away on a joined stool of unfinished pine, regarding Thomas very calmly indeed.

Then he realized that the unpleasant smell he now noticed was the same he had encountered that morning in the deserted farmhouse, and it emanated from Miles.

'Where is it?'

He blinked, realizing it was not Miles who had spoken, but the dark-bearded man. Gazing past the huge bulk of his henchman, he sought to focus on the other, whose form was half-lit by a smoky, guttering lantern on the floor beside him.

'Where is what?' he asked.

Miles leaned forward and cracked him on the ear, a hammer blow that made his head spin. Dizzily he fought the swirling lights that shot by in every direction. As they faded and the room returned slowly to normal, he made an effort to look at the tall man.

'I asked you, where is it?' the man repeated, icily calm.

'I know not what you mean,' Thomas told him, bracing himself for the next blow.

It never came. Miles peered into his eyes, then turned briefly to the tall man. No words were spoken, but Thomas gathered that even after that brief exchange, he had been believed.

The dark man thought for a moment. 'Why have you been dogging me?'

Thomas swallowed, trying to moisten his dry tongue. 'I know not what you mean—'

At once Miles hit him again, this time across his jaw, which had not yet recovered from his fight with Hawkes. For the second time that day Thomas tasted blood.

'I had not thought you so slow-witted,' the dark man was saying. 'It don't sit well with the way you thwarted me last time we met.'

Through his pain, Thomas fought to order his thoughts. The man was referring to the way he and Steer had stood up to him at Cracked Oak, and refused to hand over their catch . . . He risked a glance at Miles, whose huge bulk towered above him, but the man's expression told him nothing.

'You may beat me senseless,' he said, 'yet I know not what it is you want from me.'

The dark man gave a short laugh. 'You will not be nearly so lucky,' he said. 'By the time Miles has finished, I will know all I wish to know, and you will wish for naught but death.'

This was the truth, plain enough. Risking a quick glance about the bare little hut – it was a forester's hut, he guessed, built of mud and wattle with a roof of turf – he saw no means of escape whatsoever. He was utterly at the mercy of these men. Hence, he had only his wits.

'I'm no hero,' he muttered. 'Ask what you will, and I'll tell you . . .' Then he almost cried out, for Miles had grabbed him by the hair and banged his head against the wall.

'Of course you will tell me,' the dark man said, somewhat absently. Thomas opened his eyes to see that he had produced a pipe and was stuffing it with tobacco. Striking a flame, he lit it and puffed away for several minutes until a cloud of blue-grey smoke hung in the air.

Miles straightened, and without asking leave, moved to the far wall, which was barely a dozen feet away, and picked up a leather costrel from which he drank.

'Thirsty work,' his master observed in a matter-of-fact tone. Looking at Thomas, he added: 'You know full well we may take as long as we wish. We may eat, drink and smoke tobacco . . .' He trailed off, letting Thomas supply the implications: they could come and go, while he would merely grow weaker.

'Tell me what it is you want,' he repeated.

'The truth,' was the answer.

'About what?' Thomas countered, unable to avoid a sharpness in his tone. At once he regretted it, making a mental note to restrain himself at all costs, but it was too late. Miles stepped towards him again and dealt him a savage blow across the cheekbone. Again the room danced with light.

'You are too impatient,' the dark man said.

Thomas waited, taking slower breaths, trying to ignore the stinging on his cheek.

'I asked why you have dogged me – on the Downs, at the house called Cracked Oak, and again at the rector's.'

Thomas allowed himself a moment's thought, then said: 'You know I was charged to search for Sir Giles Buckridge's daughter . . .'

'I do,' the man smiled. 'But I hardly think she would be hiding at Doctor Parry's house. He has such a wicked reputation.'

Thomas tried to move then, for his wrists were sore, though not tied so tightly as to make them numb. His legs, still tied, were stretched out before him. A few hours of this and he would be in a sorry state.

'You think I have some reasons of my own . . .' Thomas ventured.

There was no reaction from either man. He struggled to form some kind of strategy, knowing that pretending knowledge he did not have would avail him little. Hence, should he not try to invent some plausible tale? It might buy him time . . .

'Suppose I told you I were tired of being a hired man, living on a falconer's wage . . . Suppose I decided to try and seek what you were seeking . . .'

The dark man glanced at him, then merely flicked his eyes towards Miles and back again. Immediately Miles grabbed Thomas's hair again and held it.

'Lie to me, and you'll have a cracked skull,' the other man said.

'I will not lie,' Thomas answered, tense with pain.

At a sign from his master Miles let go and straightened up, seemingly unconcerned whether he cracked skulls or not.

Once, years ago in the Low Countries, Thomas had spent four nights without food or shelter, hiding from Spanish troops. He had learned much about himself in those days; how resourceful he could be, how strong was his will to survive . . . He sought now to recapture that urge; to draw deeper upon his well of resilience.

He breathed in and took a risk. 'I know you are seeking something valuable that was hidden in the Lady Euphemia's house,' he said. 'I thought I might try to come at it myself.'

The dark-bearded man seemed to be listening with only half an ear. 'I might believe that,' he murmured. 'I still await an answer as to what you were doing at the parsonage.'

Having taken a path, Thomas decided he would stay upon it. Trying to sound sheepish, he answered: 'I sought to scare him into giving me payment to hold my tongue.'

There was a pause. 'You thought you could frighten Parry?' The man seemed close to genuine laughter.

'I think he violated Nan – the washerwoman at Chilbourne,' Thomas lied. 'Afterwards, he panicked and throttled her.'

He saw it then: both men had tensed at once, but sought to retain their outward calm. He risked a look at Miles, and saw something else in the dull brown eyes. Not fear, for this man feared nothing, but there was unease.

Of course, there could be no doubt: this was the man who had the tryst with Nan Greenwood; who had then violated her, almost in sight of the house, and killed her. *No one else hereabout would do such a thing*, Birch had said. And somehow, he had known it all along – as he knew they had killed Edmund Warren. But then, what was his horse doing at the rector's house?

The dark-bearded man was puffing on his pipe. 'So, let me lay it out. You, a liveried servant, growing tired of your lot, sought to turn thief and blackmailer all at once?' He gave a quick little smile. 'I am in difficulties with that tale.'

He glanced briefly at Miles, who, with almost a casual

174

air, snapped the back of his hand hard across Thomas's face. Then once again he gripped his hair and held it fast.

'Now I will ask once again,' said the other. 'And if I receive not an answer that sits well with the character I have formed of you, I will let Miles beat you for a while.'

Thomas's breath came fast now. He coughed, spitting blood and saliva. The sweat lay cold between his shoulders, and ran down his back.

'There is no need,' he said, managing with little effort to sound weaker than he was. 'I told you I am no hero . . . I sought some easy money, nothing more.'

The bearded man watched him, chewing on his pipe. 'What do you know about John Tyrrell?' he asked abruptly.

Thomas tried to look at him, though Miles had forced his head upwards so that he faced the roof. 'The Lady Euphemia's nephew . . .'

'I know that,' the other man said with a trace of impatience. 'I mean, what else do you know?'

Thomas hesitated, then answered: 'He is dead – the news came to Chilbourne today.'

There was a silence, and for the first time Thomas felt that he had given information that was new to the two men. At a sign from the bearded one, Miles let go of his hair and straightened up again.

'How did he die?'

Try as he might, Thomas could see no advantage yet. Knowledge, or pretended knowledge, was his only weapon here, yet he had precious little to draw on.

'Killed in a brawl in London, I heard.'

Another silence followed. Miles stooped, picked up his costrel and took another drink, and Thomas, watching from the corner of his eye, made another leap of imagination. Here was the man who had also killed Tyrrell . . . But why? What was the wayward nephew of Lady Euphemia, who had left the University and was thought to have gone away to sea, to these two?

Then at once Bartholomew Byres's words came to him. *They wanted to know of Master Tyrrell's visit here . . .*

He was clutching at straws, but what else was there? He

swallowed. 'Tyrrell hid something in the Lady Euphemia's house, years back; is that not so? That is why you held the lady and her servants prisoner while you searched . . .'

Miles lurched towards him then, and Thomas closed his eyes, not wanting to see where the blow would fall. But to his surprise the other man muttered an order, and nothing happened.

Thomas opened his eyes. The dark-bearded man's pipe had gone out, and he was examining it with what seemed to be a high degree of interest.

'You reason well,' he said finally. 'I wonder what else you have gleaned from the Lady and her servants.'

'Nothing,' Thomas said quickly. 'I am kept busy outdoors, and have little time—'

But he had displeased them again, and the next instant Miles cracked him once more across the face – seemingly harder than he intended, for a sound like the rushing of water arose in Thomas's ears, and the room faded before him.

But, as he sank into unconsciousness, a thought floated upwards and stood before him with terrible clarity: unknown to most people, the Lady Euphemia had two houses – and these men had been searching the wrong one.

Fifteen

He would not tell them – he must not. Whatever else he revealed, it could not be that. *Why?* he asked himself countless times, and always the answer came, mechanically, so that it was almost a litany: *because Lady Jane is at the Marlborough house too, and they would not scruple to harm her, abuse her, even kill her . . .*

Time had ceased to matter, save that he was sometimes aware of daylight through the uneven roof of branches and turves, and sometimes only darkness. Quickly, his corner of this little hut had become the entire world. The hours had melded into a seamless flow of pain and discomfort, hunger and thirst. He was never freed, not even to relieve himself, so that the lower half of his body was now wet and stinking. Nor was he given drink, or succour of any kind – that would merely have prolonged matters. He sensed that these men did not have unlimited time, which was why they had been at some pains to give him the opposite impression.

He sensed it, when he sensed anything, because he had begun to fear that he was not going to get out of this place alive. The first time the thought occurred he beat it away angrily, digging his fingernails sharply into his palms, forcing himself to dwell on other things. But what other things should he think upon? His daughter, Eleanor . . . Petbury, Sir Robert and Lady Margaret, the old life . . . They were only memories now – almost as far off as those of the Low Countries; part of his old self. The self that rode free on the Downs and flew falcons, and walked easily down to supper of an evening or took a mug in the Black Bear at Chaddleworth, and some nights slipped into bed with Nell . . .

177

Or was it Eliza? The memory of her body came to him with a rush of desire that helped him briefly to forget where he was, or how long he had been there. Two days? It had to be two . . . In the brief moments after he had slept, albeit fitfully, he reasoned that his absence would have been noticed; that there would be a search of some kind . . . Then the truth would beat him down: no one would look for him. From the impression he had given of late, they would merely assume he had left Chilbourne without seeking Sir Giles's approval and returned to Berkshire.

Berkshire too was becoming a memory. Lambourn Down, and the green scarp to the north that fell away to the sweet vale of the White Horse . . . How long was it since he had stood upon that vast, wondrous shape cut into the sward, and marvelled at the ancients who had made it?

Yet there were little shards of comfort, and he sought to focus upon them. The main one was that, to his relief, they had not hurt him again. Apparently content that he knew no more than he had told, they merely left him where he was as they came and went. Perhaps they reasoned that if there were anything more he would tell it of his own accord, hoping for some lessening of his plight. Or perhaps they had other intentions . . .

Early on he had tried feebly to loosen his bonds, then realized it was impossible. He could do naught but watch as they took turns to rest, sometimes taking a bite of food, standing up, often with an ear cocked towards the door. But no one came. There was no sound of hoof or human foot, only the forest birds calling.

Once he heard the dark-bearded man's voice outside, harsh and angry. But Miles's voice, by contrast, must have been very low, for he heard no response from him.

Occasionally one of them was absent for a while. Less frequently they were both gone, sometimes for hours, and those were his worst times; for he guessed that sooner or later they would move on and simply leave him or, more likely, silence him altogether. And all the while he knew he was growing weaker.

Then one time – he thought it was afternoon, but could not be sure – they went out in something of a hurry and did not come back for what seemed many hours. They had been away for long periods before, but not so long as this, and it gave him hope. He had put hope aside, but was pleased to find it was there still, and he began to laugh. Of late, perhaps during the past few hours, he had begun to feel laughter welling up from somewhere, and he distrusted it. He knew what lack of food and proper sleep could do, and it made him afraid. But hope – there it was again; no denying it, he thought, and giggled softly to himself – hope can ambush you when you least expect it.

He moved, as he had always done at odd times when they weren't looking, for he was afraid of losing the use of his limbs. There, he told himself, if you meant to conserve some morsel of strength, then you always meant to get out sooner or later – always knew you could.

But he could not; feebly he moved his upper body, and found it stiff and numb. He had not even the strength to push himself the few feet to the door. *You must*, he insisted. *Chance may not come again.* So, with a supreme effort, he forced his shoulders away from the wall, leaned forward and fell over on his side.

There he lay for what might have been a minute, or ten, his face on the floor. The warm, stale smell of earth filled his nostrils. Then he managed to pull his knees up to his chest, and tried to push himself.

He had not the strength. His boots scraped uselessly across the floor. Gritting his teeth, fighting the sense of panic and helplessness that threatened to overwhelm him, he tried again, but to no avail. Feebly he tried to move his wrists behind him, but the bonds held.

He took deep breaths, then allowed himself a shout – a cry of rage and of desperation. It came back at him, muffled by the walls of the small hut. Suddenly amused again, he realized that neither he nor his captors had ever raised their voices indoors in the whole time he had been here. In fact, Miles had never spoken . . . Perhaps he could not. Was he a deaf mute, like the young woman in the house in Marlborough? Then he remembered that she was Lady Jane, and she was no mute . . .

179

His mind had wandered again. Savagely he bit his lip until it bled, forcing himself through the pain to focus on the moment. *Well*, he thought, *you have your voice at least, you can shout for help* . . .

He tried it. 'Help! Help me!' Then he found that he was laughing again. It reminded him of a comedy some players had performed once, in the Great Hall at Petbury, years ago, before the entire household . . . Eleanor had delighted in it.

Eleanor! Of course – she was the reason he had to get out of here, to get home, the reason he had to keep trying.

He shouted again and again. He went on shouting, as loud as he could, no longer mindful of the consequences, until his throat hurt and his mouth was dry as sawdust. Only then did he stop, expecting no response.

But there *was* a response.

At first he barely heard it, thinking it was a bird of the forest. Then it came a little louder – a voice, some way off.

He drew breath sharply, his mind clearing at once. He shouted as loudly as he could: 'In the hut! Help me!'

He was dizzy from the effort, and he shook his head weakly, his ear bent towards the door, which was behind him. He struggled, trying to roll over, but he had not even the strength for that. So he shouted again.

'In the hut . . . I am tied . . . Help!'

He heard voices . . . Voices? Fear came back, then. Miles and his master must have returned, and it was over. But instead the door opened softly, timidly . . . Sunlight flooded in, and then came the sweetest sound he could have imagined: the voice of a small child.

'Father – there's a man on the floor and he is hurt!'

He tried to answer, but only a croak emerged before he sank into a sleep of exhaustion.

Later he could recall little of his discovery or his removal from the hut by the forester and his family. He was told he spoke to them, enough for them to get word to Sir Giles Buckridge, who sent Richard Hawkes and Judd with the cart to bring him to Chilbourne. There was no sign of anyone else, the forester said, nor had he heard any horses. And all the while, Thomas had been a mere four miles from the manor, beyond the old royal hunting lodge of Ludgershall, in Chute Forest, though he might as well have been in a far-off country. After his rescue things became somewhat confused, partly because it was dark by the time he was brought in, and partly because he was drifting in and out of consciousness.

He awoke later with a start, thinking he was back in his corner of the hut. But there was a light burning, and he was lying on a soft bed . . . and he could move his arms . . . He turned his head slowly to see a white-haired old man sitting beside him with an expression of calm. For a brief moment he entertained some fanciful notions of heaven, before putting a name to the face: Redmund Oakes.

'Falconer.' The old butler leaned forward and peered at him. 'Can you talk?'

Thomas swallowed, and said, 'I can, Master Oakes.'

'Good . . . I was somewhat concerned that you had damaged your voice. You have done a great deal of shouting.'

Thomas raised his hand slowly, rejoicing in the luxury of being able to do so, and saw that his wrist was bandaged. He looked about him: he was in a small, bare chamber with one window. Outside, it was still dark.

But now memories were flooding back. He tried to raise himself. Then he realized he was naked, the lower half of his body covered with a sheet.

'Not yet – you are weak.' Oakes got to his feet with some difficulty and lifted a mug to Thomas's mouth. Thirst raged through him suddenly, so he took it in his own hand, shaking a little, and drank. It was only rosewater, but it tasted like sweet wine.

He sank back, letting Oakes take the mug. 'How long have I been here . . .?' he began, but the old man waved a hand dismissively.

'Several hours – you must rest a while longer. But your hurts are not too severe – no bones broken, the slaughterman says, and he has some knowledge of such matters.'

But Thomas was restless; there seemed so much to be done. 'I must speak with Sir Giles,' he said.

'Indeed you must,' Oakes nodded. 'In the morning, when you have eaten and feel strong enough.'

'Where are my clothes?' he asked, feeling somewhat foolish.

'On the fire, I hope,' Oakes answered. 'They stank beyond belief.' He smiled a little. 'There's naught to fret about. The usher has brought fresh clothes for you – you and he are near the same size. He it was who washed you down and cleaned your wounds.'

Thomas stared in surprise. 'Hawkes?'

Oakes nodded, then murmured, 'You should not judge the man too harshly. He has many good qualities. He was once a body-servant to Sir John Hunt, until he came here and stayed . . .' He fell silent.

Thomas too said nothing; his body was sore, and matters could wait. He was alive, and safe, and there were things he could do . . . The relief was enormous. He allowed himself two brief questions.

'Whose chamber is this? And what day is it?' he asked.

'Tuesday night, the seventeenth of the month,' was the reply. 'And do not concern yourself about the chamber.'

'So,' Thomas muttered to himself, 'it was two days . . .'

Then his eyes closed, and he drifted into a sound sleep.

He slept until dawn. In the night he had woken and found food and drink on the floor by the bed, and taken both before falling asleep again. Redmund Oakes had not returned, but in the early morning he heard the sounds of the household coming to life, and stirred himself. Finding the clothes that had been left out for him, he dressed, feeling stiff and sore. But he was recovering, and despite a swollen jaw and bruises, he would be his old self again . . . Indeed, it was good to be alive.

He walked about the room and worked his tired muscles until he felt ready. Then he left it, finding himself on the top floor of the house, and walked down to the kitchen. His entrance barely caused a stir; the kitchen boy stared once, then scurried off, while the cook handed him a bowl of porridge, which he took with a grateful smile.

Clyffe grunted. 'Master says you'm to be in the Great Hall at ten o'clock.' He paused. 'There's been a coil here while you were lying in your comfy bed. Mary Henshaw upped and left last night. The Lady Euphemia don't know which way to turn.'

Thomas froze. A picture of the cool, sculptured face of Mary Henshaw rose in his mind, sounding a warning. It was time now, at last, to tell everything and face the consequences. To his surprise, he found he was looking forward to it.

But first, he would go out and see that the falcons had not suffered in his absence.

To his relief both birds had been fed, and sat contentedly on their perches. But as he turned to leave the weathering, he glanced up at the sky and stopped in his tracks.

Circling slowly, not far above him, was a familiar shape, and the thought struck him forcibly: she was no longer a ramage hawk, but was beginning to hunt for herself.

'Well, falconer, we hear you've a pretty tale to tell us. I suggest you make it brief.'

It was not Sir Giles who faced him sternly across the table in the Great Hall, but the Sheriff of Wiltshire himself, Sir Henry Willoughby. Sir Giles was there, but he seemed to have shrunk somewhat, sitting to one side as if relieved of authority – which indeed seemed to be the case. For soon Thomas found himself part of a wider sweep of events than he had imagined.

There were only men in the room: Hawkes, sitting with Redmund Oakes, and beyond them a couple of hard-faced fellows Thomas did not know, but assumed were the Sheriff's servants. Also present for some reason, permitted to sit because of his years, was the bent figure of Bartholomew Byres. The surprise for Thomas was a slight figure seated alone at one end of the table, like a forlorn prince in a fairy tale: Gervase Lambert. His part in the proceedings would no doubt now be revealed.

Thomas told them as succinctly as he could what had happened in the past few days, starting with his being over-powered by Miles near the weathering, and being taken to the hut in the forest. He told all that he remembered of his discourse with the dark-bearded man, including his own thoughts about the search for whatever had been hidden at Cracked Oak. Which of course, led to his realization that the two men had been looking in the wrong place . . . So now, trying not to flinch under the gaze of every man in the room, he was obliged to come to the part of the story that he had dreaded: the discovery of the house in Marlborough.

To his surprise, there were no cries of outrage – even from Sir Giles. Even when he talked of the banns, and his meeting with Lady Jane and Mary Henshaw, and of his short exchange with the servant Guido outside, there were no expressions of anger, or even of surprise. Instead, feeling a mixture of relief and unease, it dawned upon him that his revelations came as something of an anticlimax. Then he glanced at Gervase, sitting with his eyes lowered, and realized that at last he had told where Lady Jane was hiding.

Thomas stopped then, and stood like a penitent, eyes front, and waited.

'Well, you took your time about it,' Willoughby said coolly.

He glanced towards Sir Giles, who was looking at Thomas distractedly. 'Your decision, sir?' he muttered.

Sensing tension between the two men, Thomas was surprised when Sir Giles merely said: 'I have made none.'

Willoughby frowned. 'This man has withheld knowledge of your daughter, putting her life in danger—'

'Yes,' Sir Giles agreed absently. 'Yet I believe I know why.' He looked briefly at Gervase, who did not meet his eye. 'I wager she begged him to keep her secret, and like me he found it mighty hard to deny her – is that not so?'

He was looking at Thomas. And here, Thomas realized, was a way out: he had but to confirm that this was the case and Sir Giles would understand. He might not even be disciplined, for did not the whole of Chilbourne wish that that sweet girl be allowed to marry the young man she loved, instead of the hateful Ridley? Despite his desperate need for money, had not even Sir Giles some sympathy with the notion?

But then he sighed inwardly, knowing that he was a fool to himself, and that his plain falconer's heart would speak the truth and condemn him as it had so often done. He braced himself.

'Nay, sir,' he said, well aware of the surprise he now caused. 'I said naught because Mistress Henshaw threatened me if I spoke up.'

Willoughby leaned forward. 'Threatened you? How?'

'She said I would be accused of violating a woman of the household, sir,' Thomas answered. 'And though it is not true, she said a falconer's word would not be believed.'

Now there was something approaching outrage in the room. Sir Giles got to his feet. Willoughby was glaring. Even Redmund Oakes looked displeased, while a startled expression had appeared on the face of Gervase.

'Who is the woman you speak of?' Sir Giles's tone was harsh. He was hurt. Thomas saw the look of betrayal in his eyes and flinched. But, come what may, he knew one thing: he would not name Eliza.

The silence grew longer. Willoughby's men were on the alert, as if expecting to be called upon at any moment. Willoughby himself, angry now, was staring hard at Thomas.

'Speak, falconer, or I'll arrest you at once.'

Still Thomas stood, feeling the same tiredness he had known back in the hut, struggling to remain calm. No, he could not name Eliza. She was wayward and had a cruel streak, yet she had strength and courage as well as charm and beauty, and had demanded naught from him but honesty
. . .

'Your last chance,' Willoughby said.

Thomas blinked, feeling the cold hostility of every man in the room. He had no friends here. His fate was sealed.

A familiar voice broke the silence.

'With your leave, Sir Henry . . .'

All turned to Richard Hawkes, who had moved forward to approach the table. 'I fear you judge the falconer too harshly.' Hawkes's voice was dry and toneless. 'He merely wishes not to stain the memory of the woman who died.'

There was astonishment before a frowning Sir Giles blurted

185

out: 'You mean the washerwoman? Since when was Nan's reputation worthy of such niceties? Besides, she is dead and cannot be harmed . . .' He broke off, as if aware how coarse his words sounded. But their import was not to be disputed.

Willoughby was looking intently at Thomas. 'Is this so?' he demanded. 'Could you not have spoken and saved us all this trouble?'

Thomas swallowed. He had thrown a very brief glance at Hawkes, managing to conceal his amazement at the way the man had come to his aid. Then he saw that the reason was obvious. Hawkes knew – he must know, as he knew what sort of woman Eliza was. Yet he had protected her, for he loved her. If Thomas had ever entertained doubts about that, they had just been destroyed.

He faced Sir Henry, concealing his relief, and allowed himself one half-truth. 'Nan did spend some time with me in the stable-loft, sir,' he admitted. 'Yet naught occurred that had not her consent . . .'

Willoughby was on his feet now, red in the face from irritation or embarrassment or both. 'In God's name, man – how dare you waste my time? You think I care who you rut with? We seek a pair of murderers who have added even more outrages to their list – which indeed in your carelessness you may have contributed to!'

Thomas stared, not understanding, until Sir Giles deigned to inform him. 'Doctor Parry is dead. He was found on Monday – the day after you and the usher visited him.'

Thomas swallowed and threw another glance at Hawkes, who deliberately avoided his eye. 'Sir . . . I knew not—'

'Of course you knew not!' Willoughby thundered. 'What does a falconer know, except how to talk to birds? You even entered the house of William Jenkin and failed to notice anything odd about his absence, and he too is dead! Neck broken like Parry's, thrown down behind the barn and barely concealed with hay – yet you, we are supposed to believe, made a search of his farm!'

Thomas felt a nausea rise from his stomach, but Willoughby's anger was relentless.

'It seems plain to me that you, and you, sir, –' this with

186

a hard look at Hawkes – 'have blundered about the county for the past week, learning naught. Then when you do learn something of importance, you dare to conceal it. You are fortunate that the existence of the wedding banns in Marlborough – indeed the whole of Lady Jane's plan – has been laid bare already by Sir Giles's ward himself.' He threw a look of contempt upon Gervase, who did not react.

'Further,' Willoughby added, turning back to Thomas, 'you manage to get yourself captured by the very men we seek, who get clean away again. Indeed, they seem to have been moving from place to place under our noses with consummate ease – even, we hear, turning up at a wrestling match in full view of the entire village of East Everley, and walking off with the prize money!'

The men in the room stirred. Sir Giles seemed lost for words, for few could dispute Willoughby's concise summary of the matter. He almost flinched when the Sheriff turned to address him again.

'You should waste no more time before riding to Marlborough and bringing your daughter home, sir,' he said. 'If she were mine, I would have been a great deal more careful . . .' He broke off briefly as Sir Giles reddened, then went on: 'Moreover, I find it mighty hard to believe you had no knowledge of the existence of the Lady Euphemia's town house. And I fail to see why you did not search it sooner.'

Thomas saw the look that flickered briefly between Redmund Oakes and Richard Hawkes. Of course he knew, as they did too . . .

Sir Giles swallowed. 'I did not know that Lady Jane or Gervase knew of it . . .' he began feebly.

Willoughby snorted. But the truly shattering piece of news was yet to be delivered, and it would come from the least likely man in the room.

Willoughby was looking round, including everyone in his pronouncement. 'I now intend to raise a company large enough to put the fear of God into even those two savages we seek. Every able man – including you, falconer – will ride under my orders, and we will not rest until we have scoured every hovel, barn and hayrick in the county and discovered their whereabouts – assuming they have not fled already. Then we will lay hands upon them, and I personally will walk them to the gallows and see them hanged!'

He breathed deeply, almost purple in the face, struggling to control himself. 'And if any man dare ask what if we do not find them . . .'

There was a cough. Willoughby broke off, his head snapping round towards its source, which was familiar enough to everyone else.

All eyes upon him, Bartholomew Byres was getting slowly to his feet. He peered at Willoughby from under his white brows.

'Forgive me, sir, I must speak. For ye would waste much time . . .' He coughed again, his hands fluttering nervously about his throat. The room was tense with impatience, but for some reason every man held his tongue.

''Tis Mary Henshaw who is to blame,' the old man confessed in a shaky voice. 'She and I, for we knew what it was they sought at Cracked Oak. Even when they bound us and held us prisoner, I would not speak, for I dared not. You know not what she can do – would do . . .' He broke off, then came to the nub of his confession. 'The treasure from Drake's ship . . . It is in four saddlebags wrapped in sailcloth, and it is hidden under the floor of the house in Marlborough.'

Sixteen

He was a frail old man, yet his mind was clear, and as he told his tale, nobody in the room doubted the truth of it. Though its import made uncomfortable listening.

'They had a covenant. Mary and Master Tyrrell – the Lady Euphemia's nephew. He would visit at times ... The Lady Euphemia always indulged him, for he reminded her of the handsome gallants of her youth. If she had but known, when she let him use her house in Marlborough for his trysts, that they were young men he brought there and not maids, she would have been distressed. So none told her ... Only, Mary Henshaw saw a means to use her knowledge. She always does.'

He broke off and gave his cough, which now seemed more of a device to buy time than anything else, and turned a watery eye upon Sir Giles. 'I beg you will forgive me, sir, for I have been a base coward. I have let her rule me, and kept to myself knowledge which could have saved you much trouble ...' He was close to tears. But if some found a deal of pity for him in their hearts, Willoughby was not among them.

'Speak – the whole of it!' he said sharply. 'The law is no respecter of your years.'

'I said she – Mary – saw a means to use her knowledge,' Byres resumed quickly, shaking now. 'She it was who saw, when Master Tyrrell and his friend Will Pygot came – he was a wicked and cruel-hearted young man, I deem – she saw they had something they wished to conceal, and she watched them from a window, when first they concealed it in the oak tree. There is a hollow within it ...'

There was an intake of breath all round. 'It was in the Cracked Oak?' Sir Giles blurted. 'All the time ...'

Willoughby was staring. 'A treasure, you say – what manner of treasure do you mean?'

'A fortune, sir,' Byres said softly. 'Hived off from the *San Felipe* – a Spanish ship captured by Drake. The Queen's portion alone was said to be worth forty thousand pounds. It was moored at Plymouth . . . They overpowered the guards and took a barrel full of gold away – Pygot and Master Tyrrell. And they brought it here, and hid it—'

'Without Lady Euphemia's knowledge,' Willoughby finished dryly.

'Indeed, sir. Her ladyship's mind is elsewhere a deal of the time. Mary has no difficulty making her believe what she wants her to.' Byres glanced round at the expressions of amazement in the room. 'When Mary saw them she accosted them and threatened to tell Lady Euphemia. She said the tree was not a safe place, and bade them move it to the house in Marlborough. So they made a pact that when they came back to retrieve it, she would receive a portion . . .'

'By the good Christ.' Sir Giles sat down heavily, struggling to grasp the matter in its entirety. 'You mean to tell us that all this time you and Mary Henshaw knew what these men sought, and you stood by while they ransacked the house – even when they bound you and held your mistress hostage – and you said nothing . . .'

'You know not what Mary is, sir!' Byres raised a trembling hand towards Sir Giles. 'She is stronger than any man. She swore me to silence on pain of breaking my bones – and she would do it! She said when the time came I would have a place . . . She would set up an inn at Devizes and be her own master – that is the word she used – and I would have a seat by the fireside, and a mug every day for the rest of my life . . .' Byres gave a sob, and his frame sagged so that he almost fell. 'I am become too old for service – where would I go? Would you house me, sir – or you?'

This last was directed at Willoughby, but the High Sheriff was unshakeable in his anger. 'You admit to being a coward, yet that is too kind a word for you,' he said harshly. 'You are one of the worst men I have had to deal with.' He turned to Sir Giles, who sat with his head in his hands. 'We know where to ride to now,' he said. 'The Marlborough house.'

Sir Giles looked up, pale-faced, and nodded. Then he frowned suddenly, staring at Byres. 'Yet it was you that kept the bundle they ordered you to destroy, and showed it to me – I do not understand . . .'

Byres coughed. 'Mary ordered me to do so. She thought 'twould divert thee to hunt for the murderers of that man – the Crown Purveyor – instead of concerning yourself with what it was they sought at Cracked Oak . . .'

'We have wasted enough time.' Willoughby's tone was brisk now as he turned to the room in general. 'I charge every man to have himself geared and mounted within the half-hour, and to wait at the crossroads. We ride for Marlborough.'

But now there came a particularly loud cough from Bartholomew Byres, who took a shaky step forward. 'Sir, you must make every haste, for I fear you are too late!'

'Too late?' Sir Giles was on his feet again. 'What do you mean?'

'He means she has gone to Marlborough,' Willoughby said grimly. 'Mary Henshaw – you told me she left here last night, and none knows where. There is your answer. Now that John Tyrrell is dead, and none will come to recover the valuables – which, by the way –' this with a hard look at Sir Giles – 'are Crown property – she intends to recover the fortune for herself.' He glared at Sir Giles. 'And all the while your daughter was there, with a king's ransom under her feet!'

He looked around at the stunned expressions on the assembled faces. But Gervase Lambert was rising quickly.

'Lady Jane . . . She may be in terrible danger!'

'Indeed she may be, for which reason we will waste not a minute longer.'

Willoughby strode towards the door, his men following smartly behind him. Sir Giles, face tight with anxiety, hurried after, saying: 'Master usher, get yourself horsed – get everyone horsed!'

Hawkes hastened to obey. On his way to the door he

191

caught Thomas's eye and jerked his head. Without a word, Thomas followed him out. As he left the room he glanced behind once, and saw Byres slump brokenly into his chair, as if he would never rise from it again.

There were yet more tidings to come before the company left the crossroads. A dozen or so men, including Sir Giles, Gervase, Hawkes and Thomas, had assembled under Willoughby's command. But no sooner were they ready than one of the Sheriff's men called out, pointing towards the village. Someone was hurrying towards them on foot. As he drew close, Thomas recognized young Will Tapp.

'Sir!' he cried, nervous at the appearance of so many grim-faced men looking impatiently down at him from their skittish mounts. The sight of swords and calivers merely added to his unease.

'Whatever it is, it must wait,' Sir Giles said to the young man, but Tapp's gaze was directed at Willoughby.

'My Lord Sheriff,' he said, 'the hayward begs you to await him – he has news of those men you seek!'

'Cardmaker?' Sir Giles was impatient. 'Not now – we have no time!'

But there came a shout, and the familiar shape of the little hayward appeared, trotting towards them on the same borrowed horse he had last ridden alongside Thomas. Sir Giles turned to Willoughby, but the Sheriff raised a hand.

'Let us hear what he has to say – it cannot hurt.'

Cardmaker drew rein, somewhat out of breath. 'My Lord Sheriff, they were seen again, early this morning.' He glanced about, taking in Sir Giles and the other men he knew. 'The tall fellow and his servant, the wrestler . . .'

'Here?' Willoughby frowned. 'Which way did they go?'

'They had a woman with them. I fear for her life.'

Sir Giles turned a haggard face towards Willoughby. 'By the Christ, she has taken up with them – Mary Henshaw . . .'

Willoughby leaned forward in the saddle and addressed Cardmaker sharply. 'What did you see? Quickly now!'

'Not I, sir,' Cardmaker answered, taken aback. 'Birch, one of our village – he was out last night near the warrens on

192

some errand . . .' He hesitated, and Thomas guessed at once what kind of errand Birch had been on: clearly a damaged ankle had not stopped him making the occasional poaching foray.

'He it was saw them. They came from the direction of Chilbourne Manor, sir.' He turned to Sir Giles. 'They had a woman with them – a tall woman with grey hair . . . Only she was not one with them . . . That is . . .'

'In God's name, man, get to the nub of it!' Willoughby shouted, making Cardmaker's mount jerk with fright.

'They were leading her horse as if she were a captive, sir,' Cardmaker answered, struggling to control the reins. 'They took the Marlborough road.'

Sir Giles made a sound, almost a sob. 'Then she has told them all – and we may truly be too late!'

'Ride!' Willoughby shouted, and without waiting dug his spurs into his horse's flanks, causing it to whinny in pain. In seconds he and the entire party were galloping along the road to Marlborough, kicking up clouds of dust behind them.

Thomas, mounted on Cob, found he was in the rear. As he urged the horse forward, hoof-beats rang out behind, and he saw Cardmaker, slapping his horse's rump frantically, struggling to catch up.

'They won't mind me coming along, I wager,' he called to Thomas. 'Will they?'

Thomas ignored him, and set his face to the north.

It was a much shorter journey than the one Thomas had taken last time in the cart; well-mounted men could cover the same distance in little more than an hour. Through Savernake Forest they thundered, slowing only briefly to save their mounts, then down into the Kennett valley. Minutes later they were splashing through the ford, the houses of the great town rising before them.

The road into Marlborough was crowded, for Wednesday was market day, and folk fell back to stare at the group of armed riders who swept by in a tight-packed body on sweating horses. As they neared the square the traffic thickened and at last Willoughby raised his hand to call a halt.

'The house,' he said to Sir Giles. 'Where is it?' Then, turning abruptly to Thomas, he snapped: 'You were there last, were you not? Guide us – and quickly!'

So Thomas led the way on Cob, forcing a path through the throng of bustling townsfolk, many of whom called out, asking what was the coil. There was even a cry of 'Clubs!' from somewhere. But Willoughby turned angrily, saying they were on Sheriff's business and would not be delayed.

Past St Peter's church they rode, pressing through the narrowing lane, and turned into the street that Thomas remembered well enough. He halted outside the house and pointed.

Willoughby's men dismounted and began hammering on the door. At once windows were thrown open and heads appeared. A door opened and the woman from the next house, whom Thomas remembered, appeared in a fluster.

'By the Lord, masters – what has happened?'

Sir Giles, Hawkes and Thomas had also dismounted. Willoughby drew close to the woman, who blanched, then seeing his dress and his manner, bobbed instinctively.

'Has anyone been into this house today?' he demanded.

'Indeed, sir – there's been a deal of toing and froing here of late . . .' The woman faltered. 'I believe now they are gone.'

'Who's gone?' Willoughby asked sharply, then snapped his head aside as one of his men asked: 'May I break it, sir?'

'Break it down and be quick,' the Sheriff replied, causing the neighbour to clap a hand to her mouth in alarm. At once the door gave way with a crash, and there was a general surge through the entrance.

Thomas and Cardmaker brought up the rear, while men swarmed into every part of the house, up the stairs, and out through the passage into the back yard. There came a shout from the front parlour, where last Friday Thomas had sat nursing his aching head, and spoken with Lady Jane.

At once they pushed into the small room, only to halt abruptly. An eerie silence fell, allowing the growing hubbub of voices outside to become audible.

Using his height, Thomas peered above the men who stood motionless, crammed into the doorway and the nearer half of the room, and saw what they saw. Guido, the thin-faced servant, lay on his back in a corner, his eyes pointed at the ceiling, as vacant as only the eyes of the dead can be. On his face was an expression of dismay. Perhaps it was occasioned at least in part by the condition of the room, which reminded some of Cracked Oak – floorboards prised up and thrown aside, leaving naught but empty space below.

'Who is that?' Willoughby had not yet modulated his voice from barking commands outside, and it boomed in the room.

Sir Giles looked nauseous. 'I know not.'

'Sir . . .' Thomas began to force his way through. Men turned, making way for him as Willoughby waved him forward. 'His name was Guido, sir,' Thomas told him. 'He was the servant charged with looking after the house.'

'Jane! My Jane!' Sir Giles gazed about, anguish in his voice.

There came a muffled cry from the back of the throng, and now Gervase Lambert thrust himself forward, a look of desperation on his face. 'Your Jane?' he echoed. 'You who would marry her to a man she loathed – who is the cause of her plight! She is *my* Jane. And I will find her, be she dead or alive!'

There was silence. Sir Giles turned away. Willoughby glanced around at the man who had broken in the door, but the fellow merely shook his head.

Then came another shout, this time from upstairs. At once every man turned, and there was the thunder of boots on the narrow staircase. Thomas, waiting below, found Cardmaker beside him.

'What's this place to you?' the little man asked excitedly. 'Come to that, what's it to Sir Giles?'

Then he froze, as Thomas did, hearing a cry of agony that chilled them both. In an instant they had hurried up the stairs to crowd into another room, this time a bedchamber. The others stood about, not in a body this time, but against the walls. Thomas, fearing the worst, found his heart was beating, for what he heard, as every man had, was a woman's voice.

But it was not Lady Jane's.

Sir Giles, seemingly overcome with relief, had slumped down beside the bulky figure in voluminous skirts who lay flat on the floor beside the bed in the centre of the room. Gervase dropped to his knee nearby. All eyes were on the ash-grey face of Mary Henshaw, who regarded them calmly from her recumbent position.

'Forgive me if I do not rise, sirs,' she murmured, 'for I fear my neck is broken.'

Nobody spoke. Calmly she surveyed them, eyes flitting from one face to another, until they rested upon Willoughby.

'You have a chance to redeem yourself, woman,' the Sheriff said, coming forward. 'Tell us what has become of Lady Jane.'

'They have taken her,' was the answer.

Sir Giles bent a haggard face over her. 'Where to?'

'To Cracked Oak, of course.' A frown crossed Mary Henshaw's brow. 'Why do you linger here?'

Willoughby looked down at her. 'We came because your friend Byres has told us everything,' he answered. 'How the Queen's treasure was hidden in this house . . .'

Mary Henshaw smiled then. 'We moved it back,' she said.

There were exclamations from the men who stood about. Sir Giles turned to the Sheriff in agitation. 'We must take horse again, now!'

'Wait!' Willoughby's tone was harsh. He peered again at Mary Henshaw. 'We?' he asked. 'Who was it helped you?'

'The servant – Guido.' Her eyes wandered, then fixed upon Thomas. ''Twas the falconer's fault.'

Thomas stared but before he could form a question, Willoughby had intervened. With difficulty he lowered his bulky body to one knee beside Sir Giles. 'What do you mean? I'll have the truth now – and quickly!'

But Mary Henshaw was not to be hurried, for she was near death and knew it as well as anyone. She fixed her gaze upon the Sheriff. 'After he discovered Lady Jane was here, I knew 'twas no longer safe. We took the packs back to the last place anyone would look – the place that has already been ransacked.' She gave a hard little smile. 'It is where it was when this whole tale began: in the old oak tree.'

'But what of Jane?' Sir Giles bent over her in desperation.

'I have said,' Mary replied. She gave a little sigh, and blood appeared on her lips. Her face was deathly pale. 'You are too late,' she said.

'No!' Gervase leaned forward, his eyes blazing. 'You know what these men are – what they would do – you could not wish it upon her!'

'Wish it? Since when has what I wished been aught to the likes of you?' Mary's voice grated now. She shuddered, an involuntary motion, and every man saw the hatred in her gaze as she turned a glittering eye upon Sir Giles.

'I had a home once, and a daughter . . . Dead of plague, thirty years since . . . You think I am fit only to play nursemaid to that feeble-minded harpy, your ridiculous cousin? Only me and an old man half in his dotage to wash her linen and indulge her foolishness and applaud her every night when she plays those damned virginals. Small wonder she was dismissed from Court, for the Queen could not abide her, any more than I! After ten years I despised her with every breath in my body. After twenty I would have throttled her as she slept and danced as I did it!'

Willoughby's voice cut through the air like steel.

'You think we care for your thoughts, or your wicked soul?' he snapped. 'You have your reward, for you are dying and there's none can save you. May you find mercy when you stand before your Maker, for I have none.'

Mary Henshaw coughed, and a gout of blood spurted from her mouth and fell upon her kirtle. 'I spit upon your mercy,' she muttered. 'I curse you, as I curse all you savage, selfish men . . .' Once again, she eyed Thomas briefly. 'If he had not got himself caught by those two, I would have been gone . . . 'Twas for him they came skulking about Chilbourne, knowing he would give them away. Instead they found me. And yet –' a grotesque smile played across her features – 'still I deceived them, bringing them here, knowing the prize was already gone . . . I had not thought that the one with no ears would use me as he did.' For the first time, fear showed in her eyes. 'He cared not if I were woman or beast . . .' She coughed again, very weak now. 'Blame Parson Parry,' she muttered, so that those in the room thought her mind was failing. 'He it was pointed Miles toward poor Nan, who never harmed a soul. He it was hid them when they promised him a share of the prize – and like a fool he believed them, until they murdered his tenant and showed him what they were.'

'Parry has paid for his crimes,' Willoughby said with disgust. 'As will they.' He got stiffly to his feet, but Mary Henshaw had the last word.

'You have lost,' she said, 'for Jane is their hostage now – their lucky charm, Pepper said.'

Willoughby looked sharply at her. 'Who?'

'Simon Pepper is his name,' Mary Henshaw murmured, faintly now so that every man bent his head to hear her words. 'He it was killed Will Pygot, as his servant killed John Tyrrell . . . It's well, for death is the wages of men like they . . .' She coughed again, feebly. 'How I rejoiced to see the Lady Euphemia's grief,' she said in a voice of pure, bright malice. 'For I did mortally hate her . . .'

Then her eyes rolled until the whites showed, and she died.

Seventeen

If the ride to Marlborough had had an air of urgency about it, the ride back was one of desperation. Though Willoughby had used his authority, insisting that horses were watered and fed before they took the road south, it soon became clear that the company were to split. Those that rode the fastest mounts, and had most cause for haste, would race ahead of the rest. Sir Giles, Gervase and Richard Hawkes had soon left the rest behind – save Thomas, who was able to keep pace thanks to the spirited Cob.

Through the deep silence of Savernake Forest they rode again, then bore south-westwards towards the upper Avon valley. Sir Giles took the lead for he knew the country well, and seemed to have recovered a little now that he was on the final lap of what had become a race against time – the desperate need to reach Lady Jane before Simon Pepper and his man disappeared with her – or worse. No man dared voice his own private fears that they were, in all likelihood, already too late.

Gervase galloped close by Sir Giles. Hawkes and Thomas, riding behind, sensed a bond between the two men, united in their common purpose. The past, along with the treasure from the *San Felipe*, seemed momentarily forgotten.

Not a word had been exchanged between Thomas and Hawkes since they left Chilbourne. Now Thomas, coming up alongside him, made bold to thank him for his intervention earlier that day.

Hawkes kept his eyes on the road ahead. ''Twas not for you I did it,' he said.

'I know it,' Thomas answered. 'And my respect for you is the greater for trying to protect her . . .'

Hawkes threw him an angry look. 'You think you are the first to have . . .' He broke off, refusing to use the words.

'Let me speak,' Thomas said, 'for I now know why you are such a hard man to be with – let alone understand.'

Hawkes's eyes blazed. 'You presume to treat me as an equal?' he snapped.

It was Thomas who now kept his eyes on the road. 'Well,' he said, just loud enough to be heard above the thudding of hooves, 'if I am not, I wonder why a man like you deigned to wash the filth from my body, while I lay unconscious.'

Hawkes hesitated, then said, 'I would do the same for any member of the household who had been used as you had.'

'I doubt that,' Thomas answered. 'I believe that in some manner, you wished to redress the wrongs that stand between us.'

'Then you are a fool,' Hawkes said.

Thomas sighed. ''Tis a strange thing,' he said. 'Yet I have known men, rivals for the same woman's hand, who fought like cats in a barrel, yet each would die before they would let any real harm come to the other. Mayhap it was because they set the woman's feelings above their own – for they would not let her suffer.'

Hawkes was frowning, and his tone remained harsh. 'I told you once, you know nothing of me – or my suffering,' he muttered.

'I know you love Eliza,' Thomas said. 'And if you made bold for once to step beyond the bounds of your station, for which you seem to have such regard, you might find happiness.'

Then he gripped the rein, touched heels to Cob's flanks and urged him to greater speed, because Sir Giles and Gervase had drawn away.

It hurt him more than he expected to let Eliza go in this fashion. Perhaps she had touched his heart, too. But he had seen the look on Hawkes's face, and was content.

An hour later, they splashed across the Little Avon and clattered through the hamlet of Enford. It was now mid-afternoon and dark clouds had drifted in, blocking out the

200

sun. A breeze was blowing in off the Plain. But as they approached the lane leading to Cracked Oak there came a shout from the roadside, and the party drew rein. A small group of riders detached themselves from the shelter of a large tree and came forward. They were all villagers from East Everley, save one familiar figure, whose huge bulk straddled a small piebald pony that was normally ridden by one of the Chilbourne ladies.

'Judd!' Sir Giles paused, out of breath, the sweat standing on his brow. 'I may need you, for she is here – Lady Jane . . .'

'We heard, maister,' Judd nodded. 'Sheriff sent a man on to Chilbourne – rode so hard, he'm worn out his poor horse. Lady Kat did tell me to raise any men I could find, quick.' He indicated the others, and sniffed. 'They was nearest – I had to take what was to hand.'

Then Thomas saw, as the others did, the man who sat at the rear, one leg bound and sticking out beyond the stirrup. How Edward Birch had managed to get himself mounted, let alone ride, was anyone's guess.

'Well, I am grateful to you all,' Sir Giles said, looking at each man. 'But have a care, and obey my orders, for we face a terrible foe.'

'We know that, sir,' Judd muttered. 'We saw 'ee at the wrestling – the one with no ears.' He glanced at Birch, who looked away, then added: 'There's horses in there, sir.' He gestured towards Cracked Oak. Sir Giles looked at Hawkes, and at Gervase. Without a word he urged his mount forward.

They dismounted at the entrance to the lane, leaving Edward Birch to hold the horses. He made no protest, since it was obvious he would be little use in a fight. But as Thomas handed Cob's rein to him he caught Birch's eye, and saw the light of anger there.

'I'd sorely like to get my revenge for this,' he said, jerking his head at his broken foot. Thomas made no reply.

Now a silence seemed to have fallen, and a trace of fear showed on the faces of the villagers. They were eight in all – Judd and three men from East Everley, as well as Sir Giles, Gervase, Hawkes and Thomas. And though they carried an array of weapons between them, they were wary, knowing something of the people they were up against. Sir Giles and Hawkes bore swords, while Thomas had his small poniard, but the others had only what they could lay hands on when Judd gathered them together: billhooks, knives and stout sticks. Gervase Lambert also wore a sword, but knowing what he did of the young man, Thomas doubted his proficiency with it.

They moved forward, fanning out across the lane and on to the grass on either side as the house came into view. There was no one in sight, but there were horses – several of them, and for a moment the party held back, suddenly afraid that they might face considerably more then two men.

It was Thomas who recognized the mounts first. 'It's Warren's horse, sir,' he said to Sir Giles, who was on his left, with Gervase beside him. 'And that's Parry's.'

It was indeed the rector's small grey mare, which stood watching the approaching men warily. Apart from those, there were three other horses, making five in all.

'They took them all. They need them to carry the heavy packs,' Thomas added with some relief, but Sir Giles was not listening. Instead he pointed to one of the other mounts.

'It is Jane's,' he said, in a voice of anguish. 'The one she rode when I last saw her, hawking on the Downs . . .'

Thomas stared, though he had forgotten what horse Lady Jane rode that day; it seemed a long time ago.

'So they are alone, apart from Lady Jane,' said Hawkes, on Thomas's right, breathing hard. With a glance at Sir Giles, he drew his sword.

'Soft!' Sir Giles begged. 'They may have wind of us.'

Indeed they might, Thomas thought to himself, finding his own breath coming in shorter bursts. He scanned the ruined garden, which looked as he remembered it: pits and heaps of turned earth on all sides. And there was the lightning-blackened shape of the split oak tree that had unwittingly been the witness to so much grief.

They reached the tree, still walking in a line, whereupon Hawkes examined its inside quickly.

'If anything was here, it's gone,' he said.

All eyes strayed towards the house. It looked as peaceful as it always did, save that this time the front door and all the windows were shut.

They stopped. There was no sound – not even the call of a bird. That alone ought to have been enough to warn anyone. The village men looked uneasy, and glanced towards the master of Chilbourne for leadership.

Sir Giles hesitated. 'Well, Master usher,' he said. 'What is your advice?'

Hawkes blinked. 'We should surround the house, sir,' he suggested. 'Then wait for the Lord Sheriff and his company.'

Sir Giles turned anxiously. 'But they have Jane!'

Gervase Lambert spoke. 'We must get inside, before . . .' He broke off, a frantic look on his face.

Judd called from some yards off. 'I could get round the back, maister . . .'

'Nay – I begin to fear the worst.' Hawkes was looking uneasily at Sir Giles. 'They must know we're here.'

'Of course they know,' Thomas said. He had first-hand knowledge of the man he now knew as Simon Pepper, not to mention his fearsome servant. And it was stretching credence beyond breaking point to think that they had failed to observe the arrival of such a large party; they were barricaded inside the house.

Turning to Sir Giles, he spoke up. 'Might it not be best if you drew their attention, sir?' he asked. 'Called for them to lay down their arms, meanwhile one or two well-armed men could move through the trees, then skirt round the back. There's a window I know can be forced.'

Sir Giles nodded. 'Wise enough counsel . . .'

'Yet rash,' Hawkes snapped, looking irritably at Thomas. 'They might do anything—'

He was interrupted by a crash of glass, and every man's head turned towards the house. An upstairs window had been broken. As they stared there came a cry, and the blur of a figure beyond the casement, which disappeared at once.

'Jane!' Gervase Lambert cried. 'She was trying to call out to me!' He ran towards the door, found it locked and began beating frantically upon it.

Thomas faced Sir Giles. 'Too late for any feints now, sir,' he said. 'May I take the back?'

'I'll come with 'ee,' Judd said. And without waiting, both men hurried round the side of the house. As they went they heard Sir Giles calling to the others to find something to break down the door.

Thomas, followed by the slower-moving Judd, gained the back and hurried through the kitchen garden. The door was closed, and when he tried it, he found it wedged from inside. The window John Steer had once climbed through was likewise fastened. But now there came noise from within – a shout, and the banging of a door.

'I'll bust 'ee,' Judd said, coming up behind Thomas, puffing a little. With his elbow he smashed the window in easily, cleared the remaining shards away, put his huge hands on the frame and then turned aside in consternation.

'Jesu! I'll never get in 'ere!'

'I can,' Thomas said, and climbed through.

He dropped to the ground and almost fell over, for the floor was cluttered with debris. He was in the wrecked kitchen, still in the state he had last seen it. Glancing about, he picked his way out into the passage and found the back door, which was bolted and wedged with a wall-timber under the latch. Knocking the beam aside, he unbolted the door and wrenched it open. As he did so, some instinct made him duck – just in time, for a billet whistled past his ear and cracked against the door frame. Whirling round, he found himself face to face with Miles.

But Judd appeared at the back door then, and Miles turned, moving rapidly for such a heavy man, and ran back along the passage. Soon his footfalls sounded on the stairs.

Judd strode into the house, his big frame blocking the light. ''Twas 'ee!' he exclaimed.

'It was,' Thomas replied, breathing hard, 'and he almost broke my skull.'

More footsteps sounded from above, and there came a shout that froze both men as they stood – a woman's voice.

'They've got 'er up there,' Judd muttered.

Thomas hurried to the foot of the stairs, with Judd

204

following. They grew aware of shouting from outside, and the thudding of sword-hilts on the stout timbers of the front door.

Thomas looked, and saw no key in the huge lock. 'Tell them we can't unlock it,' he shouted to Judd. 'Open the windows – break them if you have to!'

Judd looked about, found a broken stool and at once began smashing windows. Leaving him to the task, Thomas began ascending the stairs. He moved slowly, his senses taut, peering upwards and seeing no sign of anyone. *Wait*, his inner voice told him. *Wait for the others . . . But what if they are too late?* he asked himself – and found no answer.

The great staircase creaked alarmingly. Above and ahead was the wide passage, at the end of which was the Lady Euphemia's main receiving chamber. Doors on either side were closed. As before, he had to pick his way carefully over loose boards. Then, as he reached the top of the stairs, there came a commotion from below. Listening with half an ear, he was aware that the breaking of glass had ceased, and the other men were piling into the house.

Footfalls sounded below him, and there came a shout from Gervase Lambert. Thomas turned as the young man, showing more courage than expected, began hurrying up the stairs.

But he should not have looked away.

Too late again, he told himself, hearing the sound behind him and to his left. Time seemed to have slowed. *Who could possibly match Miles?* he thought, memories of the wrestling match flooding back – then worse ones of the hut, and the expressionless face of the heavy man in his skullcap bending over him. All this came to him as he found himself pinioned, picked up like a child, and hurled fully across the passage, to fall with a sickening thud against the far wall.

Through a semi-daze he tried to sit up, and found that he could, though pains shot through his shoulder. At least he hasn't broken my neck like the others, he thought . . . then several things happened at once, and he was merely a spectator.

The first he saw was Gervase Lambert, sword in hand, leaping up the stairs two at a time. Above him was Miles, like a rock, barring his way. With a cry the young man jabbed wildly with his blade, then gaped as Miles dodged it easily, caught it with his bare left hand and yanked it out of his grasp, heedless of the hideous cut it made across his palm. Blood ran from his hand, which he ignored; he merely threw the sword upwards, caught the handle with his right hand, and lunged at Gervase.

Gervase drew back, but the thrust caught him in his side, thankfully away from any vital organ. He cried out as Miles withdrew the dripping weapon, a red stain appearing at once on his fine emerald-green doublet. Then as he sat weakly on the floor the big man raised his arm for the kill.

Thomas shouted, struggling to his feet and fumbling for his dagger. But there came more shouts from the stairs: Sir Giles, Hawkes and the others. Miles hesitated briefly, then turned and ran along the passage. Reaching the door at the end, he pushed it open and disappeared.

Hawkes was the first to gain the landing, taking in the situation quickly. He glanced from Gervase to Thomas and back. 'Help him!' he shouted to the men behind. Then leaving Gervase he moved towards Thomas, who was leaning against the wall, recovering his senses. Pain shot through his shoulder.

'In there,' Thomas said, pointing towards the far door.

'Can you walk?' Hawkes asked.

Thomas nodded. 'She's alive – we heard her scream . . .' Sir Giles came up, panting, another man behind him. The other two stooped to lift Gervase, and bore him off down the stairs.

Thomas and Hawkes eyed each other. An unseen, unspoken current darted between them before they turned and moved towards the door to the main chamber. Behind them, Sir Giles called out anxiously.

They reached the door, tried it, and were not surprised to find it bolted, or wedged shut. Hawkes stepped back and heaved his shoulder against it, but it held fast.

'There isn't time to batter it down,' Thomas said, but Hawkes had turned to Sir Giles.

'Sir – your wheel lock . . .'

Thomas had not noticed Sir Giles's hand pistol. Uneasily,

206

the master of Chilbourne came forward. Pointing the barrel at the lock, he discharged it.

There was a split-second scrape of the wheel and then the roar of the old gun was deafening, with the crash of the ball penetrating the wood. Acrid smoke filled the passageway. Wafting it aside, coughing, Hawkes thrust at the door again, but it held.

There came a scream from within.

'Break it, for the Lord's sake – hurry!' Sir Giles threw himself at the door, but it still held.

'It's barred,' Thomas said, glancing back towards the stairs. A large form was moving deliberately towards them.

'I'll thank 'ee to move aside, Thomas,' Judd said.

Nobody argued, and all stood clear as Judd took a breath, ran at the door as fast as his legs would permit, and crashed into it. With a dreadful splitting noise, the huge hinges came away from the frame and the door fell in, landing on the floor of the room with a loud bang. Dust flew everywhere.

Thomas and Hawkes stepped through the doorway. Behind came Sir Giles, Judd and another villager from East Everley, a small man nervously holding a little cudgel. Gingerly they peered through the dust and smoke.

From nowhere a shape appeared, huge and menacing. Thick arms picked up Hawkes, his sword arm flailing uselessly, and threw him hard against the wall, where he landed in a heap. Then as the other men span round, there came an ear-splitting report from across the room. Beside him, Thomas saw Sir Giles slump to the floor with a groan.

'Father!' Lady Jane Buckridge screamed, for she was there, cowering against a wall beside the dust-covered form of Lady Euphemia's precious virginals. But as Thomas, poniard in hand, glanced towards her, she pointed. Whirling round, he saw a kneeling figure in the far corner, dark-bearded, struggling to reload a small caliver at speed. But he had not enough time, and as Thomas ran at him he realized it, threw the useless weapon aside and sprang to his feet. A blade flashed in his hand.

Now they faced each other, half-crouching, ignoring events near the doorway, from whence came cries and scuffling.

Whatever struggle had commenced on the other side of the large room was no longer their concern.

Breathing hard, putting aside his pain, Thomas feinted with his dagger, then pulled back as the other man lunged at him in turn. Looking into the eyes of his opponent, he was reminded of the man's cold, deliberate gaze during the endless hours he had been at his mercy. And as the thought entered his mind, the other gave it voice.

'I should have killed you when I had the chance.'

Thomas said nothing, merely kept his poniard forward, seeking an opportunity, one eye on the other's blade. Even as he darted a glance at the other's eyes, waiting for a sign, Simon Pepper slashed at him, so close that the point scraped his canvas jerkin. Using the other man's body movement to help him, Thomas dodged aside and stabbed at the arm, knowing at once that he had struck home. Pepper grunted as the blade sank into his flesh.

But he was quick – too quick, Thomas thought, for as he withdrew his poniard the man kicked out, knocking Thomas's legs from under him. With a vain attempt at stabbing in reply, Thomas fell back, managing to break the worst of his fall with his free hand.

Dimly he was aware of movement and cries of pain from across the room, but he could only keep his eyes on his assailant, managing to duck aside as Pepper stabbed downwards. This time red pain seared through his upper arm as the blade struck.

Dizzily, clenching his teeth, Thomas struggled to rise, then fell back in agony as the muscle in his shoulder gave way. Warm blood welled from his arm. Desperately he took his poniard in his left hand, but then realized the other man was no longer going to trouble himself with Thomas, for he had other matters to attend to.

Across the room, it was a grim sight. Sir Giles lay where he had fallen, semi-conscious, moaning, a raw wound in his shoulder, near the neck. Close by him, the villager with the cudgel lay in a crumpled posture, very still. Even from that distance Thomas could see that he was dead.

Slowly the curious scene came into sharper focus. Near

the door, Hawkes was on all fours, hurt and out of breath. His sword lay where he had dropped it, beyond his reach. And looming over him now, one sleeve red with blood, was Miles, arm raised – he still had Gervase's sword.

'If you kill him,' Thomas shouted, 'I'll kill you!'

Miles hesitated, glancing unhurriedly towards Thomas. Without a word, he drew back his foot and kicked Hawkes in the side. Hawkes cried out and fell heavily on his face. Then Miles walked over to Thomas, looking utterly determined. Thomas caught his breath, looking up, still holding his poniard and feeling like a child with a stick. The face was as he remembered it: untroubled by pain, fear or remorse, fringed with the black leather thongs that held the skullcap in place. Thomas looked at him, and saw his own death.

But he saw something else too – more exactly, he was aware that there were other people in the room, whom he had almost forgotten. One was Lady Jane, white with terror, sobbing, sitting hunched beside the wall. The other . . . The other, of course, was Pepper, and he was standing by an open casement. For the first time Thomas saw the heavy-looking packs, wrapped in stained cloth and bound with straps. There were several of them in the corner, and Pepper was throwing them out of the window.

And now came something Thomas had not heard before. Miles spoke.

'Don't do that,' he said.

Ignoring him, Pepper picked up another package and tossed it through. Thomas even heard it land with a soft thud.

'I said don't,' Miles repeated. His voice was low, and very gruff. He was half-turned away, and just below the neck of his shirt Thomas could see an ugly scar on his throat. He wondered why he had never noticed it before.

Pepper picked up the last pack and threw it down. Then he turned back, as if for one final look around.

'You're leaving me,' Miles muttered, so low as to be almost inaudible.

Pepper smiled. 'There's a time for everything,' he said, placing a hand on the window frame and preparing to heave himself through it.

Miles padded towards him in the unsettling manner that reminded Thomas of the way he had moved on the wrestling field. Blood dripped from his hand. In the other he still carried the sword.

Pepper glanced back and put his boot on the threshold.

'You'll not go,' Miles said.

Pepper had one leg through the window.

'I said not,' Miles repeated.

Pepper heaved the other leg through, put his hands overhead and flexed himself, intending to push himself out.

Miles dropped the sword with a clang, took hold of Pepper with both hands and pulled him back into the room.

Pepper fell to the floor with a cry, catching himself on one of the loose boards that lay everywhere. As he struggled to rise, Miles put his hands under his arms and lifted him to his feet. Pepper spun round, trying to dodge away.

'You great, foul bladder,' he hissed in a voice of pure contempt. 'It's over – can you not see that?' At once, his poniard appeared in his hand.

With similar speed, Miles scooped up Pepper's hand in a firm grip, then grabbed his upper arm in a rough approximation of the wrestling hold Thomas had seen Birch use. He watched from his sitting position, weak with pain and fatigue, as Miles calmly broke Pepper's arm. The crack of the bone was like that of a dry branch.

Pepper screamed and staggered, his arm falling limply to his side. The poniard clattered to the floor.

'You always said you'd stand with me,' Miles said.

Pepper kicked out, his face a white blur above his heavy beard. But Miles dodged the kick easily, leaned forward and picked him up, then raised him high above his head as if he were a heavy log.

'You wished to go out,' Miles said, 'so I will oblige thee.'

And he carried Pepper, struggling impotently and screaming in rage and agony, to the window and threw him out of it. There came one last, blood-chilling cry, and a dull thud from below. Then a ghastly silence.

But Miles did not bother to look out; he merely turned and walked deliberately back towards Thomas.

Eighteen

Thomas rolled aside with difficulty, drawing breath sharply as fresh pain shot through his shoulder. Something was broken. He laughed inwardly. *You think that matters now?* he asked himself as he struggled to a sitting position, back against the wall. Feebly he looked round for something that would serve as a weapon, but there were only loose floor-boards within reach, and he doubted if he could even lift one. The room came into sharp focus again. Lady Jane sat where she had been – but her eyes were closed, as if she had fallen into a faint. Near the door lay Sir Giles and the dead man. Hawkes, groaning, was struggling to get on to all fours again. He looked up and locked eyes with Thomas, perhaps recalling a foolish fight in a dusty barn.

A vague thought was nagging at the back of Thomas's mind. Then, as Miles started towards him, it came to him. Where was Judd?

He had been in the rear when they stepped through the doorway, but in the flurry that followed, Thomas had lost sight of him. Odd, he thought now, to lose sight of someone as big as Judd . . . Idly, as though he had all the time in the world, he marvelled at the way the slaughterman had smashed the door down in one charge.

Miles was now standing over him. Then came another scream, and he realized that Lady Jane was conscious after all.

'Animal!' she shrieked.

A frown spread slowly across Miles's broad face. He turned. 'I'm a man,' he told her with an edge of warning to his voice.

'Animal, is what 'er said,' a thick voice behind snarled.

Thomas looked round. Judd was standing in the doorway, blood about his mouth and on his shirt, a sheen of sweat on his forehead. He took a step forward.

Miles moved quickly, sideways into the centre of the room. Judd took another step. There the two men faced each other like two prize bulls.

'I slaughter animals, 'tis my craft,' Judd said. When Miles made no answer, he added, 'But I do 'ee quick – without pain. When I slay you, it'll not be painless.'

Still Miles said nothing.

'You killed my Nan,' Judd said very quietly, and for the first time Thomas saw a look of uncertainty flicker across Miles's face.

'Best get her ladyship out, falconer,' Judd said to Thomas, without looking at him.

Thomas got painfully to his feet. Without a word he moved towards Lady Jane, who scrambled up, suddenly alert, and started for the doorway. 'Run, my lady' he told her, then turned back into the room.

Hawkes was on his knees, hugging himself. Guessing that some of his ribs were cracked, Thomas did not attempt to help him up. Feebly he looked round for Hawkes's sword, but then Judd's voice came to him.

'Stay back, Thomas,' he said over his shoulder in a hard voice. 'This beast is mine.'

Thomas could do naught but obey, for Judd's tone brooked no argument. Helplessly, he and Hawkes watched the two giants fight to the death.

There was some circling, followed by one or two lunges, each man careful not to let the other gain a hold. Both were bloodied and slightly out of breath; Miles from his recent exertions, Judd seemingly having been knocked out in the brief struggle by the doorway. When he bared his teeth, several of them appeared to be missing.

Suddenly, as though at some unseen signal, both men leaned into each other and locked arms. Miles grunted as his left hand, oozing blood from the deep sword-cut, grasped Judd's shoulder. Then it became an embrace, from which there would be no release until one fell.

Miles hooked his leg around Judd's, but Judd held on fast so that if he fell the other would fall with him – which was what soon happened. The next moment both of them had toppled in a massive, untidy heap that made the floor shake. Then they were indeed like two animals, struggling in a fight to the finish, grasping at each other, fists flailing and connecting and flailing again. They moved so quickly for two big men that Thomas and Hawkes had difficulty at times seeing who was on top.

But if Miles was a brute who cared only for his survival, Judd was fuelled by rage – rage at the death of his Nan. Thomas recalled in a flash the sight of his face under the tree at Chilbourne as he howled with grief . . . Now it became plain that he cared not if he died. He would be avenged, and that was enough.

Somehow Miles got back on his feet, breathing fast, twisting Judd's leg, trying to break it as he had once broken Edward Birch's. But Judd, Thomas now saw, was a champion. Had he fought on Lammas night, he would have taken the prize. Pushing himself upwards on his hands, he kicked Miles hard in the side.

Miles grunted and doubled over, though he still held on. Judd kicked him again, on the thigh this time, then managed to grab Miles by the leg. With a mighty effort he lifted his opponent's foot clear of the floor, and shoved him backwards.

Miles fell like a carthorse, close to the wall, among loose floorboards. And though he quickly rolled over and raised himself, he was hurt. For a second he paused, resting on one knee, looking balefully at Judd.

Judd padded forward, breathless and dripping with sweat, looking as if he would kick Miles again. But instead he reached down, ripped the leather skullcap from the man's head and threw it away.

Miles snarled, his fearful scars a lurid purple. Struggling to stand up, he made a grab for Judd's leg, but Judd stepped back quickly. As he did so he took hold of Miles's injured left hand and bent it back with full force.

Thomas looked away briefly, hearing the crunch of the

wrist as it broke. Miles's bellow was like that of a wounded beast. Struggling to his feet, he made a futile grab at Judd, then fell forward clumsily, his elbow crashing through the ruined floor. Daylight showed from below.

Judd was winning – the thought made Thomas's spirits soar. He glanced at Hawkes, who was still kneeling, his face white with pain, but he returned Thomas's gaze, and a faint smile of hope showed.

But it was not over. Judd had taken hold of Miles's large head, whereupon Miles, one hand bloody and useless, grasped Judd between the legs and twisted. Now it was Judd's turn to cry – a roar of pain that shook the rafters. He fell forward, and both men were again on the floor, locked in a final embrace. This time, as they gouged and beat at each other, it was clear that only one would get up.

Thomas could hear other voices now. He turned round, having all but forgotten Sir Giles and the rest of the men. Now he saw that Lady Jane had not run away: she was kneeling in the doorway beside her father, cradling his head and weeping, her soft fawn-coloured kirtle streaked with blood and dirt. Sir Giles's eyes were closed, but his chest still rose and fell.

At last others were there: the remaining two men from East Everley, one gripping a billhook, the other an oak billet. One called out, but Thomas shook his head. 'Help master Hawkes,' he said tiredly. 'Leave the other to Judd.'

So it was that, spectators all, they watched the final moments of what would be Judd's last wrestling bout – if that savage fight could be dignified by the term at all. Both men, exhausted now, were caught in a terrible struggle, reduced to biting and grasping at any part of the other's body. It was a dreadful sight. Momentarily one would appear the victor, then the other, each aware of how vulnerable he now was through his weakness.

The end finally came, as it must. Miles, grunting now with rage and pain, blood on his face and hands, had risen to a sitting position, his great arms wrapped round Judd's body as though he were a baby While his left hand hung free, his right worked its way slowly along his other arm, tightening by tiny degrees.

Judd was blowing like a huge frog, red-faced, his bruises showing bright vermilion, his hair flattened to his skull with grease and sweat. Thomas and the others, rooted where they stood, watched in dismay as the slaughterman's ribs bent inwards. A fraction more and they would crack; any further, one or more would break, and perhaps puncture a lung ...

Then a rib did break, and the report was like a muffled gunshot. Judd exhaled, expelling a huge gout of air that blew Miles's thin hair back. Like two lovers locked in a grim parody of a passionate hug, they hissed their last breath into each other's faces. Judd had locked his own arms about Miles's bulk, but he was too late, and too weak, to exert the same pressure.

The watchers flinched to a man, wanting to intervene but unsure how. There came another sickening crack, but it was unclear now whose rib it was. Miles tightened his grasp, ignoring his own pain, his breath hoarse, willing himself to keep the pressure on until the end – and he was succeeding. Judd now saw his own end and gave a sudden shout of harsh laughter, for he cared not.

He let go of Miles, his big mouth wide in a grotesque smile. A puzzled look flitted across Miles's features, but he did not relax his hold for a second – which was to be his downfall, for with the last of his strength, Judd wrenched his hands free, put them firmly about Miles's neck, and rotated his wrists.

There was a crack like a splitting rock, then a gurgle. Miles's head fell back like a doll's, his neck broken, his arms dropping to his sides. For what seemed like several seconds he remained sitting upright, even as Judd pulled himself free and sat back, too weak to stand. Then the life went from Miles's body, and he lay on his back, the same puzzled look on his face, his eyes wide open.

Judd merely sat and looked at him. Slowly he turned his bruised and blood-streaked face towards the other men, who stood in shocked silence. Thomas was trying to staunch the bloodflow from his upper arm; Hawkes was on his feet now, supported between the other men, and Lady Jane, pale-faced and silent, was still cradling her father's head.

They had all become vaguely aware of a thudding coming up the stairs and along the passage. Now Edward Birch appeared in the doorway. He froze, short of breath, silently taking in the scene. Then he looked at Judd, who stared back at him from the floor.

'You're the best,' Birch said quietly. 'Always were.'

Judd tried to smile, but gave a little cough instead. Hawkes cried out, even as Thomas moved forward, his heart thudding, dropping to his knee beside Judd.

Judd gazed at him as his eyes began to glaze over, and for the first time Thomas saw the dark blood that filled his mouth.

'Guess he'm over,' Judd whispered. Blood spilled from his lips and ran down his throat.

Thomas took his big hand and held it. 'I guess it is.'

'See Nan get a proper burial.' His voice was very faint.

'I swear it,' Thomas said.

Judd smiled at him with his eyes, even as they dulled, and a last sigh came from his mouth. He remained leaning forward in a sitting position, beside the body of his last opponent, on the blood-spattered floor. But he was dead.

Willoughby's men arrived only minutes afterwards, drawing their tired horses to a halt in front of the near-derelict house – but it was immediately clear that they were somewhat late. As they dismounted, a silence fell at the sight of the little group of men standing around a prone figure beside the wall. It lay beneath the open window, from which folk had in times past heard the sound of the Lady Euphemia playing her virginals.

They had gathered about the still form of Simon Pepper, lying twisted as he had fallen, his neck and back broken. Scattered around him were the packs that had been the cause of so many men's deaths.

Sir Giles gave the most reason for concern. He had been carried outside and lain on the grass, Lady Jane still at his side. Indeed, she had never left it. But it was Birch, with some rudimentary knowledge of injuries, who sat down with difficulty beside the master of Chilbourne to examine his wound. There was considerable relief when he looked up and made an announcement.

'The ball has missed the bone and passed through, my lady,' he told Lady Jane. 'The flesh is sorely damaged, but he should recover.'

Willoughby, breathing easier, began to assert his authority. He looked somewhat sheepishly at Hawkes, who was standing painfully to one side, and at Thomas, whose arm now bore a bloodstained bandage.

'You should have waited for us,' he said, though his tone carried little conviction. 'Yet, I suppose it was the lady you thought of . . .' He broke off, glancing towards Gervase Lambert, who was sitting beside the famous cracked oak tree. Someone had fashioned a heavy bandage and wound it about him.

As every man watched, uncertain what to do next, Lady Jane left her father and hurried to Gervase. With a sob she dropped to her knee and fell against him. Feebly the young man placed an arm about her, and held her.

Men looked away then in some embarrassment, and there was soon much milling about as the Sheriff issued his orders. Litters were to be made quickly to take Sir Giles and Gervase back to Chilbourne. Someone was despatched to send word to Marlborough and summon the barber-surgeon, while others were assigned the grisly task of removing bodies.

Thomas walked over to Hawkes, who managed a grim smile. But there was a look of respect in his eyes. 'You have acted with much courage,' he said. 'And got yourself a goodly scratch doing it.' He nodded towards the bandage. But as Thomas returned his smile feebly, the usher frowned. 'You have suffered worse injury,' he muttered.

'My shoulder,' Thomas said. 'I fear something is broken.'

'Then it shall be mended,' the other said. 'As all your hurts shall . . .' He broke off and placed a hand gently on Thomas's arm. 'Anything I can, I will do,' he said softly.

Thomas nodded, then half-turned as John Cardmaker walked up to him in a state of some excitement.

'What sights – and what terrible things have occurred!' he exclaimed. 'The whole county will talk of it.' He jerked his head towards Edward Birch, who had moved idly towards the body of Simon Pepper, now covered with a blanket.

'What's 'ee to do with it all?' he muttered, frowning.

'He has played his part well enough,' Thomas said, and walked away towards Cob.

It was evening by the time they returned to Chilbourne. Word had been sent ahead and beds prepared for Gervase and Sir Giles; Lady Katherine herself would minister to them, assisted by her daughters. But first there was a tearful reunion before the Great House as Lady Jane was welcomed home by her mother and sisters, weeping piteously. At once they hurried indoors, arms about each other, Lady Katherine calling for a chamber with a hot tub to be prepared.

It seemed to Thomas that there were more servants than before, for reasons he did not yet understand. But it transpired that word had spread rapidly to East Everley and the villages beyond, and some former employees had returned at once to the manor to be a part of things – wages or no. Cardmaker was right. All across the Downlands, there was only one topic of conversation: how a terrible battle had been fought at Cracked Oak over some bags of gold, and how the murderers of the Crown Purveyor and the rector had been killed – and above all, how Judd Chalkhill had fought the brute who took the prize on Lammas night, and died in the process.

Thomas and Hawkes, thrown together by events they could barely have imagined, sat in the warm kitchen and waited their turn for treatment. Clyffe the cook, half-drunk, brought them food and ale, but apart from slaking their thirst they ate little. Soon they were both asleep.

To Clyffe's displeasure, Edward Birch appeared at the back door later that night to ask after Thomas. His wife, Frances, was one of those now attending Lady Katherine.

'I guess you think you're due a mug and a supper too, for helping the master out,' Clyffe said.

Birch eyed him. 'I expect naught from you,' he answered. 'I wanted to speak with the falconer.'

Thomas opened his eyes. He was slumped on a seat against the wall beside Hawkes, who was snoring softly.

'How is the foot, master?' he murmured.

Birch limped over to him, his crutch scraping on the stone-flagged floor. 'Don't pay that any mind,' he said. 'You've suffered worse, from what I hear.'

'I will live.' Thomas smiled. 'Yet, if you would help me, I need someone to look to my birds. They need food and water . . .' He grimaced. 'They must wait for their exercise.'

Birch sat down heavily beside him. 'I will look to them,' he said.

Thomas smiled his thanks then turned as Hawkes stirred beside him. The usher started suddenly, looked about, then grunted with pain. 'I should not be here,' he mumbled. 'There are duties . . .'

'Best stay there, Master Hawkes,' Clyffe said, coming forward. 'Your ribs will take time to mend.'

Hawkes was taking in the situation. 'Why has our friend naught to drink?' he demanded suddenly, gesturing towards Birch. 'He has earned a mug, at the very least.'

Clyffe snorted, but went to the ale barrel and filled a mug, which he then brought over. Birch took it with a broad smile.

'Your health, Master wrestler,' he said, and took a deep pull.

Clyffe snorted again, and moved about his business. A woman appeared then, demanding hot water, and he was soon shouting to the kitchen boy to stoke up the fire.

Birch watched for a moment, then, without looking at Thomas, said, 'It's another matter I would speak about.'

Thomas looked expectantly at him, but the other shook his head slightly. 'Not here,' he muttered.

'It sounds a serious matter,' Thomas said.

Birch nodded, then turned as all of them did, for the door had opened and the stooped figure of Redmund Oakes appeared.

Thomas had seen nothing of the butler all day. Now as he came forward, he saw strain and sadness about the old man's eyes.

'Master Oakes,' Hawkes said in a voice taut with pain. 'You will make my apology to Lady Katherine . . .'

'Stay, friend Richard.' Oakes waved a hand dismissively. 'You must go to your chamber and rest. The barber-surgeon will attend you . . .' He broke off, looking at Thomas. 'You too, falconer – the master sends word he is in your debt, and will see you rewarded.'

Thomas gave a half-smile, sensing the wry amusement of every man in the room. Sir Giles's habit of promising rewards he could not deliver was only too well known.

'He is conscious then, Master Oakes?' he asked. 'That is good news indeed.'

'He is weak, but the barber-surgeon says he will mend,' Oakes replied. 'Likewise Master Gervase – he lost much blood, but the wound is staunched and bound, and he is a young man . . .' He trailed off, then glanced about at the company in general. 'Unlike poor Bartholomew Byres,' he said. When all eyes turned upon him, he gave the news. 'He died of a seizure where he sat, in the Great Chamber, less than an hour after you left this morning.'

There was a silence. In the far corner, Clyffe took a generous pull from his mug.

'Sad news,' Hawkes muttered.

Oakes lowered his eyes. 'I fear the Lady Euphemia will be hard-pressed to bear it. She has retired to her chamber, and will not come forth.'

He turned to go, then added: 'Perhaps some good may come of so much ill, for the Lady says she will never return to Cracked Oak, but will put the house up for sale . . . Mayhap Sir Giles will share a little in the proceeds.' He moved slowly to the door, and went out.

Hawkes rose stiffly and looked down at Thomas. 'Stay here, or use the chamber where you were taken when they brought you from the forest,' he said. 'Whatever you will.'

Thomas nodded his thanks. He and Birch sat in silence while the usher too went out.

Birch hesitated a moment, then said: 'It was to do with proceeds, the matter I would speak with you about.'

Thomas glanced about. Clyffe was berating the poor kitchen boy beside the fireplace. 'None can hear us now,' he said.

Birch took a pull from his mug, and looked deliberately at the floor. 'Yet, I will not tell much,' he said. 'Only, ask yourself how many packs of Spanish gold did the Lord Sheriff recover from Cracked Oak.'

Thomas frowned at him. 'There were five,' he replied.

'One more than Byres told.'

'Indeed,' Birch nodded, rather quickly. And now Thomas sensed rather than saw that he was holding in his excitement. 'Five,' Birch repeated. 'And they are Crown property, to be taken under guard to London, and restored to her glorious majesty, bless her little bald head.'

He turned then to Thomas and smiled, exactly as he had smiled upon him in the hayfield, that sunny morning when they first met.

'So nobody knows about the sixth,' he said.

Nineteen

The next day was to be one of the most momentous within the living memory of anyone at Chilbourne – even Redmund Oakes, who in his last years would sit in the chimney corner and speak at length about it to anyone who would listen.

It began quietly enough. The weather was fair, and Thomas was up by mid-morning, refreshed but sore, his left arm in a sling. A crack in the collarbone, the barber-surgeon had said with a sniff, and told him to rest it. But at once he went out to the weathering, relieved to see that Birch was as good as his promise, and had fed and watered Tamora and the lanner falcon.

Birch . . . He could not forget the man's words from last night, and they troubled him. Even one of those heavy packs, assuming the accounts he had heard were true, was worth a small fortune, and the man had simply taken it! His boldness, not to mention his cunning, defied belief. Once again Thomas found himself the repository of information he would rather not have had. Was Birch offering him a share, in return for his silence? But then why mention it at all? He had said nothing more about it last night before taking his leave.

Although Thomas did not yet know it, the answer would soon be forthcoming. The first sign that events were moving apace came when he was summoned to attend Lady Katherine in the Great Chamber after dinner.

He entered the room to find it filled with voices. Sunlight streamed through the high windows. Seated about the table, where the remains of a late dinner still lay, was Lady Katherine, with her daughters Emma and Margaret on either side. Close by sat Lady Jane and Gervase, looking at last

222

like a couple. It warmed his heart to see them so content in each other's company.

On the other side of Gervase sat Eliza. As Thomas came forward she glanced at him once, then looked away. As always, he could discern nothing from her expression.

Seated at the end of the table beside Redmund Oakes he found Hawkes, smartly dressed, his officious manner restored. But at sight of Thomas he rose stiffly and stepped forward to greet him. Servants came and went, among them Frances Birch, who threw Thomas a brief look of – what? Recognition? Or conspiracy? He looked away uncomfortably, and at once made his bow before Lady Katherine.

Lady Katherine smiled – and Thomas was reminded of the way she had looked out on the Downs with the breeze in her face. 'Sir Giles has asked me to convey his thanks, falconer,' she said. 'You have done more than should be expected for one of your duties. Indeed, it seems we are all in your debt.'

Embarrassed, Thomas merely inclined his head.

'There is much to be done,' Lady Katherine continued, 'yet I am so filled with relief that my dear daughter is restored to me . . .' She broke off, looking at Lady Jane. When she resumed, it was not Thomas she was addressing, but the entire company. 'Sir Giles will be abed for some days – perhaps weeks,' she said. 'He has authorized me to order matters in his absence.'

Thomas saw it now: a suppressed joy behind her eyes. She had dreamed of such a moment. Was that why Lady Jane seemed so calm?

'The banns announcing the wedding of Lady Jane and Master Lambert will be read for the third and final time on Sunday, at St Peter's church in Marlborough,' Lady Katherine said. A silence had fallen. Looking about, she added: 'The wedding will be permitted.'

There was a chorus of approval from many voices – the loudest being Emma's and Margaret's – though clearly the matter was already known to them and to others. But Lady Katherine raised a hand, calling for quiet. 'First, though, there are sadder affairs – the burial of our servants, and the

223

servants of the Lady Euphemia.' She glanced at Thomas. 'Falconer, you are free to return to your master at Petbury at any time, and I will see that you do not leave empty-handed.' Thomas bowed, his heart lifting, but she had not finished. 'Yet I would ask you, for my sake, to stay for the burial of Judd Chalkhill. The usher –' this with a glance at Hawkes – 'thinks you will not wish to refuse.'

Thomas nodded. 'I will stay, my lady,' he said.

Lady Katherine smiled her approval. Talk began to rise again about the table. With a sigh, Thomas made as if to retire, but at that moment the door opened, and heads turned in surprise. A servant was showing in Edward Birch, who stood uncomfortably inside the doorway. He had discarded the clumsy crutch, though his ankle was still bound, and had made an effort to look his best in a clean shirt and breeches, his hair smoothed flat. Yet his rough manner was such that most looked askance at him.

Hawkes came forward, and his demeanour was not unkind. 'Master Birch?'

'I beg leave to speak with her ladyship,' Birch said.

Hawkes looked surprised, and turned towards Lady Katherine, who was staring intently at the bold intruder.

'Alone, if you please, sir,' Birch said stoutly, though he fumbled with the woollen cap in his hands.

Hawkes blinked, but Lady Katherine was on her feet, some instinct telling her that she should hear the man. Walking around the table, she gestured to the others to finish their meal, and moved towards Birch.

The villager bowed clumsily. 'I have a most important matter for your ladyship, for your ears alone – I beg you to hear it.'

Lady Katherine hesitated, then said: 'I insist upon Master Hawkes being present.'

Birch frowned slightly, then ducked his head in acquiescence. 'Then for my part I ask that the falconer be present.'

Lady Katherine was taken aback. 'I cannot imagine what this pertains to,' she said, somewhat uneasily.

Birch moistened his dry lips. 'My lady, I have the means to help you – to help us all.'

Hawkes too was looking uncomfortable. But, coming quickly to a decision, Lady Katherine said: 'We will go to the West Chamber.' And so, watched curiously by those at the table, she allowed Hawkes to open the door for her, then led the way out of the hall.

They walked along the wide passage to a small chamber that Thomas had never seen. It was simply furnished, with a writing desk and some straight-backed chairs, and one or two faded hangings. Hawkes saw the Lady Katherine seated, then at once took up a protective position beside her. Birch, walking awkwardly, came in last and stopped before her. Thomas stood to one side.

'Well?' Lady Katherine fixed the villager with a stare.

'I have the means to relieve your debts, my lady,' Birch said simply.

There was a stunned silence.

'How dare you . . .' Hawkes began, his face flushed with anger, but Lady Katherine held up a hand.

'And how might such a man as you do that?' she asked in a neutral tone.

Birch swallowed, then seized the moment. 'The Spanish treasure, my lady, the gold that was hidden at Cracked Oak – as you'll know it is now restored to the Crown. And, as far as folk think in London – and indeed everywhere else – that's the end of the matter. Master Sheriff was mighty pleased, it seemed to me, that there was five packs and not four like he'd been told . . . I do hear he'll have a small share in the reward himself, if Her Majesty feels generous . . .'

Hawkes eyes blazed. 'You rogue!' he cried. 'You make so bold to speak to her ladyship in this manner—'

'Master usher.' Lady Katherine's voice was firm. 'Will you allow the man to come to the point before condemning him?' She turned back to Birch. 'Your name?' she enquired.

'Edward Birch, my lady, of East Everley. I did help with your harvest.'

Thomas kept all expression from his face, only marvelling at the man's nerve.

'Then finish your tale, Edward Birch,' Lady Katherine said.

''Tis a tale with a happy ending, my lady.' Birch paused, threw a swift glance at Thomas and went on. 'For the truth is, there were not five packs. I was standing beside the corpse of the . . . Well, when they lifted his body, there was another pack lying underneath him. Seemed he fell upon it. So I . . . The tip of my crutch . . . I am lame, and had my crutch then, my lady. Well, to come to the end of it, I pushed the pack under the horse blanket they'd used to cover him. No one saw, and none bothered about an old blanket, so I just took it away to the horse I was riding, and . . .' He trailed off and shrugged.

Hawkes and Thomas exchanged looks of disbelief; though while the usher's was occasioned by the news itself, Thomas was merely amazed that the man should tell it to Lady Katherine.

But she and Birch were looking each other in the eye, as though they were equals. 'So,' the lady said after a while, somewhat shakily, 'you have confessed before witnesses to a felony that would bring you to the gallows.'

'I believe I have, my lady,' Birch said.

Lady Katherine's chest rose as she breathed in heavily. 'Hence, what is to prevent me from having you arrested and held at the Sheriff's pleasure?' she enquired.

'You wouldn't get to keep the money,' Birch replied.

Hawkes bristled, but controlled his anger. 'Do you realize what you say – and what you have done?' he demanded. 'Not to mention the risk you have taken . . .'

'That I do, Master Hawkes,' Birch said, looking him straight in the eye. 'But for a prize that big, a man may take a chance.'

Lady Katherine remained composed, but each man heard the tension in her voice as she asked: 'Where is the . . . the prize, Master Birch? And how big is it exactly?'

'It's safe, where none could find it, my lady,' Birch answered. 'As for its worth – I don't calculate too well, and I know not the value of Spanish gold pieces. Only I believe they're what they call double-ducats, and there are hundreds of them.'

The silence this time was filled with possibilities. Hawkes

glanced suddenly at Lady Katherine, then looked away. Thomas could not discern what was in his mind.

'So . . .' The lady's voice was clear, but rather low. 'Tell me how much it is you want.'

Birch smiled. 'I want none of it, my lady. At least, not for myself.'

Lady Katherine stared.

'But,' Birch added, 'before I turn it over to your ladyship, in good time – by night, I'd suggest – I would ask that some of it be used in certain ways.' When Lady Katherine merely waited, he said, 'First, I would beg a place for myself and my wife Frances at Chilbourne for the rest of our days. She is a good servant, and her sister Alys would make a good washerwoman, and fill Mistress Nan's shoes. And I would be slaughterman here, in place of Judd.'

Lady Katherine gazed in surprise. 'You want work? That is all?'

'It'll do for me, my lady,' was the reply. 'Though there is one more thing that is of greater import.' He paused to include Hawkes. 'That some of the money be used to start a school for the children of East and West Everley. Such as Doctor Parry should have done, only he didn't. That would be a fitting use, my lady, wouldn't you say?'

Lady Katherine met his eye. 'I suppose it would. And the remainder?'

'I have said. 'Twould put an end to most of your troubles, would it not? Dowries, and such . . .' He broke off, having said all there was to say.

Hawkes was staring, dumbfounded at the man's boldness.

'And in return for these things, you would swear to keep silent for the rest of your days?' Lady Katherine asked, somewhat hoarsely.

Birch raised an eyebrow. 'Silent about what, my lady?'

Lady Katherine let out a breath. Thomas admired her self-control, while marvelling at the enormity of the secret he had just been privy to.

Then Hawkes spoke up suddenly in a tone Thomas had never heard him use before his master or mistress.

'What of my silence, my lady?'

Lady Katherine turned slowly, and met his eye. 'Your silence, Master usher?'

'Yes. Would it surprise you to know there are things I too might desire?'

Thomas felt a smile spreading slowly across his face. He hid it at once.

Lady Katherine looked at the usher for what seemed a long time. Then she relaxed. 'I imagine you propose to deprive me of my woman-in-waiting,' she said mildly.

Hawkes swallowed and nodded.

Thomas spent that afternoon outdoors, exercising Tamora near the house, glad to feel the warm sun on his face. In the distance, sheep dotted the pastures where the hay and corn crop had been. Closer, horses twitched their tails in the paddock. It would not be long now before he could return home.

At the house there was still more bustle. Funeral arrangements were in hand for both Bartholomew Byres and Mary Henshaw, whose body had been brought from Marlborough. Lady Euphemia herself had been seen about the house, but she seemed to forget where she was, and kept asking for Mary. Finally she had been placated by Lady Jane with the promise that her virginals were to be brought from Cracked Oak and installed in her chamber, where she could play them whenever she liked.

The gossip was that the Lady Euphemia's town house would have to be sold to satisfy Her Majesty's exchequer, whose representatives would be turning their attention to Chilbourne. How Sir Giles and Lady Katherine proposed to pay their debts was a complete mystery – especially as the news had spread that the Lady Jane's betrothal to Stephen Ridley was annulled, and she was to marry her childhood sweetheart.

To Thomas's surprise and embarrassment as he now came down the slope above the house, a brightly dressed group walked forth to meet him: the three Buckridge sisters, and behind them, Eliza.

He made his bow with difficulty, one arm in its sling and

the other carrying the hooded Tamora. The group was not composed entirely of women – Lady Jane had Gervase on her arm.

'We never did go forth with our falconry lessons, Thomas,' he said with a faint smile. The young man walked stiffly, for his body was bound up tightly beneath his bright satin doublet. But the lines of strain were gone from his eyes; indeed, he glowed with happiness.

'I venture that does not weigh heavily upon you, sir,' Thomas answered. Tamora twitched slightly under her hood.

'I will not forget what you did,' Gervase said, drawing closer to him. 'When my book of airs is taken up by the Queen I shall send you news of it, with a token of my gratitude.'

Thomas bowed. When he straightened, Lady Jane was looking directly at him. He blanched, reminded at once of how she had looked back in the room of the house in Marlborough.

'I too would thank you, Thomas,' she said. 'And ask pardon for any hard words . . .' She broke off, looking away.

Thomas smiled back and shook his head. 'Nay, my lady – to see you free and happy is reward enough.'

There came a stifled laugh as Margaret hid her face behind Emma. Lady Jane turned and at her look the two younger sisters hurried off, Margaret's shoulders shaking as she went.

'She still thinks you are handsome, for a falconer,' Jane said. To Thomas's consternation she darted forward and kissed his cheek. Before he could react, she had tugged Gervase's arm, and the two were walking back towards the house.

Which left only Eliza.

Some yards separated them but she seemed unwilling to shorten the distance, so Thomas moved towards her, and, knowing he was in full view of the house, made his bow.

'I will not kiss you,' Eliza said quietly. 'You have more than enough memories of how I taste.'

He took a breath, wanting to reach out and draw her to him.

'Yes,' she said, divining his thoughts once again. 'I would

like to clasp you too. But I may not.' She smiled a warm smile that disarmed him. 'Did you know that I am to have a dowry after all?' she asked. 'A small one, perhaps, but it shall serve. As will my husband-to-be.'

'You deserve happiness,' Thomas began, but saw the look in her eye, and stopped. 'Would you still see me hang?' he asked.

She paused, then said: 'If I were a widow one day, and you were not too old, would you come and seek me out?'

He nodded.

'Then you are as big a liar as I,' she murmured.

She turned suddenly, shading her eyes and looking towards the house. A figure had appeared, standing near the door to the kitchens, upright and motionless.

'You had better go to him,' Thomas said.

She turned to him, an odd look on her face. Was it sadness, or resignation, or both?

'I've changed my mind,' she said suddenly. Then, as Thomas looked startled, laughed aloud in girlish delight. 'I will kiss you after all,' she said, and did.

After which, he could only watch as she turned her back and walked away from him, towards the man she would now marry.

That evening events took a different turn when, to general dismay, Stephen Ridley came sweeping into Chilbourne on his fine horse, attended by several servants.

Thomas was honoured that night, having been invited to join the entire household at supper in the Great Chamber. The high table was full, and the lower ones too. Clyffe, it seemed, had excelled himself in producing the nearest to a feast that the manor had seen in months. Where had he found money to buy such good fare at short notice? folk asked one another before falling to with alacrity.

Until, that was, the interruption of Ridley, flanked by his lackeys, caused a major stir in the hall. Clearly the news had reached Marlborough.

All eyes were upon him as he strode to the table and made his bow to Lady Katherine, taking in the rest of the company with an impatient glance. Lady Katherine rose slightly, and made a token curtsey.

'I rejoice that your daughter is found, and restored to you safely, Lady Katherine,' he said loudly. 'Our prayers have been answered.' He glanced at Lady Jane, deliberately ignoring Gervase beside her. 'Now matters may be as they were,' he added. 'And I would call back the hard words that stood between us – I was but concerned for the happiness of my betrothed . . .'

Nobody spoke, though there was a subdued muttering from the lower tables.

'For she is still my betrothed,' Ridley said, with a hard expression.

Thomas, seated on the end table nearest the door, looked at the retinue of liveried attendants that stood in a stiff-necked body behind Ridley. Among them was John Steer. Feeling his eyes upon him, Steer turned his head and saw Thomas, then looked away at once.

'But what of the lawsuit, friend Stephen?' Lady Katherine's clear voice rang out in the room, causing all eyes to rest upon her.

Ridley cleared his throat in embarrassment. 'I have instructed my lawyers to suspend proceedings . . .' he began.

But Lady Katherine was not listening. 'You may have heard that my husband was hurt in an unfortunate affray yesterday,' she said. 'As you see, I am here in his place.'

'Indeed, Lady Katherine,' Ridley replied briskly. 'And I will visit Sir Giles shortly, to pay my respects.'

'Respects?' Lady Katherine sat totally erect now. 'The last time you were in his company, I recall, you showed scant respect for him. Or for anyone else.'

Ridley swallowed, feeling the hostility of every member of the Chilbourne household, high-born and low. 'You will recall the circumstances . . .' he began.

'I recall them well enough,' Lady Katherine answered. She glanced then at Lady Jane, whose eyes were lowered. But Gervase Lambert was rising to his feet.

'Sit down, sir!' Lady Katherine snapped. Gervase sat down. 'Master Ridley,' Lady Katherine resumed. The silence was now so intense that Thomas could hear larks calling from the Downs above the paddock. Ridley opened his mouth, then closed it again. There was a glassy look in his eye.

'The wedding between you and my daughter will not take place,' Lady Katherine announced. 'She is betrothed to Master Lambert, and the banns have been read—'

'They have not,' Ridley retorted, and everyone heard the menace in his tone. 'I have spoken with the rector of St Peter's,' he added. 'The man owes me one or two favours. When I explained the circumstances, he agreed that the final banns will not be read. And, moreover, no such wedding shall take place in his church.'

'No matter,' Lady Katherine said after a moment. 'They may be read in East Everley church, once the bishop has appointed a new rector.'

Ridley's jaw dropped. 'You truly mean to defy me thus?' he said.

Lady Katherine glanced to one side. Richard Hawkes had risen from his place beside Eliza and was coming forward. 'Permit me to guide you to the door, sir,' he murmured, the picture of cool efficiency.

Ridley stared at him, then at the room in general. 'You defy me?' he shouted, suddenly red in the face. 'You know who I am, and what I can do?' Then he looked up sharply, for Lady Jane had got to her feet.

'I would never have married you, sir,' she said quietly. 'I would rather die first.' Then she sat down, her eyes lowered.

Ridley turned with a baleful look at Lady Katherine, surrounded by her family and servants. 'You will all regret this, more than you can imagine,' he breathed. 'I will re-instruct my lawyers, and call in all debts . . .' Spittle ran down his chin now. His rage was terrible, but impotent, and he knew it. There were mutterings from the men in the room as he turned at last to his retinue.

'Come!' he bellowed, and strode to the door. His men followed – save one. Thomas felt his heart swell as he saw the diminutive figure of John Steer suddenly isolated in the centre of the room. Ridley had almost reached the door before one of his men noticed and tugged at his sleeve. He looked round angrily.

'Steer!' he roared.

'With your leave sir,' Steer said, just loud enough to be audible, 'I am quitting your service. As of now.'

Ridley took a step towards him, purple with rage. At the same time, Thomas rose and came forward. The two falconers exchanged a brief glance, then stood together, facing the apoplectic figure, bulky in his richly faced robes. For what seemed like a long moment, nobody moved.

Then, suddenly aware that he had lost, Ridley uttered an oath and stormed out. 'Leave then, and be damned!' he called as he left.

Hawkes waited a moment, then closed the door firmly. There was a short silence. John Steer approached the high table and bowed timidly before Lady Katherine.

'Will you be wanting a falconer, my lady,' he asked, 'once Thomas has gone home?'

Lady Katherine smiled, and laughed suddenly. Then, as if a dam had broken, there came a roar of joyful laughter from the entire company, followed by a deafening round of applause. It would have been audible out in the stable yard, where no doubt Ridley and his party were taking horse.

Steer ducked his head and looked at Thomas in fright.

Later that night, the two falconers walked up to the weathering. The hawks watched eagerly as they put fresh water out, then tore at the scraps that Thomas threw down.

'I meant to tell her ladyship that she shouldn't be too afraid of Master Stephen's threats,' Steer said. 'I know a deal too much about his affairs. He's not that big a fool.'

'I thought as much,' Thomas replied.

A bright moon shone, and a breeze ruffled the beech trees close by. Suddenly Steer looked up and pointed. 'There's a falcon,' he said. 'A young passage hawk.'

Thomas followed his outstretched arm and saw the bird, perched on a low branch, peering at them. His heart leaped.

'The ramage hawk!' he exclaimed. 'She's come back.'

Steer looked dumbfounded. 'After all this time?' he

muttered. Then he turned to Thomas with a rueful expression. 'I guess that'll be my task now, to tame her,' he said.

Thomas gazed at him and nodded solemnly. 'So it will,' he said.